D1110468

NIGHT OF
THE FOX

SOUTH ST. PAUL PUBLIC LIBRARY
106 3rd Ave No.
South St. Paul, MN 55075

Night of the Fox

Jack Higgins

OPEN ROAD

INTEGRATED MEDIA

NEW YORK

SOUTH ST. PAUL PUBLIC LIBRARY
106 3rd Ave No.
South St. Paul, MN 55075

South St Paul Pu 5.975

For Vivienne Mylne

FOREWORD

Having lived in Jersey for many years I was always fascinated by the history of the island under Nazi occupation. British citizens under the rule of the third Reich: now there was a story. The historical details of the book are authentic. There was a small prison camp in Jersey for Allied soldiers and airmen, some of whom where American, and the Slaton Sands disaster which starts the book was real enough. More American soldiers were killed in training because of an attack by German E-boats than died on Omaha Beach on D-Day. The historical background to the book came from a dear friend, Vivienne Mylne, who went to Oxford University and later became Professor of French Literature at Canterbury. She loved to alarm colleagues at high table by referring to her time in prison. How this came about was as follows. Her father was a Methodist minister who arrived with his family in Jersey as the war started. He felt it his duty to stay on under the Occupation and he and Vivienne operated an illegal radio and spread the BBC news to all their friends. A local woman with a grudge against the family betrayed them to the Gestapo. In fact, the Gestapo as such did not operate in Jersey. The Secret Field Police handled security matters but a number of their operatives were Gestapo men on secondment.

Vivienne was sentenced to a three-year prison sentence in France, commuted to one year because of health problems, and she returned to Jersey by convoy very much as described in the book. She gave me a copy of her diary which I followed so closely that within the time scale of the story if it rains on Tuesday it is because Vivienne's diary said so. The character of Martineau, the middle-aged Oxford philosophy don recruited by the SOE because he speaks fluent German and can play a good Nazi, was based on a real Oxford don I had the privilege of meeting during my university days who had been recruited in middle age, taught how to kill, dropped into France by parachute and so on. Finally he was gravely wounded in a hand-to-hand encounter with a German agent, smuggled back to England and awarded the Distinguished Service Order. All this I allocated to Martineau, a case of fiction imitating life. *Night of the Fox* was filmed as a four-hour mini series for television with that great film actor George Peppard playing Martineau, exactly right as to age and attitude. All in all, this is one of my favourite books and it has been translated into thirty-five languages.

The German Occupation of the British Channel Islands during the Second World War is a matter of fact. Although mention is made of certain political and military leaders within the historical context of the period, it must be stressed that this is a work of fiction, nor is any reference intended to living persons.

I

THE ROMANS USED TO think that the souls of the departed stayed near their tombs. It was easy to believe that on a cold March morning, with a sky so black that it was as if night was about to fall.

I stood in the granite archway and looked in at the graveyard. The notice board said *Parish Church of St. Brelade* and the place was crammed with headstones and tombs, and here and there a granite cross reared up. There was a winged angel on the far side, I noticed that, and then thunder rumbled on the horizon and rain swept in across the bay.

The porter at the hotel had given me an umbrella and I put it up and ventured in. On Sunday in Boston I'd never heard of the British Channel Islands off the coast of France or the Island of Jersey. Now it was Thursday and here I was having traveled halfway round the world to seek the final answer to something that had taken three years out of my life.

The church was very old and built of granite. I moved toward it through the tombstones, pausing to look out over the bay. The tide was out and there was a fine sweep of golden sands extending to a concrete seawall and I could see my hotel.

I heard voices and, turning, saw two men in cloth caps, sacks over their shoulders, crouching under a cypress tree by the far wall of the graveyard. They stood up and moved away, laughing together as if at some joke, and I noticed they were carrying spades. They disappeared around the back of the church and I crossed to the wall.

There was a freshly dug grave, covered with a tarpaulin although the tree gave it some protection from the rain. I don't think I've ever felt so excited. It was as if it had been waiting for me and I turned and moved through the headstones to the entrance of the church, opened the door and went inside.

I'd expected a place of darkness and gloom, but the lights were on and it was really very beautiful, the vaulted ceiling unusual in that it was constructed of granite, no evidence of wooden beams there at all. I walked toward the altar and stood for a moment, looking around me, aware of the quiet. There was the click of a door opening and closing. A man approached.

He had white hair and eyes of the palest blue. He wore a black cassock and carried a raincoat over one arm. His voice was dry and very old and there was a hint of Irish to it when he spoke. "Can I help you?"

"Are you the rector?"

"Oh, no." He smiled good-humoredly. "They put me out to grass a long time ago. My name is Cullen. Canon Donald Cullen. You're an American?"

"That's right." I shook hands. He had a surprisingly firm grip. "Alan Stacey."

"Your first visit to Jersey?"

"Yes," I said. "Until a few days ago I never knew the place existed. Like most Americans, I'd only heard of *New* Jersey."

He smiled. We moved toward the door and he carried on, "You've chosen a bad time of the year for your first visit. Jersey can be one of the most desirable places on earth, but not usually during March."

"I didn't have much choice," I said. "You're burying someone here today. Harry Martineau."

He had started to pull on his raincoat and paused in surprise. "That's right. I'm performing the ceremony myself, as a matter of fact. Two o'clock this afternoon. Are you a relative?"

"Not exactly, although I sometimes feel as if I am. I'm an assistant professor of philosophy at Harvard. I've been working on a biography of Martineau for the past three years."

"I see." He opened the door and we went out into the porch.

"Do you know much about him?" I asked.

"Very little, besides the extraordinary way he met his end."

"And the even more extraordinary circumstance of his last rites," I said. "After all, Canon, it isn't often you get to bury a man forty years after his death."

The bungalow was at the other end of St. Brelade's Bay, close to L'Horizon Hotel where I was staying. It was small and unpretentious, but the living room was surprisingly large, comfortable and cluttered, two walls lined with books. Sliding windows opened to a terrace and a small garden, the bay beyond. The tide was rushing in, the wind lifting the sea into whitecaps, and rain rattled against the window.

My host came in from the kitchen and put a tray on a small table by the fire. "I hope you don't mind tea."

"Tea will be fine."

"My wife was the coffee drinker in the family, but she died three years ago. I could never abide the stuff myself."

He filled my cup and pushed it toward me as I sat down on the other side of the table from him. The silence hung between us. He raised his cup and drank very precisely, waiting.

"You're very comfortable here," I said.

"Yes," he said. "I do very well. Lonely, of course. The great weakness of all human beings, Professor Stacey, is that we all need somebody." He refilled his cup. "I spent three years in Jersey as a boy and grew to love the place very much."

"That would be easy enough." I looked out at the bay. "It's very beautiful."

"I returned on holiday on many occasions. When I retired, I was a canon of Winchester Cathedral. Our only son moved to Australia many years ago, so …" He shrugged.

"Jersey seemed an obvious choice as my wife had owned this bungalow for many years. A legacy from an uncle."

"That must have been convenient."

"Yes, especially with the housing laws the way they are here." He put down his cup, took out a pipe and started to fill it from a worn leather pouch. "So," he said briskly. "Now you know all about me. What about you and friend Martineau?"

"Do you know much about him?"

"I'd never heard of the man until a few days ago when my good friend, Dr. Drayton, came to see me, explained the circumstances in which the body had been recovered and told me it was being shipped from London for burial here."

"You're aware of the manner of his death?"

"In a plane crash in 1945."

"January 1945, to be precise. The RAF had a unit called the Enemy Aircraft Flight during the Second World War. They operated captured German planes to evaluate performance and so on."

"I see."

"Harry Martineau worked for the Ministry of Economic Warfare. In January 1945, he went missing when traveling as an observer in an Arado 96, a German two-seater training plane being operated by the Enemy Aircraft Flight. It was always believed to have gone down in the sea."

"And?"

"Two weeks ago it was found during excavations in an Essex marsh. Work on the building site was halted while an RAF unit recovered what was left."

"And Martineau and the pilot were still inside?"

"What was left of them. For some reason the authorities kept a low profile on the affair. News didn't filter through to me until last weekend. I caught the first plane out. Arrived in London on Monday morning."

He nodded. "You say you've been working on a biography of him. What makes him so special? As I told you, I'd never even heard his name before."

"Nor had the general public," I said. "But in the thirties, in academic circles..." I shrugged. "Bertrand Russell considered him one of the most brilliant and innovative minds in his field."

"Which was?"

"Moral philosophy."

"An interesting study," the canon said.

"For a fascinating man. He was born in Boston. His father was in shipping. Wealthy, but not outrageously so. His mother, although born in New York, was of German parentage. Her father taught for some years at Columbia then returned to Germany in 1925 as professor of surgery at Dresden University." I got up and walked to the window, thinking about it as I peered out. "Martineau went to Harvard, did a doctorate at Heidelberg, was a Rhodes scholar at Oxford, a Fellow of Trinity College and Croxley Professor of Moral Philosophy by the age of thirty-eight."

"A remarkable achievement," Cullen said.

I turned. "But you don't understand. Here was a man who was questioning everything. Turning his whole field upside down. And then the Second World War broke out and the rest is silence. Until now, that is."

"Silence?"

"Oh, he left Oxford, we know that. Worked for the Ministry of Defence and then the Ministry of Economic Warfare, as I told you. Many academics did that. But the tragedy was that he seems to have stopped working altogether in his chosen field. No more papers and the book he'd been writing for years was left unfinished. We've got the manuscript at Harvard. Not a line written after September nineteen thirty-nine."

"How very strange."

I went back and sat down. "We have all his papers in the Harvard Library. What really intrigued me on going through them was a personal thing."

"And what was that?"

"When I finished high school at eighteen, instead of going straight to Harvard I joined the Marines. Did a year in Vietnam until a bullet in the left kneecap sent me home for good. Martineau did the same sort of thing. Joined the American Expeditionary Force in the last few months of the First World War, underage, I might say, and served as an infantry private in the trenches in Flanders. I was fascinated by the fact that in turning from what we'd gone through, we'd both sought another answer in the same way."

"From the hell of war to the cool recesses of the mind." Canon Cullen knocked out his pipe in the hearth. "I can't remember who said that. Some war poet or other."

"God save me from those," I said. "Nam cost me a permanently stiff left leg, three years in the hands of psychiatrists and a failed marriage."

The clock on the mantelpiece struck twelve. Cullen got up, moved to the sideboard and poured whisky from a cut glass decanter into two glasses. He brought them back and handed me one. "I was in Burma during the war myself, which was bad enough." He sipped a little whisky and put down his glass on the hearth. "And so, Professor, what about the rest?"

"The rest?"

"Priests are supposed to be ingenuous souls who know nothing of the reality of life," he said in that dry, precise voice. "Rubbish, of course. Our business is confession, human pain, misery. I know people, Professor, after fifty-two years as an ordained priest, and one learns to know when they are not telling you everything." He put a match to his pipe and puffed away. "Which applies to you, my friend, unless I'm very much mistaken."

I took a deep breath. "He was in uniform when they found him."

He frowned. "But you said he was working for the Ministry of Economic Warfare."

"German Luftwaffe uniform," I said. "Both he and the pilot."

"Are you certain?"

"I have a friend from the Vietnam days in the Marines called Tony Bianco. He's with the CIA at our embassy in London. They get to know things, these people. I had problems with the Ministry of Defence the other day. They were giving very little away about Martineau and that plane."

"Your friend checked up for you?"

"And found out something else. The newspaper report about that Arado being from the Enemy Aircraft Flight. That's suspect, too."

"Why?"

"Because they always carried RAF rondels. And according to Bianco's informant, this one still had Luftwaffe markings."

"And you say you couldn't get any more information from official sources?"

"None at all. Ridiculous though it may seem, Martineau and that flight are still covered by some wartime security classification."

The old man frowned. "After forty years?"

"There's more," I said. "I had this kind of problem last year when I was researching. Ran into roadblocks, if you know what I mean. I discovered that Martineau was awarded the Distinguished Service Order in January 1944. One of those awards that appears in the list without explanation. No information about what he'd done to earn it."

"But that's a military award and a very high one at that. Martineau was a civilian."

"Apparently civilians have qualified on rare occasions, but it all begins to fit with a story I heard when researching at Oxford three years ago. Max Kubel, the nuclear physicist, was a professor at Oxford for many years and a friend of Martineau's."

"Now I *have* heard about him," Cullen said. "He was a German Jew, was he not, who managed to get out before the Nazis could send him to a concentration camp?"

"He died in nineteen seventy-three," I said. "But I managed to interview the old man who'd been his manservant at his Oxford college for more than thirty years. He told me that during the big German offensive in nineteen forty that led to Dunkirk, Kubel was held by the Gestapo under house arrest at Freiburg, just across the German border from France. An SS officer arrived with an escort to take him to Berlin."

"So?"

"The old boy, Howard his name was, said that Kubel told him years ago that the SS officer was Martineau."

"Did you believe him?"

"Not at the time. He was ninety-one and senile, but one has to remember Martineau's background. Quite obviously he could have passed for a German any time he wanted. He not only had the language but had the family background."

Cullen nodded. "So, in view of more recent developments you're prepared to give more credence to that story?"

"I don't know what to think anymore." I shrugged. "Nothing makes any sense. Martineau and Jersey, for example. To the best of my knowledge he never visited the place and he died five months before it was freed from Nazi occupation." I swallowed the rest of my whisky. "Martineau has no living relatives, I know that because he never married, so who the hell is this Dr. Drayton of yours? I know one thing. He must have one hell of a pull with the Ministry of Defence to get them to release the body to him."

"You're absolutely right." Canon Cullen poured me another Scotch whisky. "In all respects, but one."

"And what would that be?"

"Dr. Drayton," he said, "is not a he, but a she. Dr. Sarah Drayton, to be precise." He raised his glass to toast me.

I am the resurrection and the life, saith the Lord: he that believeth in me, though he were dead, yet shall he live.

Cullen sounded even more Irish as he lifted his voice bravely against the heavy rain. He wore a dark cloak over his vestments and one of the funeral men stood beside him holding an umbrella. There was only one mourner, Sarah Drayton, standing on the other side of the open grave, an undertaker behind her with another umbrella.

She looked perhaps forty-eight or fifty although, as I discovered later, she was sixty, small and with a figure still trim in the black two-piece suit and hat. Her hair was short, expertly cut and iron gray. She was not in any way conventionally beautiful, with a mouth that was rather too large and hazel eyes above wide cheekbones. It was a face of considerable character with an impression of someone who had seen the best and worst that life had to offer, and there was an extraordinary stillness to her. If I had seen her only in passing, I'd have turned for a second look. She was that sort of woman.

She ignored me completely and I stayed back under what shelter the trees provided, getting thoroughly damp in spite of my umbrella. Cullen concluded the service, then moved toward her and spoke briefly. She kissed him on the cheek and he turned and moved away toward the church, followed by the funeral men.

She stayed there for a while at the graveside and the two gravediggers waited respectfully a few yards away. She still ignored me as I moved forward, picked up a little damp soil and threw it down on the coffin.

"Dr. Drayton?" I said. "I'm sorry to intrude. My name is Alan Stacey. I wonder if I might have a few words? I'm not a reporter, by the way."

Her voice was deeper than I had expected, calm and beautifully modulated. She said, without looking at me, "I know very well who you are, Professor Stacey. I've been expecting you at any time these past three years." She turned and smiled and suddenly looked absolutely enchanting and about twenty years of age. "We really should get out of this rain before it does us both a mischief. That's sound medical advice and for free. My car is in the road outside. I think you'd better come back for a drink."

The house was no more than five minutes away, reached by a narrow country lane along which she drove expertly at considerable speed. It stood in about an acre of well-tended garden surrounded by beech trees through which one could see the bay far below. It was Victorian from the look of it, with long narrow windows and green shutters at the front and a portico at the entrance. The door was opened instantly as we went up the steps by a tall, somber-looking man in a black alpaca jacket. He had silver hair and wore steel-rimmed glasses.

"Ah, Vito," she said as he took her coat. "This is Professor Stacey."

"Professore." He bowed slightly.

"We'll have coffee in the library later," she said. "I'll see to the drinks."

"Of course, Contessa."

He turned away and paused and spoke to her in Italian. She shook her head and answered fluently in the same language. He went through a door at the rear of the hall.

"Contessa?" I asked.

"Oh, don't listen to Vito." She dismissed my query politely, but firmly. "He's a terrible snob. This way."

The hall was cool and pleasant. Black and white tiled floor, a curving staircase and two or three oil paintings on the wall. Eighteenth-century seascapes. She opened a double mahogany door and led the way into a large library. The walls were lined with books, and French windows looked out to the garden. There was an Adam fireplace with a fire burning brightly in the basket grate and a grand piano, the top crammed with photos, mostly in silver frames.

"Scotch all right for you?" she asked.

"Fine."

She crossed to a sideboard and busied herself at the drinks tray. "How did you know who I was?" I asked. "Canon Cullen?"

"I've known about you since you started work on Harry." She handed me a glass.

"Who told you?"

"Oh, friends," she said. "From the old days. The kind who get to know things."

It made me think of Tony Bianco, my CIA contact at the embassy, and I was immediately excited. "Nobody seems to want to answer any of my questions at the Ministry of Defence."

"I don't suppose they would."

"And yet they release the body to you. You must have influence?"

"You could say that." She took a cigarette from a silver box, lit it and sat in a wing chair by the fire, crossing slim legs. "Have you ever heard of SOE, Professor?"

"Of course," I said. "Special Operations Executive. Set up by British Intelligence in 1940 on Churchill's instructions to coordinate resistance and the underground movement in Europe."

" 'Set Europe ablaze,' that's what the old man ordered." Sarah Drayton flicked ash in the fire. "I worked for them."

I was astonished. "But you can't have been more than a child."

"Nineteen," she said. "In 1944."

"And Martineau?"

"Look on the piano," she said. "The end photo in the silver frame."

I crossed to the piano and picked the photo up and her face jumped out at me, strangely unchanged except in one respect. Her hair was startlingly blond and marcelled—that's the term I think they used to use. She wore a little black hat and one of those coats from the wartime period with big shoulders and tight at the waist. She also wore silk stockings and high-heeled shoes and clutched a black patent-leather bag.

The man standing next to her was of medium height and wore a leather military trenchcoat over a tweed suit, hands thrust deep into the pockets. His face was shadowed by a dark slouch hat and a cigarette dangled from the corner of his mouth. The eyes were dark, no expression to them at all, and his smile had a kind of ruthless charm. He looked a thoroughly dangerous man.

Sarah Drayton got up and joined me. "Not much like the Croxley Professor of Moral Philosophy at Oxford there, is he?"

"Where was it taken?" I asked.

"In Jersey. Not too far from here. May nineteen forty-four. The tenth, I think."

"But I've been in Jersey long enough to know that it was occupied by the Germans at that time," I said.

"Very much so."

"And Martineau was here? With you?"

She crossed to a Georgian desk, opened a drawer and took out a small folder. When she opened it I saw at once that it contained several old photographs. She passed one to me. "This one I don't keep on top of the piano for obvious reasons."

She was dressed pretty much as she had been in the other photo and Martineau wore the same leather trenchcoat. The only difference was the SS uniform underneath, the silver death's-head badge in his cap. "Standartenführer Max Vogel," she said. "Colonel, to you. He looks rather dashing, doesn't he?" She smiled as she took it from me. "He had a weakness for uniforms, Harry."

"Dear God," I said. "What is all this?"

She didn't answer, but simply passed me another photo. It was faded slightly, but still perfectly clear. A group of German officers. In front of them stood two men on their own. One was Martineau in the SS uniform, but it was the other who took my breath away. One of the best-known faces of the Second World War. Field Marshal Erwin Rommel. The Desert Fox himself.

I said, "Was that taken here too?"

"Oh yes." She put the photos back in the desk and picked up my glass. "I think you could do with another drink."

"Yes. I believe I could."

She got me one, handed the glass to me, and we moved to the fire. She took a cigarette from the box. "I should stop, I suppose. Too late now. Another bad habit Harry taught me."

"Do I get an explanation?"

"Why not?" she said, and turned as rain drummed against the French windows. "I can't think of anything better to do on an afternoon like this, can you?"

LONDON 1944

2

IT STARTED, IF ONE can ever be certain where anything starts, with a telephone call received by Brigadier Dougal Munro at his flat in Haston Place, ten minutes' walk from the London headquarters of SOE in Baker Street. As head of Section D at SOE he had two phones by his bed, one routed straight through to his office. It was this that brought him awake at four o'clock on the morning of April 28, 1944.

He listened, face grave, then swore softly. "I'll be right over. One thing, check if Eisenhower is in town."

Within five minutes he was letting himself out of the front door, shivering in the damp cold, lighting the first cigarette of the day as he hurried along the deserted street. He was at that time sixty-five, a squat, powerful-looking man with white hair, his round, ugly face set off by steel-rimmed spectacles. He wore an old Burberry raincoat and carried an umbrella.

There was very little of the military in either his bearing or his appearance, which was hardly surprising. His rank of brigadier was simply to give him the necessary authority in certain quarters. Until 1939, Dougal Munro had been an archaeologist by profession. An Egyptologist, to be more precise, and fellow of All Souls at Oxford.

For three years now, head of Section D at SOE. What was commonly referred to in the trade as the dirty tricks department.

He turned in at the entrance of Baker Street, nodded to the night guard and went straight upstairs. When he went into his office, Captain Jack Carter, his night duty officer, was seated behind his desk. Carter had a false leg, a legacy of Dunkirk. He reached for his stick and started to get up.

"No, stay where you are, Jack," Munro told him. "Is there any tea?"

"Thermos flask on the map table, sir."

Munro unscrewed the flask, poured a cup and drank. "God, that's foul, but at least it's hot. Right, get on with it."

Carter now got up and limped across. There was a map of the southwest of England on the table, concentrating mainly on Devon, Cornwall and the general area of the English Channel.

"Exercise Tiger, sir," he said. "You remember the details?"

"Simulated landings for Overlord."

"That's right. Here in Lyme Bay in Devon there's a place called Slapton Sands. It bears enough similarities to the beach we've designated Utah in the Normandy landings to make it invaluable for training purposes. Most of the young Americans going in have no combat experience."

"I know that, Jack," Munro said. "Go on."

"Last night's convoy consisted of eight landing craft. Five from Plymouth and three from Brixham. Under naval escort, of course. They were to do a practice beach landing at Slapton."

There was a pause. Munro said, "Tell me the worst."

"They were attacked at sea by German E-boats, we think the Fifth and Ninth Schnellboote Flotillas from Cherbourg."

"And the damage?"

"Two landing craft sunk for certain. Others torpedoed and damaged."

"And the butcher's bill?"

"Difficult to be accurate at the moment. Around two hundred sailors and four hundred and fifty soldiers."

Munro said. "Are you trying to tell me we lost six hundred and fifty American servicemen last night? Six hundred and fifty and we haven't even started the invasion of Europe?"

"I'm afraid so."

Munro walked restlessly across the room and stood at the window. "Has Eisenhower been told?"

"He's in town, sir, at Hayes Lodge. He wants to see you at breakfast. Eight o'clock."

"And he'll want the facts." Munro turned and went to his desk. "Were there any Bigots among those officers lost?"

"Three, sir."

"Dear God, I warned them. I warned them about this," Munro said. "No Bigot to in any way undertake hazardous duty."

Some months previously it had become regrettably clear that there were serious breaches of security, in some cases by high-ranking American officers, in connection with the projected invasion of Europe. The Bigot procedure had been brought in as an answer to the situation. It was an intelligence classification above Most Secret. Bigots knew what others did not—the details of the Allied invasion of Europe.

"The three are missing so far," Carter said. "I've got their files."

He laid them on the desk and Munro examined them quickly. "Stupid," he said. "Unbelievably stupid. Take this man, Colonel Hugh Kelso."

"The engineering officer?" Carter said. "He's already visited two of the Normandy beaches by night, courtesy of Four Commando, to check on the suitability of the terrain for vehicles."

"Sword Beach and Utah Beach." Munro groaned. "For God's sake, Jack, what if he was picked up by one of those E-boats? He could be in enemy hands right now. And they'll make him talk if they want to, you know that."

"I don't think it's likely that any of those missing were picked up by the Germans, sir. The captain of the destroyer *Saladin,* which was one of the escorts, said the E-boats attacked at a range of fifteen hundred meters, then got the hell out of it fast. Typical hit and run. A lot of darkness and confusion on both sides. And the weather isn't too good. Wind force five to six and freshening, but I'm informed that the way the currents are in Lyme Bay, most of the bodies will come ashore. Already started."

"Most, Jack, most." Munro tapped the map on the table. "The Germans know we're coming. They're expecting the invasion. They're ready for it. Hitler's put Rommel himself in charge of all coastal fortifications. But they don't know where and they don't know when." He shook his head, staring down at the map. "Wouldn't it be ironic if the greatest invasion in history had to be called off because one man with all the right information fell into the wrong hands."

"Not likely, sir, believe me," Carter said gently. "This Colonel Kelso will come in on the tide with the rest of them."

"God help me, but I pray that he does, Jack. I pray that he does," Dougal Munro said fervently.

But at that precise moment, Colonel Hugh Kelso was very much alive, more afraid than he had ever been in his life, cold and wet and in terrible pain. He lay huddled in the bottom of a life raft in several inches of water about a mile offshore from the Devon coast, a contrary current carrying him fast toward Start Point on the southernmost tip of Lyme Bay, and beyond Start Point were the open waters of the English Channel.

Kelso was forty-two, married with two daughters. A civil engineer, he had been managing director of the family firm of construction engineers in New York for several years and had a high reputation in the field. Which was why he'd been drafted into the Engineering Corps in 1942 with the immediate rank of major. His experience with the engineering problems involved in beach landings on various islands in the South Pacific had earned him a promotion and a transfer to SHAEF Headquarters in England to work on the preparation for the invasion of Europe.

He'd taken part in Exercise Tiger on the request of the commanding officer for one reason only. The American 1st Engineer Special Brigade was one of the units assigned to take the beach designated as Utah during the coming Normandy landings, and Hugh Kelso had actually visited Utah Beach six weeks previously, under cover of darkness, guarded by British commandos. Slapton Sands was as close to the terrain as they could get. It had seemed sensible to seek his opinion, which was why he'd sailed on LST 31 from Plymouth.

Like everyone on board, Kelso had been taken totally by surprise by the attack. A considerable number of flares had been noticed in the distance which had been assumed to be from British MTBs. And then the first torpedo had struck and the night had become a living hell of burning oil and screaming men. Although Kelso didn't know it then, 413 men were killed from LST 31 alone. In his own case, he was blown off his feet by the force of the explosion and slammed against a rail, toppling into the water. His life jacket kept him afloat, of course, but he lost consciousness, coming to his senses to find himself being towed through the icy water.

The flames were a hundred yards away and in the reflected light he was aware only of an oil-soaked face.

"You're okay, sir. Just hang on. There's a life raft here."

The life raft loomed out of the darkness. It was the new model of inflatable developed from Pacific experience. A round, fat orange sphere riding high in the water and intended to carry as many as ten men. There was a canopy on top to protect the occupants from wind and weather, the entrance flap standing open.

"I'll get you in, sir, then I'll go back for some more. Come on, up you go."

Kelso felt weak, but his unknown friend was strong and muscular. He pushed hard, shoving Kelso in headfirst through the flap. And then Kelso was aware of the pain in his right leg, like a living thing and worse than anything he had ever known. He screamed and fainted.

When he came to, he was numb with cold and it took him a few moments to work out where he was. There was no sign of his unknown friend. He felt around in the darkness, then peered out through the open flap. Spray dashed in his face. There was no light anywhere, only the dark and the wind and the sound of the sea running. He checked the luminous dial of his waterproof watch. It was almost five o'clock and then he remembered that these life rafts carried an emergency kit. As he turned to feel for it, the pain started in his leg again. He gritted his teeth as his hands found the emergency kit box and got the lid open.

There was a waterproof flashlight in a clip on the inside of the lid and he switched it on. He was alone, as he had thought, in the orange cave, about a foot of water slopping around him. His uniform trousers were badly torn below the right knee, and when he put his hand inside gingerly he could feel the raised edges of bone in several places.

There was a Verey pistol in the box and he fingered it for a moment. It seemed the obvious thing to send up one of its parachute distress flares, but then he paused, trying to make his tired brain think straight. What if the German naval units that had attacked them were still in the area? What if it was the enemy that picked him up? He couldn't take that chance. He was, after all, a Bigot. In a matter of weeks an armada of six thousand ships would sail across the narrow waters of the English Channel and Kelso knew time and place. No, better to wait until dawn.

The leg was really hurting now and he rummaged in the box and found the medical kit with its morphine ampules. He jabbed one in his leg and, after a moment's hesitation, used another. Then he found the bailer and wearily started to throw water out through the open flap. God, but he was tired. Too much morphine perhaps, but at least the pain had dulled and he dropped the bailer and pulled the plastic zip at the entrance and leaned back and was suddenly asleep.

On his right, a few hundred yards away, was Start Point. For a while he seemed to be drifting toward the rocks and then a contrary current pulled him away. Ten minutes later, the life raft passed that final point of land and a freshening wind drove it out into the cold waters of the English Channel.

Eisenhower was seated in the Regency bow window of the library at Hayes Lodge having breakfast of poached eggs, toast and coffee when the young aide showed Dougal Munro in.

"Leave us, Captain," the general said and the aide withdrew. "Difficult to smile this morning, Brigadier."

"I'm afraid so."

"Have you eaten?"

"I haven't eaten breakfast for years, General."

For a moment, Eisenhower's face was illuminated by that famous and inimitable smile. "Which shows you aren't an old military hand. You prefer tea, don't you?"

"Yes, General."

"You'll find it on the sideboard behind you—special order. Help yourself, then tell me what you know of this wretched business. My own people have already given me their version, but I've always had considerable respect for your people at SOE, you know that."

Munro helped himself to the tea and sat in the window seat and gave Eisenhower a brief resume of the night's events.

"But surely the naval escorts should have been able to prevent such a thing happening," the general said. "On the other hand, I hear the weather wasn't too good. It's past belief. I visited Slapton myself only three days ago to see how the exercises were going. Went down by special train with Tedder and Omar Bradley."

"Most of the crews of your LSTs are new to those waters, and the English Channel at the best of times can be difficult." Munro shrugged. "We've had torpedo boats from the Royal Navy hanging around off Cherbourg regularly during these exercises because Cherbourg, as the General knows, is the most important E-boat base on the French coast. There was a sea mist and the Germans obviously slipped out with their silencers on and probably with their radar sets switched off. They do more than forty knots, those things. Nothing afloat that's faster and they boxed rather cleverly on their approach. Fired off parachute flares so the people in the convoy assumed they were ours."

"Goddammit, you never assume anything in this game. I'm tired of telling people that." Eisenhower poured another coffee, stood up and went to the fire. "Bodies coming ashore by the hundred, so they tell me."

"I'm afraid so."

"Needless to say, this whole thing stays under wraps. We're going to arrange for some kind of mass grave down there in Devon for the time being. At least it's a defense area under military rule, which should help. If this got out, so close to the invasion, it could have a terrible effect on morale."

"I agree." Munro hesitated and said carefully, "There is the question of the Bigots, General."

"Who should never have been there in the first place. No one knows the regulations on Bigots better than you."

"It could be worse, sir. There were three in all. Two of the bodies have already been recovered. The third, this man." Munro took a file from his briefcase and pushed it across. "Is still missing."

Eisenhower read the file quickly. "Colonel Hugh Kelso." His face darkened. "But I know Kelso personally. He checked out two beaches in Normandy only weeks ago."

"Utah and Sword. On those occasions he had commandos nursing him and he also had an L pill with him, just in case he was caught. As the General knows, the cyanide in those things kills instantaneously."

Eisenhower pushed the file across. "He knows, Brigadier, both when we're going and where. The implications are past belief."

"We've men on the beaches around Slapton looking for him now, General. I've little reason to doubt that his body will turn up with the rest of them."

"Don't try to make me feel good," Eisenhower told him sharply. "Some of those bodies will never come in on the tide. I know that and so do you, and if Kelso is one of them, we can never be certain that he wasn't picked up by the enemy."

"That's true, General," Munro admitted because there wasn't really anything else he could say.

Eisenhower walked to the window. Rain dashed against the pane. "What a day," he said morosely. "One thing's for sure. I can only think of one man who'll have a smile on his face this morning."

At that very moment Adolf Hitler was reading a report on the Slapton Sands affair in the map room of his underground headquarters known as Wolf's Lair, near Rastenburg, deep in the forests of East Prussia.

Most of those important in the Nazi hierarchy were present. Heinrich Himmler, Reichsführer of the SS and Chief of both State and Secret Police, Josef Goebbels, Reichsminister for Propaganda, Reichsleiter Martin Bormann, Secretary to the Führer among other things, and Oberführer Rattenhuber, Himmler's Chief of Security and Commander of the SS guard at Rastenburg.

Hitler almost danced with delight and crumpled the thin paper of the message in one hand. "So, our Navy can still strike, and hard, right in the enemy's own backyard! Three ships sunk, and hundreds of casualties." His eyes sparked. "A bad morning for General Eisenhower, gentlemen."

There was general enthusiasm. "Good news indeed, my Führer," Goebbels said and delivered his usual high laugh.

Bormann, who had been the first to see the message, said quietly, "If we can do this to them off the coast of Devon, my Führer, all things are possible off the coast of France."

"They won't even get ashore," Himmler put in.

"Probably not," Hitler said, in high good humor. "But now, gentlemen, to the purpose of our meeting." They grouped around the circular table and he tapped the large-scale map of France. "The Westwall proceeds, I think." He turned to Bormann. "The report on Army Group B which I asked for? Has it arrived?"

Bormann turned inquiringly to Rattenhuber who said, "I've just had a report from the airfield. The courier, a Captain Koenig, landed five minutes ago. He's on his way."

"Good." Hitler seemed abstracted now, as if somehow alone as he stared down at the map. "So, gentlemen, where do we start?"

On December 26, 1943, a remarkable and gifted young German officer, Colonel Klaus von Stauffenberg, reported for a meeting at Rastenburg with a time bomb in his briefcase. Unfortunately, the meeting did not take place, as the Führer had already departed for Bavaria for the Christmas holiday. In spite of having lost his left eye and right hand in action, von Stauffenberg was Chief of Staff to General Olbricht of the General Army Office and the center of a conspiracy of army generals whose aim was to assassinate the Führer and save Germany from disaster.

His own abortive attempt at Christmas 1943 was only one of many that had failed. Yet there was no shortage of volunteers to the cause, as witness Captain Karl Koenig traveling in the rear of the military car from the airfield to Wolf's Lair on that gray April morning with the papers from Berlin that Hitler had requested. He was in a highly nervous state, which was hardly surprising when one considered the time bomb carefully placed in the false bottom of the briefcase. He had told the pilot at Rastenburg airfield to be ready for a quick turnaround and his fingers trembled as he lit a cigarette.

The SS driver and guard in front stared woodenly ahead, and as time passed, Koenig's nervousness increased. There were minefields on either side in the gloomy woods, electric fences, guards patrolling everywhere with savage dogs and three gates to pass through to reach the inner compound. Still, time to arm the bomb. Once done, it would give him exactly thirty minutes, they had told him.

He reached for the lock on the left-hand strap of the briefcase and depressed it. There was an immediate and very powerful explosion which killed Koenig and the two guards instantly and blew the car apart.

Hitler was beside himself with rage, pacing up and down in the map room. "Again and yet again they try." He turned on Rattenhuber. "And you, Oberführer? What about you? Sworn to protect my personal safety."

"My Führer," Rattenhuber stammered. "What can I say?"

"Nothing!" Hitler stormed and turned on the rest of them. "You say nothing of use to me—not any of you."

In the shocked silence, it was Himmler who spoke, his voice dry and precise. "That there has been negligence here is true, my Führer, but surely we see further proof, in the failure of this dastardly attempt, of the certainty of your own destiny. Further proof of Germany's inevitable victory under your inspired guidance."

Hitler's eyes blazed, his head went back. "As always, Reichsführer, you see. The only one who does." He turned on the others. "Get out, all of you. I wish to talk to the Reichsführer alone."

They went without a murmur, Goebbels the last one to leave. Hitler stood staring down at the map desk, hands clasped behind him. "In what way may I serve my Führer?" Himmler asked.

"There is a plot, am I not right?" Hitler said. "A general conspiracy to destroy me, and this Captain Koenig was simply an agent?"

"Not so much a general conspiracy as a conspiracy of generals, my Führer."

Hitler turned sharply. "Are you certain?"

"Oh, yes, but proof—that is something else."

Hitler nodded. "Koenig was an aide of General Olbricht. Is Olbricht one of those you suspect?" Himmler nodded. "And the others?"

"Generals Stieff, Wagner, von Hase, Lindemann. Several more, all being closely watched."

Hitler stayed remarkably cool. "Traitors each and every one. No firing squad. A noose each when the time comes. No one higher, though? It would seem our field marshals are loyal at least."

"I wish I could confirm that, my Führer, but there is one who is heavily suspect. I would be failing in my duty not to tell you."

"Then tell me."

"Rommel."

Hitler smiled a ghastly smile that was almost one of triumph, turned and walked away and turned again, still smiling. "I think I expected it. Yes, I'm sure I did. So, the Desert Fox wishes to play games."

"I'm almost certain of it."

"The people's hero," Hitler said. "We must handle him carefully, wouldn't you say?"

"Or outfox him, my Führer," Himmler said softly.

"Outfox him. Outfox the Desert Fox." Hitler smiled delightedly. "Yes, I like that, Reichsführer. I like that very much indeed."

Hugh Kelso slept until noon and when he awakened, he was sick. He turned over in the violently pitching life raft and pulled down the zip of the entrance flap. His heart sank. There was nothing but sea, the life raft twisting and turning on the angry waves. The sky was black, heavy with rain and the wind was gusting 5 or 6, he could tell that. Worst of all, there wasn't a hint of land anywhere. He was well out in the English Channel, so much was obvious. If he drifted straight across, wasn't picked up at all, he'd hit the coast of France, possibly the Cherbourg Peninsula. Below that, in the Gulf of St. Malo, were the Channel Islands. Alderney, Guernsey and Jersey. He didn't know much about them except that they were British and occupied by the enemy. He was not likely to be carried as far south as that, though.

He got the Verey light out, and fired an orange distress flare. There was seldom any German naval traffic in the Channel during daylight. They tended to keep to the inshore run behind their minefields. He fired another flare and then water cascaded in through the flap and he hurriedly zipped it up. There were some field rations in the emergency kit. He tried to eat one of the dried fruit blocks and was violently sick and his leg was on fire again. Hurriedly, he got another morphine ampule and injected himself. After a while, he pillowed his head on his hands and slept again.

Outside, the sea lifted as the afternoon wore on. It started to get dark soon after five o'clock. By that time the wind was blowing sou'westerly, turning him away from the French coast and the Cherbourg Peninsula so that by six o'clock he was ten miles to the west of the Casquets Light off the island of Alderney. And then the wind veered again, pushing him down along the outer edge of the Gulf of St. Malo toward Guernsey.

Kelso was aware of none of these things. He awakened around seven o'clock with a high temperature, washed his face with a little water to cool it, was sick again and dropped into something approaching a coma.

In London, Dougal Munro was working at his desk, the slight scratching of his pen the only sound in the quiet of the room. There was a knock at the door and Jack Carter limped in with a folder in one hand. He put it down in front of Munro.

"Latest list from Slapton, sir."

"Anything on Kelso?"

"Not a thing, sir, but they've got every available ship out there in the bay looking for the missing bodies."

Dougal Munro got up and moved to the window. The wind moaned outside, hurling rain against the pane. He shook his head and said softly, "God help sailors at sea on a night like this."

3

AS COMMANDER OF ARMY Group B, Field Marshal Erwin Rommel was responsible for the Atlantic Wall defenses, his sole task to defeat any Allied attempt to land in northern France. Since taking command in January of 1944 he had strengthened the coastal defenses to an incredible degree, tramping the beaches, visiting every strongpoint, impressing his own energetic presence on everyone from divisional commanders to the lowliest private.

His headquarters seemed permanently on the move so that no one could be sure where he was from one day to the next. He had an uncomfortable habit of turning up in his familiar black Mercedes accompanied only by his driver and his most trusted aide from Afrika Korps days, Major Konrad Hofer.

On the evening of that fateful day at about the time Hugh Kelso was somewhere in the general area of the Casquets Light, west of Alderney, the field marshal was sitting down to an early dinner with the officers of the 21st Parachute Regiment in a chateau at Campeaux some ten miles from St. Lo in Normandy.

His primary reason for being there was sound enough. The High Command, and the Führer himself, believed that the invasion, when it came, would take place in the area of the Pas de Calais. Rommel disagreed and had made it clear that if he were Eisenhower, he would strike for Normandy. None of this had done anything for his popularity among the people who counted at OKW, High Command of the Armed Forces, in Berlin. Rommel didn't give a damn about that anymore. The war was lost. The only thing that was uncertain was how long it would take.

Which brought him to the second reason for being in Normandy. He was involved in a dangerous game and it paid to keep on the move, for since taking command of Army Group B he had renewed old friendships with General von Stulpnagel, military governor of France, and General Alexander von Falkenhausen. Both were involved, with von Stauffenberg, in the conspiracy against Hitler. It had not taken them long to bring Rommel around to their point of view.

They had all been aware of the projected assassination attempt at Rastenburg that morning. Rommel had sent Konrad Hofer by air to Berlin the previous day to await events at General Olbricht's headquarters, but there had been no news at all. Not a hint of anything untoward on the radio.

Now, in the mess, Colonel Haider, commanding the regiment, stood to offer the loyal toast. "Gentlemen—to our Führer and total victory."

"So many young men," Rommel thought to himself, "and what for?" But he raised his glass and drank with them.

"And now, Field Marshal Erwin Rommel, the Desert Fox himself, who does our mess so much honor tonight."

They drained their glasses, then applauded him, cheering wildly, and Rommel was immensely touched. Colonel Haider said, "The men have arranged a little entertainment in your honor, Field Marshal. We were hoping you might be willing to attend."

"But of course." Rommel held out his glass for more champagne. "Delighted."

The door opened at the back of the mess and Konrad Hofer entered. He looked tired and badly needed a shave, his field gray greatcoat buttoned up to his neck.

"Ah, Konrad, there you are," Rommel called. "Come and have a glass of champagne. You look as if you could do with it."

"I've just flown in from Berlin, Field Marshal. Landed at St. Lo."

"Good flight?"

"Terrible, actually." Hofer swallowed the champagne gratefully.

"My dear boy, come and have a shower and we'll see if they can manage you a sandwich." Rommel turned to Colonel Haider. "See if you can delay this little show the men are putting on for half an hour."

"No problem, Field Marshal."

"Good—we'll see you later then." Rommel picked up a fresh bottle of champagne and two glasses and walked out followed by Hofer.

As soon as the bedroom door was closed, Hofer turned in agitation. "It was the worst kind of mess. All that fool Koenig managed to do was blow himself up outside the main gate."

"That seems rather careless of him," Rommel said dryly. "Now calm yourself, Konrad. Have another glass of champagne and get under the shower and just take it slowly."

Hofer went into the bathroom and Rommel straightened his uniform, examining himself in the mirror. He was fifty-three at that time, of medium height, stocky and thick-set with strong features, and there was a power to the man, a force, that was almost electric. His uniform was simple enough, his only decorations the Pour le Mérite, the famous Blue Max, won as a young infantry officer in the First World War, and the Knight's Cross with Oak Leaves, Swords and Diamonds, both of which hung around his neck. On the other hand, one hardly needed anything else if one had those.

Hofer emerged in a bathrobe toweling his hair. "Olbricht and a few more up there are in a blue funk and I don't blame them. I mean the Gestapo or the SD could be on to this at any time."

"Yes," Rommel conceded. "Himmler may have started life as a chicken farmer, but whatever else you may say about him he's no fool. How was von Stauffenberg?"

"As determined as ever. He suggests you meet with Generals von Stulpnagel and Falkenhausen within the next few days."

"I'll see what I can do."

Hofer was back in the bathroom pulling on his uniform again. "I'm not so sure it's a good idea. If Himmler does have his suspicions about you, you could be under close surveillance already."

"Oh, I'll think of something," Rommel said. "Now hurry up. The men are laying on a little show for me and I don't want to disappoint them."

The show was presented in the main hall of the chateau. A small stage had been rigged at one end with some makeshift curtains. Rommel, Hofer and the regimental officers sat down in chairs provided at the front; the men stood in the hall behind them or sat on the grand staircase.

A young corporal came on, bowed and sat down at the grand piano and played a selection of light music. There was polite applause. Then he moved into the song of the Fallschirmjäger, the paratroopers' own song, sung everywhere from Stalingrad to North Africa. The curtains parted to reveal the regimental choir singing lustily. There was a cheer from the back of the hall and everyone started to join in, including the officers. Without pause, the choir moved straight into several choruses of *We March Against England,* an unfortunate choice, Rommel told himself. It was interesting to note that no one tried singing the *Horst Wessel.* The curtain came down to a storm of cheering and several instrumentalists came on, grouped themselves around the pianist and played two or three jazz numbers. When they were finished, the lights went down and there was a pause.

"What's happening?" Rommel demanded.

"Wait and see, Herr Field Marshal. Something special, I assure you."

The pianist started to play the song that was most popular of all with the German forces, *Lili Marlene.* The curtains parted to reveal only a pool of light on a stool in the center of the stage from a crude spotlight. Suddenly, Marlene Dietrich stepped into the light straight out of *Blue Angel,* or so it seemed. Top hat, black stockings and suspenders. She sat on the stool to a chorus of wolf whistles from the men and then she started to sing *Lili Marlene,* and that haunting, bittersweet melody reduced the audience to total silence.

A man, of course, Rommel could see that, but a brilliant impersonation and he joined in the applause enthusiastically. "Who on earth is that?" he asked Colonel Haider.

"Our orderly room corporal, Berger. Apparently he used to be some sort of cabaret performer."

"Brilliant," Rommel said. "Is there more?"

"Oh, yes, Herr Field Marshal. Something very special."

The instrumentalists returned and the choir joined them in a few more numbers. There was another pause when they departed and then a steady, muted drum roll. The curtain rose to reveal subdued lighting. As the choir started to sing the song of the Afrika Korps from the side of the stage, Rommel walked on. And it was quite unmistakably he. The cap with the desert goggles, the white scarf carelessly knotted at the neck, the old leather greatcoat, the field marshal's baton in one gloved hand, the other arrogantly on the hip. The voice, when he spoke, was perfect as he delivered a few lines of his famous battlefield speech before El Alamein.

"I know I haven't offered you much. Sand, heat and scorpions, but we've shared them together. One more push and it's Cairo, and if we fail... well, we tried—together."

There was total silence from the body of the hall as Colonel Haider glanced anxiously at Rommel. "Field Marshal, I hope you're not offended."

"Offended? I think he's marvelous," Rommel said and jumped to his feet. "Bravo!" he called and started to clap and behind him, the entire audience joined in with the chorus of the Afrika Korps song, cheering wildly.

In the makeshift dressing room next to the kitchen, Erich Berger slumped into a chair and stared at himself in the mirror. His heart was beating and he was sweating. A hell of a thing for any actor to perform in front of the man he was taking off, and such a man. A name to conjure with. The most popular soldier in Germany.

"Not bad, Heini," he said softly. "Mazel tov." He took a bottle of schnapps from the drawer, drew the cork and swallowed some.

A Yiddish phrase on the lips of a corporal in a German Fallschirm-jäger regiment might have seemed strange to anyone who had overheard. His secret was that he wasn't Erich Berger at all, but Heini Baum, Jewish actor and cabaret performer from Berlin and proud of it.

His story was surprisingly simple. He had performed with success in cabaret all over Europe. He had never married. To be frank, his inclinations ran more toward men than women. He had persisted in living in Berlin, even as the Nazis came to power, because his aging parents had always lived there and would not believe that anything terrible could ever happen. Which it did, of course, though not for a long time. As an entertainer, Baum was of use to the Reich. He still had to wear his Star of David on his coat, but a series of special permits kept him afloat and his parents with him, while all around them their friends were taken away.

And then there was the fateful night in 1940 when he had arrived at the end of his street, coming home from cabaret, in time to see the Gestapo taking his mother and father from their house. He had turned and run, like the coward he was, pausing only in a side street to tear the Star of David from his coat. He was forty-four years of age and looked ten years younger on a good day. Nowhere to go, for his papers told the world he was a Jew.

So, he'd caught a train to Kiel with the wild idea that he might be able to get a ship from there to somewhere—anywhere. He'd arrived just after one of the first of the devastating RAF raids on that city, had stumbled through the chaos and flames of the city center, searching for shelter as the RAF came back for a second go. Lurching down into a cellar, he'd found a man and a woman and a twelve-year-old girl dead, all from the same family he learned when he examined their identity cards. Erich Berger, his wife and daughter. And one thing more. In Berger's pocket were his call-up papers, ordering him to report the following week.

What better hiding place could a Jew who was afraid to be a Jew find? Sure, he was ten years older than Berger, but it wouldn't show. To change the photos on the two identity cards was simple enough so that the body he dragged out to leave in the rubble of the street to be found later was that of Heini Baum, Jew of Berlin. It had been necessary to obliterate most of the dead man's face with a brick, just to help things along, but after what he'd been through that part was easy.

How ironic that it was the paratroops he'd been inducted into. He'd been everywhere. Crete, Stalingrad, North Africa, a nice flashy hero in his Luftwaffe blouse and baggy paratroopers' pants and jump boots, with the Iron Cross Second and First Class to prove it. He took another pull at the schnapps bottle, and behind him the door opened and Rommel, Colonel Haider and Hofer entered.

It was midnight and Hugh Kelso had never been happier, up at Cape Cod at the summer bungalow, sitting on the veranda in the swing seat, reading a book, a cool glass to his hand and Jane, his wife, was calling, on her way up from the beach, her face shaded by a sun hat, the good legs tanned under the old cotton dress, and the girls in swimming suits and carrying buckets and spades, voices faint on the warm afternoon air. Everyone so happy. So very happy. He didn't feel cold anymore, didn't really feel anything. He reached out to take Jane's hand as she came up the steps to the veranda and the voices faded and he came awake, shaking all over.

It was pitch dark and the sea wasn't as rough, and yet he seemed to be moving very fast. He pulled down the zip on the flap with stiff fingers and peered out. Only a slight phosphorescence as the water turned over and a vast darkness. His eyes were weary, sore from the salt water. For a wild moment he thought he saw a light out there. He shook his head, closed then opened his eyes again. A mistake, of course. Only the never-ending night. He zipped up the flap, lay back and closed his eyes, trying to think of Jane and his two daughters. Perhaps they would come back again?

Although he didn't know it, he had already drifted something like seventy miles since leaving Lyme Bay on the Devon coast and his eyes had not deceived him. What he had just seen through the darkness was a momentary flash of light as a sentry at the German guard post on Pleinmont Point on the southwest corner of the island of Guernsey had opened a door to go out on duty. To the southeast, perhaps thirty miles away, was Jersey, the largest of the Channel Islands. It was in this general direction that the freshening wind bore him as he slept on.

Rommel leaned on the mantelpiece and stirred the fire with his boot. "So, the others would like me to talk with von Stulpnagel and Falkenhausen?"

"Yes, Herr Field Marshal," Hofer said. "But as you point out, one must take things very carefully at the moment. For such a meeting, secrecy would be essential."

"And opportunity," Rommel said. "Secrecy and opportunity." The clock on the mantelpiece chimed twice and he laughed. "Two o'clock in the morning. The best time for crazy ideas."

"What are you suggesting, Herr Field Marshal?"

"Quite simple, really. What is it now, Saturday? What if we arranged a meeting next week at some agreed rendezvous with von Stulpnagel and Falkenhausen while I was actually supposed to be somewhere else? Jersey, for example?"

"The Channel Islands?" Hofer looked bewildered.

"The Führer himself suggested not two months ago that I inspect the fortifications there. You know my feelings about the military importance of the islands. The Allies will never attempt a landing. It would cause too many civilian casualties. British civilian casualties, I might add."

"And yet they tie up the 319 Infantry Division," Hofer said. "Six thousand troops in Jersey alone. Ten thousand service personnel in all, if you include Luftwaffe and Navy people."

"And yet we've poured so much into them, Konrad, because the Führer wants to hang onto the only piece of British territory we've ever occupied. The strongest fortifications in the world. The same number of strongpoints and batteries as we have to defend the entire European coast from Dieppe to St. Nazaire." He turned and smiled. "The Führer is right. As commander of the Atlantic Wall, I should certainly inspect such an important part of it."

Hofer nodded. "I see that, Herr Field Marshal, but what I don't see is how you can be in two places at once. Meeting with Falkenhausen and Stulpnagel in France and inspecting fortifications in Jersey."

"But you saw me in two places earlier this evening," Rommel said calmly, "both in the audience and on stage at the same time."

The room was so quiet that Hofer could hear the clock ticking. "My God," he whispered. "Are you serious?"

"Why not? Friend Berger even fooled me when he came on stage. The voice, the appearance."

"But would he be intelligent enough to carry it off? There are so many things he wouldn't know how to handle. I mean, being a Field Marshal is rather different from being an orderly room clerk," Hofer said.

"He seems intelligent enough to me," Rommel told him. "He's obviously talented and a brave soldier to boot. Iron Cross First and Second Class. And you mustn't forget one important thing."

"What's that, Herr Field Marshal?"

"He'd have you at his shoulder every step of the way to keep him straight." Suddenly Rommel sounded impatient. "Where's your enthusiasm, Konrad? If you're that worried, I'll give you a few days to prepare him. Let's see, it's Saturday now. How about descending on Jersey next Friday. I'm only thinking of thirty-six hours or so. Back in France on Saturday night or Sunday at the latest. If Berger can't carry it off for that length of time, I'll eat my hat."

"Very well, Herr Field Marshal. I'll notify the Channel Islands that you'll be arriving next Friday."

"No, you won't," Rommel said. "We box more cleverly than that. Who's the commander-in-chief?"

"Major General Count von Schmettow. His headquarters are in Guernsey."

"I've met him," Rommel said. "Good officer."

"With a reputation for being pro-English, which didn't do him any good in some quarters," Hofer said.

"On the other hand, the fact that he's Field Marshal von Rundstedt's nephew certainly helped there. Who's military commander in Jersey?"

"I'll check." Hofer took a file from his briefcase and worked his way down a unit situation list. "Yes, here we are. Colonel Heine is military commander."

"And civil administration?"

'The important people there are Colonel Baron von Aufsess and Captain Heider."

"And the inhabitants themselves? Who are their representatives?"

'There's an organization called the Superior Council of the States of Jersey. The president is the bailiff of the island. A man called Alexander Coutanche."

"Good," said Rommel. "This is what we do. Send General von Schmettow a signal ordering him to hold a coordinating meeting in Guernsey to consider the implications for the islands of the invasion of France threatened this summer."

"And you want them all there?"

"Oh, yes. Military commander Jersey, the civil affairs people, the bailiff and his lot, and whoever's in charge of the Navy and Luftwaffe contingents in the islands."

"Which will leave only junior officers in command."

"Exactly."

"There's not too much flying in and out of the Channel Islands these days. The RAF are far too active in that area. It's usual to travel between the islands by sea and at night."

"I know," Rommel said. "I've taken advice on that point from Naval Headquarters in Cherbourg. Tell von Schmettow to call his meeting for next Saturday. In the circumstances they must travel either Thursday night or in the early hours of Friday to make sure they get there. I'll fly in on Friday morning in the Storch."

"A risky flight, Herr Field Marshal."

"For you, Konrad, and Berger, of course, not for me." Rommel smiled with a kind of ruthless charm. "The first thing they'll know about my arrival is when you ask the tower for permission to land at the airfield."

"And what will von Schmettow think?"

"That the whole thing has been a deliberate ploy so that I can make a snap inspection of the military situation in the island and its defenses."

"That's really rather clever," Hofer said.

"Yes, I think it is." Rommel started to unbutton his tunic. "In the meantime, I'll meet with Falkenhausen and Stulpnagel at some quiet spot and get on with it." He yawned. "I think I'll go to bed. See that signal goes to von Schmettow in Guernsey tomorrow. Oh, and speak to Colonel Haider first thing in the morning. Tell him I'm much taken with Corporal Berger and want to borrow him for a while. I don't think he'll make any difficulties."

"I doubt it, Herr Field Marshal," Hofer said. "Sleep well," and he went out.

Dougal Munro slept on a small military bed in the corner of his office at Baker Street that night. It was about three o'clock in the morning when Jack Carter shook him gently awake. Munro opened his eyes instantly and sat up. "What is it?"

"Latest lists from Slapton, sir. You asked to see them. Still over a hundred bodies missing."

"And no sign of Kelso?"

"I'm afraid not. General Montgomery isn't too happy, but he has had an assurance from the Navy that the E-boats couldn't have picked survivors up. They were too far away."

"The trouble with life, Jack, is that the moment someone tells you something is impossible, someone else promptly proves that it isn't. What time is first light?"

"Just before six. That should make a big difference to the final search."

"Order a car for eight o'clock. We'll take a run down to Slapton and see for ourselves."

"Very well, sir. Are you going back to sleep?"

"No, I don't think so." Munro stood up and stretched. "Think I'll catch up on some paperwork. No peace for the wicked in this life, Jack."

At six o'clock on that same morning, Kelso came awake from a strange dream in which some primeval creature was calling to him from a great distance. He was very, very cold, feet and hands numb, and yet his face burned and there was sweat on his forehead.

He unzipped the flap and peered out into the gray light of dawn, not that there was anything much to see for he was shrouded in a sea fog of considerable density. Somewhere in the distance, the beast called again, only now he recognized it for what it was—a foghorn. Although he didn't know it, it was the Corbiere Light on the tip of the southernmost coast of Jersey, already behind him as the current swept him along. He sensed land, could almost smell it and, for a little while, came back to life again.

He could hear waves breaking on an unseen shore, and then the wind tore a hole in the curtain and he glimpsed cliffs, concrete gun emplacements on top. The place, although it meant nothing to Kelso, was Noirmont Point, and as the sea fog dropped back into place, the current carried him into St. Aubin's Bay, close inshore.

There were waves taking him in, strange, twisting currents carrying him round. At one side, a wave broke sending spray high in the air, and all around him was white foam, rocks showing through. And then there was a voice, high and clear, and the fog rolled away to reveal a small beach, rocks climbing steeply to a pine wood above. There was someone there, a man running along the shore, in woolen cap, heavy reefer coat and rubber boots.

The life raft slewed broadside in the surf, lifted high and smashed against rocks, pitching Kelso headfirst through the flap into the water. He tried to stand up, his scream as his right leg collapsed under him drowned by the roaring of the surf, and then the man was knee-deep in water, holding him. It was only then that he realized it was a woman.

"All right, I've got you. Just hang on."

"Leg," he mumbled. "Leg broken."

He wasn't sure what happened after that, and he came to in the shelter of some rocks. The woman was dragging the landing craft out of the water. When he tried to sit up, she turned and came toward him. Kelso said as she knelt down, "Where am I, France?"

"No," she said. "Jersey."

He closed his eyes for a moment and shivered. "You're British, then?"

"I should hope so. The last I heard of my husband, he was a major in the Tanks Corps serving in the Western Desert. My name's Helen de Ville."

"Colonel Hugh Kelso."

"American Air Force, I suppose? Where did your plane come down?"

"It didn't. I'm an army officer."

"An army officer? But that doesn't make sense. Where on earth have you come from?"

"England. I'm a survivor of a ship that was torpedoed in Lyme Bay." He groaned suddenly as pain knifed through his leg and almost lost his senses.

She opened his torn trouser leg and frowned. "That's terrible. You'll have to go to hospital."

"Will that mean Germans?"

"I'm afraid so."

He clutched at the front of her reefer coat. "No—no Germans."

She eased him back down. "Just lie still. I'm going to leave you for a little while. I'm going to need a cart."

"Okay," he said. "But no Germans. They mustn't get their hands on me. You must promise. If you can't do that, then you must kill me. See, there's a Browning pistol here."

He plucked at it and she leaned over him, face set, and took the pistol from its holster on his left thigh. "You're not going to die and the Jerries aren't going to have you either—that's the only promise I'm prepared to give. Now wait for me."

She slipped the pistol into her pocket, turned and hurried away. He lay there on that fog-shrouded shore, trying to get his bearings, and then the leg started to hurt again and he remembered the morphine in the emergency kit. He began to crawl toward the life raft. That, of course, was very definitely the final straw, and he plunged into darkness.

4

HELEN DE VILLE LEFT the cart track which was the usual way
down to the beach and took a shortcut, scrambling up the steep hillside through the pine trees. She was strong and wiry, not surprising
after four years of enemy occupation and the food restrictions that
had caused her to lose nearly thirty pounds in weight. She often joked
that it had given her back the figure she'd enjoyed at eighteen, an unlooked-for bonus at forty-two. And like most people, the lack of a car
and a public transport system meant she was used to walking many
miles each week.

She stood at the edge of the trees and looked across at the house.
De Ville Place was not one of the largest manors on the island. It had
been once in days of family glory, but a disastrous fire at the end of
the nineteenth century had destroyed one entire wing. It was very old,
constructed of Jersey granite weathered by the years. There were rows
of French windows at the front on either side of the entrance, a granite
wall dividing the house from a courtyard at one side.

She paused, taking her time, for there was an old Morris sedan
parked in the courtyard, one of those requisitioned by the enemy. For
two years now she'd had German naval officers billeted on her. They

came and went, of course, sometimes staying only a night or two when E-boats of the 5th Schnellboote Flotilla came over from Guernsey.

Mostly they were regulars, young officers serving with various naval units based in Jersey. The war took its toll. There were often engagements with British MTBs in the area of the Channel Islands, and the RAF frequently attacked convoys to Granville, St. Malo and Cherbourg, even when they made a night run. Men died, but some survived. As she started across the lawn, the door opened and one of them came out.

He wore a white sweater, old reefer coat and seaboots and carried a duffel bag in one hand. The face beneath the salt-stained naval cap was good-humored and recklessly handsome. A bravo, this one, straight out of the sixteenth century, who wore a white top to his cap, usually an affectation of German U-boat commanders, but then Lieutenant Guido Orsini was a law unto himself, an Italian on secondment to the German Navy, trapped in the wrong place at entirely the wrong time when the Italian government had capitulated. Helen de Ville had long since given up pretending that she felt anything but considerable affection for him.

"Morning, Guido."

"Helen, cara mia." He blew her a kiss. "I'm the last, as usual."

"Where to today?"

"Granville. Should be fun in this fog. On the other hand, it keeps the Tommies at home. Back tomorrow. Do you want to go into St. Helier? Can I give you a lift?"

"No thanks. I'm looking for Sean."

"I saw the good General not ten minutes ago coming out of the south barn with a felling axe and walking down toward his cottage. See you tomorrow. I must fly. Ciao, cara."

He went through the small gate to the courtyard. A moment later, she heard the Morris start up and drive away. She crossed the courtyard herself, went through a field gate and ran along the track through trees. Sean Gallagher's cottage stood by a stream in a hollow. She could see him now in old corduroy pants and riding boots, the sleeves of the checked shirt rolled up above muscular arms as he split logs.

"Sean!" she called and stumbled almost falling.

He lowered the axe and turned, pushing a lock of reddish brown hair from his eyes as he looked toward her. He dropped the axe and reached out to catch her as she almost fell again.

Sean Martin Gallagher was fifty-two and, as an Irish citizen, officially neutral in this war. He had been born in Dublin in 1892, his father a professor of surgery at Trinity College, a man who had taken no interest in women until, in his fiftieth year during a professional visit to Jersey, he had met a young nurse called Ruth le Brocq. He'd married her within a month and taken her back to Dublin.

She'd died in childbirth the following year and the boy Sean grew up spending the long summers each year in Jersey with his grandparents, the rest of the time in Dublin with his father. Sean's ambition was to be a writer, and he'd taken a degree in literature at his father's university, Trinity College. The exigencies of life made him a soldier, for as he finished college the First World War started.

He'd joined the Irish Fusiliers, a regiment that many Jerseymen served in, and by 1918 was a very old twenty-six. A major, twice wounded, and with an MC for gallantry on the Somme. As he used to say, any real experience of war came after that, fighting with the IRA in Ireland under Michael Collins' leadership, as commander of a flying column in County Mayo.

The treaty with the British government which had ended the conflict in 1922 had only proved a prelude to a bloody and vicious civil war between those elements of the IRA who refused to accept the treaty and those who chose to fight for the Irish Free State government under Collins. Sean Gallagher had chosen the Free State and found himself a general at the age of thirty, sweeping through the west of Ireland, ruthlessly hunting down old comrades.

Afterward, sick of killing, he'd traveled the world, living on money left to him by his father, writing the odd novel when he had a mind, finally settling in Jersey in 1930. Ralph de Ville had been a boyhood friend, and Helen he had loved desperately and hopelessly from the first moment they had met. His home in St. Lawrence, deep in the country, had been requisitioned by the Germans in 1940. Helen, with Ralph away serving with the British Army, needed a strong right arm, which explained his presence at the dower cottage on the estate. And he still loved her, of course, and still quite hopelessly.

The old cart had seen better days and the horse was considerably leaner than it should have been as they negotiated the track down to the beach, Sean Gallagher leading the horse, Helen at his side.

"If this goes wrong," he said gravely. "If they find out you're helping this man, it won't just be a prison sentence. It could mean a firing squad or one of those concentration camps they're talking about."

"And what about you?"

"Jesus, woman, I'm a neutral, don't I keep telling you that?" He smiled mischievously, the gray eyes full of humor. "If they want to keep that old bastard, de Valera, sweet back in Dublin, they've got to handle me with dress gloves. Mind you, after the way I chased the arse off him all over Ireland in the Civil War, he might welcome the news that they want to shoot me."

She burst out laughing. "I love you, Sean Gallagher. You always make me feel good at the worst times." She put an arm around the small, lean man's shoulders and kissed him on the cheek.

"As a brother," he said. "You love me as a brother, as you often remind me, so keep your mad passion in your pocket, woman, and concentrate. Colonel Hugh Kelso, he said, an American army officer torpedoed off Devon?"

"That's right."

"And what was all that about how the Germans mustn't get their hands on him?"

"I don't know. He was half out of his mind and his leg's in a terrible state, but at the suggestion he might have to go to hospital he went crazy. Said it would be better if I shot him."

"A fine old mess from the sound of it," Gallagher said, and led the horse down onto the fog-shrouded beach.

It was very quiet, the sea calm, so quiet that they could hear the whistle of the German military train from across the bay as it ran along the front from St. Helier to Millbrook.

Hugh Kelso lay face-down on the sand unconscious. Sean Gallagher turned him over gently and examined the leg. He gave a low whistle. "He needs a surgeon, this lad. I'll get him in the cart while he's still out. You gather as much driftwood as you can and hurry."

She ran along the beach and he lifted Kelso up, taking his weight easily, for he was surprisingly strong for a small man. Kelso groaned but stayed out, and the Irishman eased him onto the sacks in the cart and draped a few across him.

He turned as Helen came back with an armful of wood.

"Cover him with that while I see to the life raft."

It was still bumping around in the shallows, and he waded into the water and pulled it up on the sand. He looked inside, removed the emergency kit, then took out a spring-blade gutting knife and slashed at the skin of the life raft fiercely. As air rushed out, it crumpled and he rolled it up and carried it to the cart, shoving it onto the rack underneath.

Helen arrived with another armful of wood which she put in the back with the rest. "Will that do?"

"I think so. I'll stop by the paddock and we'll put the life raft down the old well shaft. But let's get moving."

They started up the track, Helen sitting on the shaft of the cart, Sean leading the horse. Suddenly there was laughter up ahead and a dog barked. The Irishman paused and took his time over lighting one of the vile French cigarettes that he smoked. "Nothing to worry about, I'll handle it," he told her.

The Alsatian arrived first, a splendid animal which barked once, then recognized Gallagher as an old friend, and licked his hand. Two German soldiers in field gray and helmets, rifles over their shoulders, came next. "Guten morgen, Herr General," they both called eagerly.

"And good morning to you two daft buggers." Gallagher's smile was his friendliest as he led the horse on.

"Sean, you're quite mad," she hissed.

"Not at all. Neither of those two lads speak a word of English. It might have been fun if they'd looked under the cart though."

"Where are we going?" she demanded. "There's no one at the Place at the moment."

It was always referred to in that way, never as a house.

"Isn't Mrs. Vibert in?"

"I gave her the day off. Remember that niece of hers had a new baby last week."

"Naughty girl," Gallagher said. "And her man away serving in the British Army. I wonder what he'll think when he comes home and finds a bouncing boy with blue eyes and blond hair called Fritz."

"Don't be cruel, Sean. She's not a bad girl. A little weak perhaps. People get lonely."

"Do you tell me?" Gallagher laughed. "I haven't exactly noticed you chasing me around the barn this week."

"Be sensible," she said. "Now where do we take him? There's the Chamber."

During the English Civil War, Charles de Ville, the Seigneur of the manor at that time, had espoused the Royalist cause. He'd had a room constructed in the roof with a secret staircase from the master bedroom known to the family over the years as the Chamber. It had saved his life during the time of Cromwell's rule when he was sought as a traitor.

"No, too awkward at the moment. He needs help and quickly. We'll take him to my cottage first."

"And what about a doctor?"

"George Hamilton. Who else could you trust? Now hang on while I get this life raft down the well."

He tugged it out and moved into the trees. She sat there, aware of her uneven breathing in the silence of the wood. Behind her, under the sacking and the driftwood, Hugh Kelso groaned and stirred.

At Slapton Sands just before noon, the tide turned and a few more bodies came in. Dougal Munro and Carter sat in the lee of a sand dune and had an early lunch of sandwiches and shared a bottle of beer. Soldiers tramped along the shoreline, occasionally venturing into the water at some officer's command to pull in another body. There were already about thirty laid out on the beach.

Munro said, "Someone once said the first casualty when war comes is truth."

"I know exactly what you mean, sir," Carter said.

A young American officer approached and saluted. "The beach is cleared of new arrivals at the moment, sir. Thirty-three since dawn. No sign of Colonel Kelso." He hesitated. "Does the Brigadier wish to view the burial arrangements? It's not too far."

"No thank you," Munro told him. "I think I can manage without that."

The officer saluted and walked away. Munro got up and helped Carter to his feet. "Come on, Jack. Nothing we can do here."

"All right, sir."

Carter balanced on his walking stick and Munro stood, hands in pockets, and looked out to sea. He shivered suddenly. "Anything wrong, sir?" Carter asked.

"Someone just walked over my grave, Jack. To be honest, I've got a bad feeling about this. A very bad feeling. Come on, let's get back to London," and he turned and walked away along the beach.

"So, Berger, you understand what I am saying to you?" Konrad Hofer demanded.

Heini Baum stood rigidly at attention in front of the desk in the office which the CO had been happy to lend to the field marshal at Campeaux. He tried to ignore the fact that Rommel stood at the window looking out into the garden.

"I'm not sure, Herr Major. I think so."

Rommel turned. "Don't be stupid, Berger. You're an intelligent man, I can see that, and a brave one." He tapped the Iron Cross First Class with the tip of his crop and the band around the left sleeve with the Gothic lettering. "The Afrika Korps cuff-title, I see. So, we are old comrades. Were you at Alamein?"

"No, Field Marshal. Wounded at Tobruk."

"Good. I'm a plain man so listen carefully. You did a wonderful impersonation of me last night, in both appearance and voice. Very professional."

"Thank you."

"Now I require a second performance. On Friday, you will fly to Jersey for the weekend accompanied by Major Hofer. You think you could fool them in Jersey for that long, Berger? King for a day? Would you like that?"

Baum smiled. "Actually, I think I would, sir."

Rommel said to Hofer. "There you are. Sensible and intelligent, just as I told you. Now make the arrangements, Konrad, and let's get out of here."

~

The cottage was built in the same kind of granite as the house. There was one large living room with a beamed ceiling and a dining table and half-a-dozen chairs in a window alcove. The kitchen was on the other side of the hall. Upstairs, there was one large bedroom, a storeroom and a bathroom.

Rather than negotiate the stairs, Gallagher had laid Kelso out on a long comfortable sofa in the living room. The American was still unconscious, and Gallagher found his wallet and opened it. There was his security card with photo, some snaps of a woman and two young girls, obviously his family, and a couple of letters which were so immediately personal that Gallagher folded them up again. He could hear Helen's voice from the kitchen as she spoke on the telephone. Kelso opened his eyes, stared blankly at him and then noticed the wallet in Gallagher's hand.

"Who are you?" He grabbed at it weakly. "Give it back to me."

Helen came in and sat on the sofa and put a hand on his forehead. "It's all right. Just be still. You're burning up with fever. Remember me, Helen de Ville?"

He nodded slowly. "The woman on the beach."

"This is a friend, General Sean Gallagher."

"I was just checking his papers," Gallagher told her. "The identity card is a little damp. I'll leave it out to dry."

She said to Kelso. "Do you remember where you are?"

"Jersey." He managed a ghastly smile. "Don't worry. I'm not quite out of my mind yet. I can think straight if I concentrate."

"All right, then, listen to me," Sean Gallagher said. "Your leg is very bad indeed. You need hospital and a good surgeon."

Kelso shook his head. "Not possible. As I told this lady earlier, no Germans. It would be better to shoot me than let them get their hands on me."

"Why?" Sean Gallagher demanded bluntly.

"She called you General. Is that true?"

"I was once in the Irish Army and I served with the Brits in the last war. Does that make a difference?"

"Perhaps."

"All right, what's your unit?"

"Engineers—assault engineers, to be precise. We lead the way in beach landings."

Sean Gallagher saw it all. "Is this something to do with the invasion?"

Kelso nodded. "It's coming soon."

"Sure and we all know that," Gallagher said.

"Yes, but I know where and I know when. If the Germans could squeeze that out of me, can you imagine what it would mean? All their troops concentrated in the right place. We'd never get off the beach."

He was extremely agitated, sweat on his forehead. Helen soothed him, easing him down. "It's all right, I promise you."

"Is George Hamilton coming?" Gallagher asked.

"He was out. I left a message with his housekeeper that you wanted to see him urgently. I said you'd cut your leg and thought it needed a stitch or two."

"Who's Hamilton?" Kelso demanded.

"A doctor," Helen said. "And a good friend. He'll be here soon to see to that leg of yours."

Kelso was shaking again as the fever took hold. "More important things to think of at the moment. You must speak to your resistance people here. Tell them to get on the radio as soon as possible and notify Intelligence in London that I'm here. They'll have to try to get me out."

"But there is no resistance movement in Jersey," Helen said. "I mean, there's a hell of a lot of people who don't care to be occupied and make life as awkward for the enemy as they can, but we don't have anything like the French Resistance, if that's what you mean."

Kelso stared at her in astonishment and Gallagher said, "This island is approximately ten miles by five. There are something like forty-five thousand civilians. A good-size market town, that's all. How long do you think a resistance movement would last here? No mountains to run to, nowhere to take refuge. Nowhere to go, in fact."

Kelso seemed to have difficulty in taking it in. "So, there's no resistance movement. No radio?"

"No links with London at all," Gallagher told him.

"Then what about France?" Kelso asked desperately. "Granville,

St. Malo. They're only a few hours away across the water, aren't they? There must be a local unit of the French Resistance in those places."

There was a significant pause, then Helen turned to Gallagher. "Savary could speak to the right people in Granville. He knows who they are and so do you."

"True."

"Guido was leaving as I came up from the beach," she said. "He told me they were trying for Granville this afternoon. Taking advantage of the fog." She glanced at her watch. "They won't have the tide until noon. You could take the van. There are those sacks of potatoes to go into St. Helier for the troops' supply depot and the market."

"All right, you've convinced me," Gallagher said. "But if I know Savary, he won't want any of this, not in his head. That means writing it down, which is taking one hell of a chance."

"We don't have any choice, Sean," she said simply.

"No, I suppose you're right." Gallagher laughed. "The things I do for England. Look after our friend here. I'll be back as soon as I can."

As he reached the door she called, "And Sean?"

He turned. "Yes?"

"Don't forget to drive on the right-hand side of the road."

It was an old joke, but not without a certain amount of truth. One of the first things the German forces had done on occupying Jersey was to change the traffic flow from the left- to the right-hand side of the road. After four years, Gallagher still couldn't get used to it, not that he drove very often. They only had the old Ford van as a special dispensation because the de Ville farmlands supplied various crops for the use of the German forces. The size of the petrol ration meant the van could be used only two or three times a week anyway. Gallagher stretched it by coasting down the hills with the engine off, and there was always a little black-market petrol available if you knew the right people.

He drove down through the tiny picturesque town of St. Aubin and followed the curve of the bay to Bel Royal, St. Helier in the distance. He passed a number of gun emplacements with a few troops in evidence, but Victoria Avenue was deserted on the run into town. One of the French trains the Germans had brought over passed him on its way to Millbrook, the only sign of activity until he reached the Grand Hotel. He checked his watch. It was just before eleven. Plenty of time to catch Savary before the *Victor Hugo* left for Granville, so he turned left into Gloucester Street and made his way to the market.

There weren't too many people about, mainly because of the weather. The scarlet and black Nazi flag with its swastika on the pole above the Town Hall entrance hung limply in the damp air. The German for Town Hall is Rathaus. It was, therefore, understandable that the place was now known as the Rat House by the local inhabitants.

He parked outside the market in Beresford Street. It was almost deserted, just a handful of shoppers and a sprinkling of German soldiers. The market itself was officially closed, open for only two hours on a Saturday afternoon. There would be enough people in evidence then, desperately hoping for fresh produce.

Gallagher got two sacks of potatoes from the van, kicked open the gate and went inside. Most of the stalls in the old Victorian Market were empty, but there were one or two people about. He made straight for a stall on the far side where a large genial man in heavy sweater and cloth cap was arranging turnips in neat rows under a sign *D. Chevalier.*

"So, it's swedes today?" Gallagher said as he arrived.

"Good for you, General," Chevalier said.

"Do you tell me? Mrs. Vibert gave me swede jam for breakfast the other day." Gallagher shuddered. "I can still taste it. Two sacks of spuds for you here."

Chevalier's eyes lit up. "I knew you wouldn't let me down, General. Let's have them in the back."

Gallagher dragged them into the room at the rear, and Chevalier opened a cupboard and took out an old canvas duffel bag. "Four loaves of white bread."

"Jesus," Gallagher said. "Who did you kill to get those?"

"A quarter pound of China tea and a leg of pork. Okay?"

"Nice to do business with you," Gallagher told him. "See you next week."

His next stop was at the troop supply depot in Wesley Street. It had originally been a garage and there were half-a-dozen trucks parked in there. There wasn't much happening, but a burly Feldwebel called

Klinger was sitting in the glass office eating a sandwich. He waved, opened the door and came down the steps.

"Herr General," he said genially.

"God, Hans, but you do well for yourself." Gallagher said in excellent German and prodded the ample stomach.

Klinger smiled. "A man must live. We are both old soldiers, Herr General. We understand each other. You have something for me?"

'Two sacks of potatoes for the official list."

"And?"

"Another sack for you, if you're interested."

"And in exchange?"

"Petrol."

The German nodded. "One five-gallon can."

"Two five-gallon cans," Gallagher said.

"General." Klinger turned to a row of British Army issue petrol cans, picked two up and brought them to the van. "What if I turned you in? You're so unreasonable."

"Prison for me and a holiday for you," Gallagher said. "They say the Russian Front's lovely at this time of the year."

"As always, a practical man." Klinger pulled the three sacks of potatoes out of the van. "One of these days a patrol is going to stop you for a fuel check, and they'll discover your petrol is the wrong color."

"Ah, but I'm a magician, my friend, didn't I tell you that?" and Gallagher drove away.

Military petrol was dyed red, the ration for agricultural use was green, and doctors enjoyed a pink variety. What Klinger hadn't discovered was that it was a simple matter to remove the dye by straining the petrol through the filter of the gas mask issued to the general public at the beginning of the war. A little green dye added afterward turned military petrol to the agricultural variety very quickly indeed.

Survival was what it was all about. This was an old island, and the Le Brocq half of him was fiercely proud of that. Over the centuries, the island had endured many things. As he passed the Pomme d'Or Hotel, German Naval Headquarters, he looked up at the Nazi flag hanging above the entrance and said softly, "And we'll still be here when you bastards are long gone."

5

GALLAGHER PARKED THE VAN at the weighbridge and walked
along the Albert Pier, going up the steps to the top section. He paused
to light one of his French cigarettes and looked out across the bay. The
fog had thinned just a little and Elizabeth Castle, on its island, looked
strange and mysterious, like something out of a fairy story. Walter Raleigh had once ruled there as governor. Now Germans with concrete
fortifications and gun emplacements up on top.

He looked down into the harbor. As always it was a hive of activity.
The Germans used Rhine barges, among other vessels, to carry supplies
to the Channel Islands. There were several moored on the far side at the
New North Quay. There were a number of craft of various kinds from
the 2 Vorpostenbootsflotille and two M40 Klasse minesweepers from
the 24th Minesweeper Flotilla. Several cargo vessels, mostly coasters,
among them the SS *Victor Hugo,* were moored against the Albert Pier.

Built in 1920 by Ferguson Brothers in Glasgow for a French firm
engaged in the coastal trade, she had definitely seen better days. Her
single smokestack was punctured in several places by cannon shell
from RAF Beaufighters in an attack on one of the night convoys from
Granville two weeks previously. Savary was the master with a crew of

ten Frenchmen. The antiaircraft defenses consisted of two machine guns and a Bofors gun, manned by seven German naval ratings commanded by Guido Orsini.

Gallagher could see him now on the bridge, leaning on the rail, and called in English, "Heh, Guido? Is Savary about?"

Guido cupped his hands. "In the café."

The hut farther along the pier which served as a café was not busy, four French seamen playing cards at one table, three German sailors at another. Robert Savary, a large, bearded man in a reefer coat and cloth cap, a greasy scarf knotted at his neck, sat on his own at a table next to the window, smoking a cigarette, a bowl of coffee in front of him.

"Robert, how goes it?" Gallagher demanded in French and sat down.

"Unusual to see you down here, Mon General, which means you want something."

"Ah, you cunning old peasant." Gallagher passed an envelope under the table. "There, have you got that?"

"What is it?"

"Just put it in your pocket and don't ask questions. When you get to Granville, there's a café in the walled city called Sophie's. You know it?"

Savary was already beginning to turn pale. "Yes, of course I do."

"You know the good Sophie Cresson well and her husband Gerard?"

"I've met them." Savary tried to give him the envelope back under the table.

"Then you'll know that their business is terrorism carried to as extreme a degree as possible. They not only shoot the Boche, they also like to make an example of collaborators, isn't that the colorful phrase? So if I were you, I'd be sensible. Take the letter. Needless to say, don't read it. If you do, you'll probably never sleep again. Just give it to Sophie with my love. I'm sure she'll have a message for me, which you'll let me have as soon as you're back."

"Damn you, General," Savary muttered and put the envelope in his pocket.

"The Devil took care of that long ago. Don't worry. You've nothing to worry about. Guido Orsini's a good lad."

"The Count?" Savary shrugged. "Flashy Italian pimp. I hate aristocrats."

"No Fascist, that one, and he's probably got less time for Hitler than you have. Have you any decent cigarettes in your bag? I'm going crazy smoking that filthy tobacco they've been importing for the official ration lately."

Savary looked cunning. "Not really. Only a few Gitanes."

"Only, the man says." Gallagher groaned aloud. "All right, I'll take two hundred."

"And what do I get?"

Gallagher opened the bag Chevalier had given him. "Leg of pork?"

Savary's jaw dropped. "My God, my tongue's hanging out already. Give me."

Gallagher passed it under the table and took the carton of cigarettes in return. "You know my telephone number at the cottage. Ring me as soon as you get back."

"All right."

Savary got up and they went outside. Gallagher, unwilling to wait, got a packet of Gitanes out, opened it and lit one. "Jesus, that's wonderful."

"I'll be off then." Savary made a move to walk toward the gangway of the *Victor Hugo.*

Gallagher said softly, "Let me down on this one and I'll kill you, my friend. Understand?"

Savary turned, mouth open in astonishment as Gallagher smiled cheerfully and walked away along the pier.

George Hamilton was a tall, angular man whose old Harris tweed suit looked a size too large. A distinguished physician in his day, at one time professor of pharmacology at the University of London and a consultant of Guy's Hospital, he had retired to a cottage in Jersey just before the outbreak of war. In 1940, with the Germans expected at any day, many people had left the island, a number of doctors among them, which explained why Hamilton, an M.D. and Fellow of the Royal College of Physicians, was working as a general practitioner at the age of seventy.

He pushed a shock of white hair back from his forehead and stood up, looking down at Kelso on the couch. "Not good. He should be in hospital. I really need an x-ray to be sure, but I'd say at least two fractures of the tibia. Possibly three."

"No hospital," Kelso said faintly.

Hamilton made a sign to Helen and Gallagher, and they followed him into the kitchen. "If the fractures were compound—in other words, if there was any kind of open wound, bone sticking through, then we wouldn't have any choice. The possibility of infection, especially after all he's been through, would be very great. The only way of saving the leg would be a hospital bed and traction."

"What exactly are you saying, George?" Gallagher asked.

"Well, as you can see, the skin isn't broken. The fractures are what we term comminuted. It might be possible to set the leg and plaster it."

"Can you handle that?" Helen demanded.

"I could try, but I need the right conditions. I certainly wouldn't dream of proceeding without an x-ray." He hesitated. "There is one possibility."

"What's that?" Gallagher asked.

"Pine Trees. It's a little nursing home in St. Lawrence run by Catholic Sisters of Mercy. Irish and French mostly. They have x-ray facilities there and a decent operating theater. Sister Maria Teresa, who's in charge, is a good friend. I could give her a ring."

"Do the Germans use it?" Helen asked.

"Now and then. Usually young women with prenatal problems, which is a polite way of saying they're in for an abortion. The nuns, as you may imagine, don't like that one little bit, but there isn't anything they can do about it."

"Would he be able to stay there?"

"I doubt it. They've very few beds and surely it would be too dangerous. The most we could do is patch him up and bring him back here."

Gallagher said, "You're taking a hell of a risk helping us like this, George."

"I'd say we all are," Hamilton told him dryly.

"It's vitally important that Colonel Kelso stay out of the hands of the enemy," Helen began.

Hamilton shook his head. "I don't want to know, Helen, so don't try to tell me, and I don't want the nuns to be involved either. As far as Sister Maria Teresa is concerned, our friend must be a local man who's had a suitable accident. It would help if we had an identity card for him, just in case."

Helen turned on Gallagher. "Can you do anything? You managed a card for that Spanish Communist last year when he escaped from the working party at those tunnels they've been constructing in St. Peter."

Gallagher went to the old eighteenth-century pine desk in the corner of the kitchen, pulled out the front drawer, then reached inside and produced a small box drawer of the kind people had once used to hide valuables. There were several blank identity cards in there, signed and stamped with the Nazi eagle.

"Where on earth did you get those?" Hamilton asked in astonishment.

"An Irishman I know, barman in one of the town hotels, has a German boyfriend, if you follow me. A clerk at the Feldkommandatur. I did him a big favor last year. He gave me these in exchange. I'll fill in Kelso's details and well give him a good Jersey name. How about Le Marquand?" He took out pen and ink and sat at the kitchen table. "Henry Ralph Le Marquand. Residence?"

He looked up at Helen. "Home Farm, de Ville Place," she said.

"Fair enough. I'll go and get the color of his eyes, hair and so on while you phone Pine Trees." He paused at the door. "I'll enter his occupation as fisherman. That way we can say it was a boating accident. And one more thing, George."

"What's that?" Hamilton asked as he lifted the phone.

"I'm going with you. We'll take him up in the van. No arguments. We must all hang together, or all hang separately." He smiled wryly and went out.

Pine Trees was an ugly house, obviously late Victorian in origin. At some time, the walls had been faced in cement which had cracked in many places, here and there, large pieces having flaked away altogether. Gallagher drove the van into the front courtyard, Hamilton sitting beside him. As they got out, the front door opened and Sister Maria Teresa came down the sloping concrete ramp to meet them. She wore a simple black habit, a small woman with calm eyes and not a wrinkle to be seen on her face though she was in her sixties.

"Dr. Hamilton." Her English was good, but with a pronounced French accent.

"This is General Gallagher. He manages de Ville Place where the patient is employed."

"We'll need a trolley," Gallagher said.

"There's one just inside the door."

He got it and brought it to the back of the van. He opened the doors, revealing Kelso lying on an old mattress, and they eased him out onto the trolley.

Sister Maria Teresa led the way inside, and as he pushed the trolley up the ramp, Gallagher whispered to Kelso, "Don't forget, keep your trap shut, and if you have to moan in pain, try not to sound American."

Hamilton stood in the operating theater examining the x-ray plates which young Sister Bernadette had brought in. "Three fractures," Sister Maria Teresa said. "Not good. He should be in hospital, Doctor, but I don't need to tell you that."

"All right, Sister. I'll tell you the truth," Hamilton said. "If he goes down to St. Helier they'll want to know how it happened. Our German friends insist on it. You know what sticklers for detail they are. Le Marquand was fishing illegally when the accident took place."

Gallagher cut in smoothly, "Which could earn him three months in jail."

"I see." She shook her head. "I wish I had a bed to offer, but we're quite full."

"Any Germans about?"

"Two of their girlfriends," she said calmly. "The usual thing. One of the army doctors handled that yesterday. Major Speer. Do you know him?"

"I've worked with him on occasion at the hospital," Hamilton said. "I've known worse. Anyway, Sister, if you'd care to assist me, you and Sister Bernadette, we'll get started."

She eased him into a robe and he went to scrub up at the sink in the corner. As Sister Bernadette helped him on with rubber gloves, he said to Maria Teresa, "A short-term anesthetic only. Chloroform on the pad will do." He moved to the operating table and looked down at Kelso. "All right?"

Kelso, gritting his teeth, nodded and Hamilton said to Gallagher. "You'd better wait outside."

Gallagher turned to leave, and at that moment, the door opened and a German officer walked in.

"Ah, there you are, Sister," he said in French, then smiled and changed to English. "Professor Hamilton, you here?"

"Major Speer," Hamilton said, gloved hands raised.

"I've just looked in on my patients, Sister. Both are doing well."

Speer was a tall, handsome man with a good-humored, rather fleshy face. His greatcoat hung open, and Gallagher noticed an Iron Cross First Class on the left breast and the ribbon for the Russian Winter War. A man who had seen action.

"Anything interesting, Doctor?"

"Fractures of the tibia. An employee of General Gallagher here. Have you met?"

"No, but I've heard of you many times, General." Speer clicked his heels and saluted. "A pleasure." He moved to the x-rays and examined them. "Not good. Not good at all. Comminuted fracture of the tibia in three places."

"I know hospitalization and traction should be the norm," Hamilton said. "But a bed isn't available."

"Oh, I should think it perfectly acceptable to set the bones and then plaster." Speer smiled with great charm and took off his greatcoat. "But, Herr Professor, this is hardly your field. It would be a pleasure to take care of this small matter for you."

He was already taking a gown down from a peg on the wall and moved to the sink to scrub up. "If you insist," Hamilton said calmly. "There's little doubt this is more your sort of thing than mine."

A few minutes later, Speer was ready, leaning down to examine the leg. He looked up at Sister Maria Teresa. "Right, Sister, chloroform now, I think. Not too much and we'll work very quickly."

From the corner, Gallagher watched, fascinated.

Savary wasn't feeling too pleased with life as he walked along the cobbled streets of the walled city in Granville.

For one thing, the trip from Jersey in the fog had been lousy, and he was distinctly unhappy at the situation Gallagher had placed him in. He turned into a quiet square. Sophie's Bar was on the far side, a chink of light showing here and there through the shutters. He walked across, slowly and reluctantly, and went in.

Gerard Cresson sat in his wheelchair playing the piano, a small man with the white intense face of the invalid, black hair hanging almost to his shoulders. He'd broken his back in an accident on the docks two years before the war. Would never walk again, not even with crutches.

There were a dozen or so customers scattered around the bar, some of them seamen whom Savary knew. Sophie sat on a high stool behind the marble counter, bottles ranged behind her against an ornate mirror, and read the local newspaper. She was in her late thirties, dark hair piled high on her head, black eyes, the face sallow like a gypsy's, the mouth wide and painted bright red. She had good breasts, the best Savary had ever seen. Not that it would have done any good. With a knife or a bottle she was dynamite, and there were men in Granville with scars to prove it.

"Ah, Robert, it's been a long time. How goes it?"

"It could be worse, it could be better."

As she poured him a cognac, he slipped the letter across. "What's this?" she demanded.

"Your friend Gallagher in Jersey uses me as a postman now. I don't know what's in it and I don't want to, but he expects an answer when I return. We sail tomorrow at noon. I'll be back." He swallowed his cognac and left.

She came round the counter and called to one of the customers, "Heh, Marcel, look after the bar for me."

She approached her husband who had stopped playing and was lighting a cigarette. "What was that all about?"

"Let's go in the back and find out."

She pulled his wheelchair from the piano, turned and pushed him along the bar to the sitting room at the rear. Gerard Cresson sat at the table and read Gallagher's letter, then pushed it across to her, face grave.

She read it quickly, then got a bottle of red wine and filled two glasses. "He's in a real mess this time, our friend the General."

"And then some."

Between them they had controlled the Resistance movement from Granville to Avranches and St. Malo for three years now. Gerard provided the organizing ability and Sophie was his good right arm. They were a very successful team. Had to be to have survived so long.

"You'll radio London?"

"Of course."

"What do you think?" she said. "Maybe they'll ask us to try to get this Yank out of Jersey."

"Difficult at the best of times," he said. "Not possible with the state he's in." He held out his glass for more wine. "Of course, there is a rather obvious solution. Much better for everyone in the circumstances, I should have thought."

"And what's that?"

"Send someone across to cut his throat."

There was silence between them. She said, "It's been a long war."

"Too long," he said. "Now take me to the storeroom and I'll radio London."

Major Speer turned from the sink, toweling his hands. Sister Bernadette was already mixing the plaster of Paris, and he crossed to the operating table and looked down at Kelso who was still unconscious.

"An excellent piece of work," George Hamilton said.

"Yes, I must say I'm rather pleased with it myself." Speer reached for his greatcoat. "I'm sure you can handle the rest. I'm already late for dinner at the officers' club. Don't forget to let me know how he progresses, Herr Professor. General." He saluted and went out.

Hamilton stood, looked down at Kelso, suddenly drained as he stripped off his gloves and gown. Kelso moaned a little as he started to come round and said softly, "Janet, I love you."

The American accent was unmistakable. Sister Bernadette appeared not to have noticed, but the older woman glanced sharply at Hamilton and then at Gallagher.

"He seems to be coming around," Hamilton said lamely.

"So it would appear," she said. "Why don't you and General Gallagher go to my office. One of the nuns will get you some coffee. We have some of the real stuff thanks to Major Speer. Sister Bernadette and I will put the cast on for you."

"That's very kind of you, Sister."

The two men went out and along the corridor, past the kitchen where two nuns worked, to the office at the end. Hamilton sat behind the desk and Gallagher gave him one of his Gitanes and sat in the window seat.

"The moment he came through that door will stay with me forever," the Irishman said.

"As I told you, he's not a bad sort," Hamilton commented. "And a damn fine doctor."

"You think Kelso will be all right?"

"I don't see why not. We should be able to move him in an hour or so. We'll have to watch him closely for the next few days. The possibility of infection mustn't be discounted, but there were some ampules of this new wonder drug, penicillin, in that emergency kit from his life raft. I'll start him on that if he gets the wrong sort of reaction."

"Sister Maria Teresa—she knows things aren't what they seem."

"Yes, I feel rather bad about that," George Hamilton said. "As if I've used her. She won't tell, of course. It would be contrary to every belief she holds dear."

"She reminds me of my old aunt in Dublin when I was a lad," Gallagher said. "Incense, candles and the Holy Water."

"Do you still believe, Sean?" Hamilton asked.

"Not since the first of July, nineteen sixteen, on the Somme," Gallagher said. "I was attached to a Yorkshire Regiment, the Leeds Pals. The idiots at headquarters sent those lads over the top, packs on their backs, into heavy machine-gun fire. By noon, there were around forty or so survivors out of eight hundred. I decided then that if God existed, he was having a bad joke at my expense."

"I take your point," Hamilton said gravely.

Gallagher stood up. "I think I'll sample the night air for a while," and he opened the door and went out.

George Hamilton rested his head on his arms on the desk and yawned. It had been a long day. He closed his eyes and was asleep within a couple of minutes.

It was just after ten and Dougal Munro was still working away at his desk in his office at Baker Street when the door opened and Jack Carter limped in, his face grim. He placed a signal flimsy on the brigadier's desk. "Brace yourself, sir."

"What is this?" Munro demanded.

"Message just in from our Resistance contact in Granville. That's in Normandy."

"I know where it is, for God's sake." Munro started to read and suddenly sat up straight. "I don't believe it."

Munro read the signal through again. "It couldn't be worse. There isn't a resistance movement in Jersey. No one to call on. I mean, this de Ville woman and the Gallagher man, how long can they manage, especially if he's ill? And how long can he get by on a small island like that? It doesn't bear thinking of, Jack."

For the first time since Carter had known him he sounded close to despair, uncertain which way to go. "You'll think of something, sir, you always do," Carter said gently.

"Thanks for the vote of confidence." Munro stood up and reached for his coat. "Now you'd better phone through to Hayes Lodge and get me an immediate appointment with General Eisenhower. Tell them I'm on my way."

Helen de Ville had been waiting anxiously for the sound of the van returning, and when it drove into the courtyard, at the side of de Ville Place, she ran out. As Gallagher and Hamilton got out of the van, she cried, "Is he all right?"

"Still doped up, but the leg's doing fine," Gallagher told her.

"There's no one in at the moment. They're either in Granville or at sea or at the officers' club, so let's get him upstairs."

Gallagher and Hamilton got Kelso out of the van, joined hands and lifted him between them. They followed Helen through the front door, across the wide paneled hall and up the great staircase. She opened the door of the master bedroom and led the way in. The furniture was seventeenth-century Breton, including the four-poster bed. There was a bathroom through a door on the right side of the bed, on the left, carved library shelving from wall to ceiling crammed with books. Her fingers found a hidden spring and a section swung back to disclose a stairway. She led the way up and Gallagher and Hamilton followed with some difficulty, but finally made it to a room under the roof. The walls were paneled in oak, and there was a single window in the gable end. It was comfortable enough with carpet on the floor and a single bed.

They got Kelso onto the bed and Helen said, "There's everything you need, and the only entrance is from my room, so you should be quite safe. An ancestor of mine hid here from Cromwell's people for years. I'm afraid the convenience hasn't improved since his day. It's that oak commode over there."

"Thanks, but all I want to do is sleep," Kelso said, his face tired and strained.

She nodded to Gallagher and the old doctor and they went out and downstairs. Hamilton said, "I'll get off myself. Tell Helen I'll look in tomorrow."

Sean Gallagher took his hand for a moment. "George, you're quite a man."

"All in a doctor's day, Sean." Hamilton smiled. "See you tomorrow." And he went out.

Gallagher went through the hall and along the rear passage to the kitchen. He put the kettle on the stove, and was pushing a few pieces of wood in among the dying embers when Helen came in.

"Is he all right?" he asked.

"Fast asleep already." She sat on the edge of the table. "Now what do we do?"

"Nothing we can do until Savary gets back from Granville with some sort of message."

"And what if there isn't any message?"

"Oh, I'll think of something. Now sit down and have a nice cup of tea."

She shook her head. "We've got a choice of either bramble or beet tea and, tonight, I just can't face either."

"Oh, ye of little faith." Gallagher produced the packet of China tea which Chevalier had given him that morning at the market.

She started to laugh helplessly and put her arms around his neck. "Sean Gallagher, what would I do without you?"

~

Eisenhower was in full uniform for he'd been attending a dinner party with the prime minister when he'd received Munro's message. He paced up and down the library at Hayes Lodge, extremely agitated. "Is there no way we can put someone in?"

"If you mean a commando unit, I don't think so, sir. The most heavily defended coast in Europe."

Eisenhower nodded. "What you're really saying is that it's impossible to get him out."

"No, sir, but very, very difficult. It's a small island, General. It's not like hiding someone on the back of a truck and driving three hundred miles overnight to the Pyrenees or arranging for one of our Lysanders to fly in to pick him up."

"Right, then get him across to France where you can fix those things."

"Our information is that he's not capable of traveling."

"For God's sake, Munro, everything could hang on this. The whole invasion. Months of planning."

Munro cleared his throat and nervously for him. "If worse came to worst, General, would you be willing to consider Colonel Kelso as expendable?"

Eisenhower stopped pacing. "You mean have him executed?"

"Something like that."

"God help me, but if there's nothing else for it, then so be it." Eisenhower walked up to the huge wall map of western Europe. "Six thousand ships, thousands of planes, two million men and the war in balance. If they find out our exact points of landing, they'll mass everything they've got." He turned. "Intelligence reported a Rommel speech of a few weeks ago in which he said just that. That the war would be won or lost on those beaches."

"I know, General."

"And you ask is Kelso expendable?" Eisenhower sighed heavily. "If you can save him, do. If you can't..." He shrugged. "In any case, considering what you've already said about the Jersey situation, how would you go about getting an agent in? I should think a new face would stick out like a sore thumb."

"That's true, General. We'll have to think about it."

Jack Carter, standing respectfully quiet by the fire, coughed. "There is one way, General."

"What's that, Captain?" Eisenhower inquired.

"The best place to hide a tree is in a wood. It seems to me the people who are most free to come and go are the Germans themselves. I mean, new personnel must be posted there all the time."

Eisenhower turned sharply to Munro. "He's got a point. Have you got any people capable of that kind of work?"

Munro nodded. "Here and there, sir. It's a rare skill. Not just a question of speaking fluent German, but thinking like a German and that isn't easy."

Eisenhower said, 'I'll give you a week, Brigadier. One week and I expect you to have this matter resolved."

"My word on it, sir."

Munro walked out briskly, Carter limping along behind. "Radio Cresson in Granville to relay a message to Gallagher in Jersey saying someone will be with him by Thursday."

"Are you sure, sir?"

"Of course I am," Munro said cheerfully. "That was a masterly suggestion of yours in there, Jack. Best place to hide a tree is in a wood. I like that."

"Thank you very much, sir."

"German personnel moving in and out all the time. What would one new arrival be among many, especially if provided with the right kind of credentials?"

"It would take a very special man, sir."

"Come off it, Jack," Munro said as they reached the street and the car. "There's only one man for this job. You know it and I know it. Only one man capable of playing a Nazi to the hilt and ruthless enough to put a bullet between Kelso's eyes if necessary. Harry Martineau."

"I must remind you, sir, that Colonel Martineau was given a definite promise after that business in Lyons that his services wouldn't be required again. His health alone should make it impossible."

"Nonsense, Jack. Harry could never resist a challenge. Find him. And another thing, Jack. Check SOE files. See if we've got anyone with a Jersey background."

"Men only, sir?"

"Good God, Jack, of course not. Since when have we been interested in men only in our business."

He tapped on the partition and the driver took them away from the curb.

6

THE COTTAGE IN DORSET, not far from Lulworth Cove, had been loaned to Martineau by an old friend from Oxford days. It stood in a tiny valley above the cliffs, and the way to the beach was blocked by rusting barbed wire. There had once been a notice warning of mines, not that there were any. That had been the first thing the landlord at the village pub had told Martineau when he'd moved into the area, which explained why he was walking along the shoreline, occasionally throwing stones into the incoming waves, the morning after Dougal Munro's meeting with Eisenhower at Hayes Lodge.

Harry Martineau was forty-four, of medium height, with good shoulders under the old paratrooper's camouflaged jump jacket which he wore against the cold. His face was very pale, with the kind of skin that never seemed to tan, and wedge-shaped, the eyes so dark that it was impossible to say what their true color was. The mouth was mobile, with a slight ironic smile permanently in place. The look of a man who had found life more disappointing than he had hoped.

He'd been out of hospital for three months now and things were better than they'd been for a while. He didn't get the chest pain anymore, except when he overdid things, but the insomnia pattern was terrible. He could seldom sleep at night. The moment he went to bed, his brain seemed to become hyperactive. Still, that was only to be expected. Too many years on the run, of living by night, danger constantly at hand.

He was no use to Munro anymore, the doctors had made that clear. He could have returned to Oxford, but that was no answer. Neither was trying to pick up the threads of the book he'd been working on in 1939. The war had taught him that if nothing else. So, he'd dropped out as thoroughly as a man could. The cottage in Dorset by the sea, books to read, space to find himself in.

"And where the hell have you gone, Harry?" he asked morosely as he started up the cliff path. "Because I'm damned if I can find you."

The living room of the old cottage was comfortable enough. A Persian carpet on the flagged floor, a dining table and several rush-backed chairs and books everywhere, not only on the shelves but piled in the corner. None of them were his. Nothing in this place was his except for a few clothes.

There was a sofa on each side of the stone fireplace. He put a couple of logs on the embers, poured himself a scotch, drank it quickly and poured another. Then he sat down and picked up the notepad he'd left on the coffee table. There were several lines of poetry written on it and he read them aloud.

The station is ominous at midnight. Hope is a dead letter. He dropped the notepad back on the table with a wry smile. "Admit it, Harry," he said softly. "You're a lousy poet."

Suddenly, he was tired, the feeling coming in a kind of rush, the lack of sleep catching up with him. His chest began to ache a little, the left lung, and that took him back to Lyons, of course, on that final and fatal day. If he'd been a little bit more on the ball it wouldn't have happened. A case of taking the pitcher to the well too often or perhaps, quite simply, his luck had run out. As he drifted into sleep, it all came back so clearly. Standartenführer Jurgen Kaufmann, the head of the Gestapo in Lyons, was in civilian clothes that day as he came down the steps of the Town Hall and got into the back of the black Citroën. His driver was also in civilian clothes, for on Thursday afternoons Kaufmann visited his mistress and liked to be discreet about it.

"Take your time, Karl," he said to his driver, an SS sergeant who'd served with him for two years now. "We're a little early. I said I wouldn't be there till three and you know how she hates surprises."

"As you say, Standartenführer." Karl smiled as he drove away. Kaufmann opened a copy of a Berlin newspaper which he had received in the post that morning and settled back to enjoy it. They moved through the outskirts of town into the country. It was really quite beautiful, orchards of apples on either side of the road, and the air was heavy with the smell of them. For some time Karl had noticed a motorcycle behind them, and when they turned into the side road leading to the village of Chaumont, it followed.

He said, "There's a motorcyclist been on our tail for quite some time, Standartenführer." He took a Luger from his pocket and laid it on the seat beside him.

Kaufmann turned to look through the rear window and laughed. "You're losing your touch, Karl. He's one of ours."

The motorcyclist drew alongside and waved. He was SS Feld-gendarmerie in helmet, heavy uniform raincoat, a Schmeisser machine pistol slung across his chest just below the SS Field Police metal gorget that was only worn when officially on duty. The face was anonymous behind the goggles. He waved a gloved hand again.

"He must have a message for me," Kaufmann said. "Pull up."

Karl turned in at the side of the road and braked to a halt and the motorcyclist pulled up in front. He shoved his machine up on the stand and Karl got out. "What can we do for you?"

A hand came out of the raincoat pocket holding a Mauser semi-automatic pistol. He shot Karl once in the heart, hurling him back against the Citroen. He slid down into the road. The SS man turned him over with his boot and shot him again very deliberately between the eyes. Then he opened the rear door.

Kaufmann always went armed, but he'd taken off his overcoat and folded it neatly in the corner. As he got his hand to the Luger in the right pocket and turned, the SS man shot him in the arm. Kaufmann clutched at his sleeve, blood oozing between his fingers.

"Who are you?" he cried wildly. The other man pushed up his

*goggles and Kaufmann stared into the darkest, coldest eyes he had
ever seen in his life.*

*"My name is Martineau. I'm a major in the British Army serving
with SOE."*

*"So, you are Martineau." Kaufmann grimaced with pain. "Your
German is excellent. Quite perfect."*

"So it should be. My mother was German," Martineau told him.

*Kaufmann said, "I'd hoped to meet you before long, but under
different circumstances."*

*"I'm sure you did. I've wanted to meet you for quite some time. Since
nineteen thirty-eight, in fact. You were a captain at Gestapo Headquarters in Berlin in May of that year. You arrested a young woman called
Rosa Bernstein. You probably don't even remember the name."*

*"But I recall her very well," Kaufmann told him. "She was Jewish
and worked for the Socialist Underground."*

*"I was told that by the time you'd finished with her she couldn't
even walk to the firing squad."*

*"That's not true. The firing squad never came into it. She was hanged
in cellar number three. Standard procedure. What was she to you?"*

"I loved her." Martineau raised his pistol.

*Kaufmann cried, "Don't be a fool. We can do a deal. I can save
your life, Martineau, believe me."*

*"Is that so?" Harry Martineau said, and shot him between the
eyes, killing him instantly.*

*He pushed the heavy motorcycle off its stand and rode away. He
was perfectly in control in spite of what he had just done. No emotion—nothing. The trouble was, it hadn't brought Rosa Bernstein
back, but then, nothing ever could.*

He rode through a maze of country lanes for over an hour, working
his way steadily westward. Finally, he turned along a narrow country
lane, grass growing so tall on either side that it almost touched. The
farmhouse in the courtyard at the end of the lane had seen better days,
a window broken here and there, a few slates missing. Martineau got
off the bike, pushed it up on the stand and crossed to the front door.

"Heh, Pierre, open up!" He tried the latch and hammered with his
fist and then the door opened so suddenly that he fell on his knees.

The muzzle of a Walther touched him between the eyes. The man holding it was about forty and dressed like a French farm laborer in beret, corduroy jacket and denim trousers, but his German was impeccable. "Please stand, Major Martineau, and walk inside very slowly."

He followed Martineau along the corridor into the kitchen. Pierre Duval sat at the table, tied to a chair, a handkerchief in his mouth, eyes wild, blood on his face.

"Hands on the wall and spread," the German said, and ran his hands expertly over Martineau, relieving him of the Schmeisser and the Mauser.

He moved to the old-fashioned telephone on the wall and gave the operator a number. After a while he said, "Schmidt? He turned up. Yes, Martineau." He nodded. "All right, fifteen minutes."

"Friend of yours?" Martineau inquired.

"Not really. I'm Abwehr. Kramer's the name. That was the Gestapo. I don't like those swine any more than you do, but we all have a job to do. Take your helmet and raincoat off. Make yourself comfortable."

Martineau did as he was told. Evening was falling fast outside, the room was getting quite dark. He put the helmet and coat down and stood there in the SS uniform, aware of Pierre on the other side of the table, eyes glaring wildly, leaning back in his chair, his feet coming up.

"What about a drink?" Martineau asked.

"My God, they told me you were a cool one," Kramer said admiringly.

Pierre lunged with his feet at the edge of the table ramming it into the German's back. Martineau's left hand deflected the pistol and he closed, raising his knee. But Kramer turned a thigh, raising stiffened fingers under Martineau's chin, jerking back his head. Martineau hooked Kramers left leg, sending the German crashing to the ground, going down with him, reaching for the wrist of the hand that held the pistol, smashing his fist into the side of Kramer's neck, aware of the pistol exploding between them.

There was the distinct sound of bone cracking and the German lay still, alive, but moaning softly. Martineau got to his feet feeling suddenly weak and faint, opened the table drawer, spilling its contents on the floor and picked up a breadknife. He moved behind Pierre and sliced the ropes that bound him to the chair. The old Frenchman jumped up, pulling the gag from his mouth.

"My God, Harry, I've never seen so much blood."

Martineau glanced down. The front of the SS blouse was soaked in blood. His own blood and there were three bullet holes that he could see, one of them smoldering slightly from powder burns.

He slumped into the chair. "Never mind that."

"Did you get him, Harry? Did you get Kaufmann?"

"I got him, Pierre," Martineau said wearily. "When's the pickup?"

"The old aero club at Fleurie at seven, just before dark."

Martineau looked at his watch. "That only gives me half an hour. You'll have to come too. Nowhere else for you to go now."

He got to his feet and started for the door, swaying a little, and the Frenchman put an arm around him. "You'll never make it, Harry."

"I'd better because about five minutes from now the Gestapo are going to be coming up that road," Martineau told him and went outside.

He got the bike off the stand and threw a leg across the saddle, then he kicked it into life, feeling curiously as if everything was happening in slow motion. Pierre climbed up behind and put his arms around him and they rode away, out of the yard and along the lane.

As they turned into the road at the end, Martineau was aware of two dark sedans coming up fast on his left. One of them skidded to a halt, almost driving him into the ditch. He swung the motorcycle to the right, wheels spinning as he gunned the motor, was aware of shots, a sudden cry from Pierre, hands loosening their hold as the old Frenchman went backward over the rear wheel.

Martineau roared down the road toward the canal at the far end, swerved onto the towpath, one of the Gestapo cars following close. Two hundred yards away there was a lock, a narrow footbridge for pedestrians crossing to the other side. He rode across with no difficulty. Behind him, the car braked to a halt. The two Gestapo operatives inside jumped out and began to fire wildly, but by then he was long gone.

He could never remember clearly afterward any details of that cross-country ride to Fleurie. In the end, it was all something of an anticlimax anyway. The field had been headquarters of an aero club before the war. Now it lay derelict and forlorn and long disused.

He was aware of the roaring of the Lysander's engine in the distance as he rode up to the airfield himself. He paused, waiting, and the

Lysander came in out of the darkness for a perfect touchdown, turned and taxied toward him. He got off the bike, allowing it to fall to one side. He promptly fell down himself, got up again and lurched forward. The door swung open and the pilot leaned across and shouted, "I wasn't too sure when I saw the uniform."

Martineau hauled himself inside. The pilot reached over and closed and locked the door. Martineau coughed suddenly, his mouth and chin red.

The pilot said, "My God, you're choking on your own blood."

"I've been doing that for at least four years now," Martineau said.

The pilot had other things on his mind, several vehicles converging on the other end of the runway by the old buildings. Whoever they were, they were too late. The Bristol Perseus engine responded magnificently when fully boosted. The Westland Lysander was capable of taking off from rough ground, fully loaded, in two hundred and forty yards. At Fleurie, that night, they managed it in two hundred, clearing the cars at the end of the runway and climbing up into the gathering darkness.

"Very nice," Martineau said. "I liked that." And then he fainted.

"So, he's in Dorset, is he?" Munro said. "Doing what?"

"Not very much from what I can make out." Carter hesitated. "He did take two bullets in the left lung, sir, and..."

"No sad songs, Jack, I've other things on my mind. You've had a look at my ideas on a way of getting him into Jersey? What do you think?"

"Excellent, sir. I would have thought it all pretty foolproof, at least for a few days."

"And that's all we need. Now, what else have you got for me?"

"As I understand it from your preliminary plan, sir, what you're seeking is someone to go in with him to establish his credentials. Someone who knows the island and the people and so on?"

"That's right."

"There's an obvious flaw, of course. How on earth would you explain their presence? You can't just pop up in the island after four years of occupation without some sort of an explanation."

"Very true." Munro nodded. "However, I can tell by the throb in your voice that you've already come up with a solution, so let's get on with it, Jack. What have you got?"

"Sarah Anne Drayton, sir, age nineteen. Born in Jersey. Left the island just before the war to go out to Malaya where her father was a rubber planter. He was a widower apparently. Sent her home a month before the fall of Singapore."

"Which means she hasn't been back in Jersey since when?" Munro looked at the file. "Nineteen thirty-eight. Six years. That's a long time at that age, Jack. Girls change out of all recognition."

"Yes, sir."

"Mind you, she's young."

"We've used them as young as this before, sir."

"Yes, but rarely and only in extremes. Where did you find her?"

"She was put forward for SOE consideration two years ago, mainly because she speaks fluent French with a Breton accent. Her maternal grandmother was Breton. Naturally, she was turned down because of her youth."

"Where is she now?"

"Probationer nurse here in London at Cromwell Hospital."

"Excellent, Jack." Munro stood up and reached for his jacket. "We'll go and see her. I'm sure she'll prove to be intensely patriotic."

That the Luftwaffe had been chased from British skies, the Blitz had long gone, was a tale for the front pages of newspapers only. In the spring of 1944 night attacks were renewed on London, using the JU88S with devastating results. That Sunday was no exception. By eight o'clock the casualty department at Cromwell Hospital was working flat out.

Sarah Drayton had been supposed to come off shift at six. She had now been on duty for fourteen hours without a break, but there were simply not enough nurses or doctors available. She worked on, helping with casualties laid out in the corridors, trying to ignore the crump of bombs falling in the middle distance, the sound of fire engines.

She was a small, intense girl, dark hair pushed up under her cap, her face very determined, the hazel eyes serious. Her gown was filthy, stained with blood, her stockings torn. She knelt to help the matron sedate a panic-stricken young girl who was bleeding badly from shrapnel wounds. They stood up to allow porters to carry the girl away on a stretcher.

Sarah said, "I thought night raids were supposed to be a thing of the past."

"Tell that to the casualties," the matron said. "Almost a thousand of them in March. Right, you clear off, Drayton. You'll be falling down soon from sheer fatigue. No arguments."

She walked wearily along the corridor, aware that the sound of the bombing now seemed to have moved south of the river. Someone was sweeping up broken glass, and she stepped around them and moved to the reception desk to book out.

The night clerk was talking to two men. She said, "Actually, this is Nurse Drayton coming now."

Jack Carter said, "Miss Drayton, this is Brigadier Munro and I'm Captain Carter."

"What can I do for you?" Her voice was rather low and very pleasant.

Munro was much taken with her at once, and Carter said, "Do you recall an interview you had two years ago? An Intelligence matter?"

"With SOE?" She looked surprised. "I was turned down."

"Yes, well, if you could spare us some time we'd like a word with you." Carter drew her over to a bench beside the wall, and he and Munro sat on either side of her. "You were born in Jersey, Miss Drayton?"

"That's right."

He took out his notebook and opened it. "Your mother's name was Margaret de Ville. That has a particular interest for us. Do you by any chance know a Mrs. Helen de Ville?"

"I do. My mother's cousin, although she was always Aunty Helen to me. She was so much older than I was."

"And Sean Gallagher?"

"The General? Since I was a child." She looked puzzled. "What's going on here?"

"In good time, Miss Drayton," Munro told her. "When did you last see your aunt or General Gallagher?"

"Nineteen thirty-eight. My mother died that year and my father took a job in Malaya. I went out to join him."

"Yes, we know that," Carter said.

She frowned at him for a moment, then turned on Munro. "All right, what's this about?"

"It's quite simple really," Dougal Munro said. "I'd like to offer you a job with SOE. I'd like you to go to Jersey for me."

She stared at him in astonishment, but only for a moment, and then she started to laugh helplessly and the sound of it was close to hysteria. It had, after all, been a long day.

"But, Brigadier," she said. "I hardly know you."

"Strange chap, Harry Martineau," Munro said. "I've never known anybody quite like him."

"From what you tell me, neither have I," Sarah said.

The car taking them down to Lulworth Cove was a huge Austin, a glass partition separating them from the driver. Munro and Jack Carter were in the rear, side by side, and Sarah Drayton sat on the jump seat opposite. She wore a tweed suit with pleated skirt, tan stockings and black brogues with half-heels, blouse in cream satin with a black string tie at her neck. She looked very attractive, cheeks flushed, eyes flickering everywhere. She also looked extremely young.

"It was his birthday the week before last," Carter told her.

She was immediately interested. "How old was he?"

"Forty-four."

"What they call a child of the century, my dear," Munro told her. "Born on the seventh of April, nineteen hundred. That must seem terribly old to you."

"Aries," she said.

Munro smiled. "That's right. Before the advent of our so called enlightened times astrology was a science. Did you know that?"

"Not really."

"The ancient Egyptians always chose their generals from Leos, for example."

"I'm a Leo," she said. "July twenty-seventh."

"Then you *are* in for a complicated life. Something of a hobby of mine. Take Harry, for instance. Very gifted, brilliant analytical mind. A professor in the greatest university in the world at thirty-eight. Then look at what he became in middle life."

"How do you explain that?" she demanded.

"Astrology explains it for us. Aries is a warrior sign, but very commonly those born around the same time as Harry are one thing on the surface, something else underneath. Mars decanate in Gemini, you see, and Gemini is the sign of the twins."

"So?"

"People like that can be very schizophrenic. On one level, you're Harry Martineau, scholar, philosopher, poet, full of sweet reason, but on the dark side…" He shrugged. "A cold and ruthless killer. Yes, there's a curious lack of emotion to him, wouldn't you agree, Jack? Of course, all this has been extremely useful in the job he's been doing for the past four years. Suppose that's what's kept him alive when most of the others have died."

Carter said, "Just in case you're getting a rather bad impression of Harry Martineau, two things, Sarah. Although his mother was born in the States, she was of German parentage, and Harry spent a lot of time with them in Dresden and Heidelberg as he grew up. His grandfather, a professor of surgery, was an active Socialist. He died in a fall from the balcony of his apartment. A nasty accident."

"Aided by two Gestapo thugs taking an arm and a leg each to help him on his way," Munro put in.

"And then there was a Jewish girl named Rosa Bernstein."

"Yes," Sarah put in. "I was beginning to wonder whether females had ever entered into his life. No mention of marriage."

"He met Rosa Bernstein when she did a year at an Oxford College, St. Hugh's, in nineteen thirty-two. He was spending increasing time in Europe by then. Both his parents were dead. His father had left him reasonably well off, and as an only child, he had no close relatives."

"But he and Rosa never married?"

"No," Munro said, and added bluntly: "You'll often find prejudice on both sides of the fence, my dear. Rosa's parents were Orthodox Jews, and they didn't like the idea of their daughter marrying a Gentile. She and Harry pursued what you might term a vigorous affair for some years. I knew them both well. I was at Oxford myself in those days."

"What happened?"

It was Carter who answered her. "She was active in the Socialist underground. Went backward and forward from England to Germany as a courier. In May, nineteen thirty-eight, she was apprehended, taken to Gestapo Headquarters at Prince Albrechtstrasse in Berlin. A good address for a very bad place. There, she was interrogated with extreme brutality and, according to our information, executed."

There was a long silence. She seemed abstracted, staring out of the window into the distance. Munro said, "You don't seem shocked? I find that strange in one so young."

She shook her head. "I've been nursing for two years now. I deal with death every day of my life. So Harry Martineau doesn't particularly care for Germans?"

"No," Carter said. "He doesn't like Nazis. There's a difference."

"Yes, I can see that."

She stared out of the window again, feeling restless, on edge, and it was all to do with Martineau, this man she had never met. He filled her mind. Would not go away.

Carter said, "One thing we didn't ask. I hope you don't mind my being personal, but is there anyone in your life at the moment? Anyone who would miss you?"

"A man?" She laughed harshly. "Good heavens, no! I never work less than a twelve-hour daily shift at the Cromwell. That leaves one just about enough time to have a bath and a meal before falling into bed." She shook her head. "No time for men. My father's in a Japanese prison camp. I've an old aunt in Sussex, his elder sister, and that's about it. No one to miss me at all. I'm all yours, gentlemen."

She delivered the speech with an air of bravado and an illusion of calm sophistication that in one so young was strangely moving.

Munro, unusually for him, felt uncomfortable. "This is important, believe me." He leaned forward, put a hand on her arm. "We wouldn't ask you if it wasn't."

She nodded. "I know, Brigadier, I know." She turned and stared out of the window again at the passing scenery, thinking about Martineau.

He awoke with a dull ache just behind the right eye and his mouth tasted foul. Only one answer to that. He pulled on an old tracksuit and grabbed a towel, left by the front door and ran down to the sea.

He stripped and ran out through the shallows, plunging through the waves. It wasn't even a nice morning, the sky the color of slate gray, and there was rain on the wind. Yet quite suddenly, he experienced one of those special moments. Sea and sky seemed to become one. For a little while all sounds faded as he battled his way through the waves. Nothing mattered. Not the past or the future. Only this present moment. As he turned on his back, a herring gull fled overhead and it started to rain.

A voice called out, "Enjoying yourself, Harry?"

Martineau turned toward the shore and found Munro standing there in old tweed coat and battered hat, holding an umbrella over his head. "My God," he said. "Not you, Dougal?"

"As ever was, Harry. Come on up to the cottage. There's someone I'd like you to meet."

He turned and walked back across the beach without another word. Martineau floated there for a while, thinking about it. Dougal Munro wasn't just paying a social call, that was for sure, not all the way from London. Excitement surged through him and he waded out of the water, toweled himself briskly, pulled on the old tracksuit and ran across the beach and up the cliff path. Jack Carter was standing on the porch, watching the rain and smoking a cigarette.

"What, you too, Jack?" Martineau smiled with real pleasure and took the other man's hand. "Does the old sod want me to go back to work?"

"Something like that." Carter hesitated, then said, "Harry, I think you've done enough."

"No such word in the vocabulary, Jack, not until they nail down the lid and put you six feet under." Martineau brushed past Carter and went inside.

Munro was sitting by the fire, reading the notepad he'd found on the table. "Still writing bad poetry?"

"Always did." Martineau took the pad from him, tore off the top sheet, crumpled it up and tossed it into the fireplace. It was then that he became aware of Sarah Drayton standing in the kitchen doorway.

"I'm making tea for everyone. I hope that's all right, Colonel Martineau. I'm Sarah Drayton."

She didn't bother holding out her hand, for it would have trembled too much. She was aware that she was close to tears and her stomach was hollow with excitement, throat dry. *Coup de foudre,* the French called it. The thunderclap. The best kind of love of all. Instant and quite irrevocable.

And at first, he responded, brushing a lock of black hair back from the white forehead, his face illuminated by a smile of great natural charm, and then the smile faded and he turned on Munro, anger in his voice, as if seeing everything.

"My God, what a bastard you are, Dougal. So now we're using schoolgirls?"

Hugh Kelso's adventures did not take long in the telling, but when he was finished, Munro carried on.

"The other month we knocked off a man called Braun in Paris. Jack has the details. I think you'll find it interesting."

"What was he, Gestapo?" Martineau asked.

"No, SD." Carter turned to Sarah Drayton sitting on the other side of the fire. "That's the Secret Intelligence Department of the SS, responsible only to Himmler himself. More powerful than any other organization in Germany today."

"Go on about Braun," Martineau said.

"Well, according to his papers, he was RFSS." Carter turned again to Sarah. "That means Reichsführer SS. It's a cuff title that members of Himmler's personal staff wear on their uniform sleeve." He took a paper from the file he was holding and offered it to Martineau. "It seems Braun was a kind of roving ambassador, empowered to make his own investigations wherever he pleased."

"With supreme authority over everyone he came into contact with," Munro said. "Read that letter."

Martineau took it from its envelope and unfolded it.

It was on excellent paper, the heading embossed in black.

DER REICHSFÜHRER—Berlin, 9 November 1943
ss—sturmbannführer
braun erwin, ss-nr 107863

This officer acts under my personal orders on business of the utmost importance to the Reich. All personnel, military and civil, without distinction of rank, must assist him in any way he sees fit.

H. HIMMLER

A remarkable document in itself. Even more astonishing was that it was countersigned across the bottom: *Adolf Hitler, Führer und Reichskanzler.*

"He obviously had a certain amount of influence," Martineau said dryly, handing it back to Carter.

Munro said, "Well the bastard's dead now, but our Paris people got some useful information out of him before he left."

"I bet they did," Martineau said, and lit a cigarette.

"He has a dozen or so of these special envoys floating around Europe, putting the fear of God into everyone wherever they turn up. All highly secret. Nobody knows who they are. I've got our forgery department preparing a complete set of papers for you. SD identity card and a copy of that letter and whatever else you need. Name of Max Vogel. We thought we'd give you a little rank, just to help the ship along, so it's Standartenführer." He turned to Sarah, "Colonel to you."

"I get the picture," Martineau said. "I arrive on Jersey's fair shore and frighten the hell out of everyone."

"You know as well as I, dear boy, that there's nothing more frightening than a schoolmaster in a leather overcoat turned revolutionary. Lenin for a start. And you must admit, you do a very good Nazi, Harry."

"And the child?" Martineau inquired. "Where does she fit in?"

"You need someone with you to establish your credentials with Mrs. de Ville and this chap Gallagher. Sarah is related to one and knows the other. Another thing, she was last in Jersey six years ago, aged thirteen—all plaits and ankle socks, I shouldn't wonder. Still herself enough for Helen de Ville and Gallagher to recognize, but different enough to pass as a stranger with other people, especially when we've finished with her."

"And what's that supposed to mean?"

"Well, there's a fair trade in ladies of the night between France and Jersey."

"You mean whores? You're not suggesting she play one of those?"

"Most senior German officers in France have French girlfriends. Why should you be any different? To start off, Sarah speaks excellent French with a Breton accent because that's what her grandmother was.

By the time our people at Berkley Hall have finished with her, changed her hair color, got her into the right clothes—"

"You mean, turned her into a little French tart?" Martineau interrupted.

"Something like that. Perfect cover for her."

"And when are we supposed to go in?"

"Day after tomorrow. A Lysander drop near Granville. Two-hour flight, Harry. Piece of cake. Sophie Cresson will meet you. Afterward, you use your authority to cross to Jersey on one of the night boats from Granville. Once over there, you make it up as you go along. You've got till Sunday at the outside."

"And what if it's impossible to get him out? What then?"

"Up to you."

"I see. I play executioner for you again?" He turned on Sarah. "What do you think about all this?"

He was angry, the face whiter than ever, the eyes very dark. "Oh, I don't know," she said. "It sounds as if it could be rather interesting."

In a sense, the flippancy of her remarks was an attempt to control her feelings, and when she turned and moved to the table to pour more tea into her cup, her hand shook slightly. The death of her mother had sent her to live with her father on a plantation deep in the Malayan jungle. A life of discomfort and considerable danger, an extraordinary upbringing for a girl of thirteen, and yet she'd loved every minute of it. In moments of the greatest danger, she seemed to come alive. The hospital by night, the bombing, the casualties who needed her. Once again, she'd loved every minute of it.

And now this. It was not just sexual desire, although she was enough of a woman to know that she wanted Martineau. But that was only part of it. It was what this strange, intense, tortured man offered. The promise of danger, excitement of a kind she had never even dreamed of before.

"Rather interesting? Dear God!" Martineau poured himself a scotch. "Have you read any of the works of Heidegger, Jack?"

"I'm familiar with them."

"An interesting man. He believed that for authentic living what was necessary was the resolute confrontation of death."

"That sounds fine by me," Munro said.

"Really?" Martineau laughed harshly. "As far as I'm concerned, it's idiots like that who made me give up on philosophy." He raised his glass and toasted them all. "Here we go then. Berkley Hall next stop."

7

THE FIRING RANGE AT Berkley Hall was in the basement. The armorer was an Irish Guards staff sergeant named Kelly, long past retirement and back in harness only because of the war. The place was brightly lit at the target end where cutout replicas of charging Germans stood against sandbags. Kelly and Sarah Drayton were the only people on the firing line. They'd given her battle dress to wear, slacks and blouse of blue serge, the kind issued to girls in the Women's Auxiliary Air Force. She'd tied her hair up and tucked it inside the peaked cap, leaving her neck bare. It somehow made her look very vulnerable.

Kelly had various weapons laid out on the table. "Have you ever fired a handgun before, miss?"

"Yes," she said, "in Malaya. My father was a rubber planter. He used to be away a great deal so he made sure I knew how to use a revolver. And I've fired a shotgun a few times."

"Anything here that looks familiar?"

"That revolver." She pointed. "It looks like the Smith and Wesson my father owned."

"That's exactly what it is, miss," Kelly said. "Obviously in more normal circumstances you'd be given a thorough grounding in weaponry as part of your course, but in your case, there just isn't time. What I'll do is show you a few things, just to familiarize you with some basic weapons you're likely to come across. Then you can fire a few rounds and that will have to do."

"Fair enough," she said.

"Rifles are simple," he said. "I won't waste your time with those. Here we've got two basic submachine guns. The British Sten in standard use with our own forces. This is a Mark 11S. Silenced version, developed for use with the French Resistance groups. Thirty-two rounds in that magazine. Automatic fire burns out the silencer, so use it semiautomatic or single burst. Like to have a go?"

It was surprisingly light and gave her no problems at all when she fired it from the shoulder, the only sound being the bolt reciprocating. She tore a sandbag apart to one side of the target she aimed at.

"Not much good," she said.

"Few people are with these things. They're good at close quarters when you're up against several people and that's all," Kelly told her. "The other submachine gun's German. An MP40. Popularly known as the Schmeisser. The Resistance use those a lot too."

He went through the handguns with her then, both the revolvers and the automatics. When she tried with the Smith & Wesson, arm extended, she only managed to nick the shoulder of the target once out of six shots.

"I'm afraid you'd be dead, miss."

As he reloaded, she said, "What about Colonel Martineau? Is he any good?"

"You could say that, miss. I don't think I've ever known anyone better with a handgun. Now, try this way." He crouched, feet apart, holding the gun two-handed. "See what I mean?"

"I think so." She copied him, the gun out in front of her in both hands.

"Now squeeze with a half breath of a pause between each shot."

This time, she did better, hitting the target once in the shoulder and once in the left hand.

"Terrific," Kelly said.

"Not if you consider she was probably aiming for the heart."

Martineau had come in quietly behind them. He wore a dark polo neck sweater and black corduroy pants and he came to the table and examined the guns. "As I'm going to have to look after this infant and as time is limited, do you mind if I take a hand?"

"Be my guest, sir."

Martineau picked up a pistol from the table. "Walther PPK, semi-automatic. Seven-round magazine goes in the butt, like so. Pull the slider back and you're in business. It's not too large. You wouldn't notice it in your handbag, but it will do the job and that's what matters. Now come down the range."

"All right."

They moved so close that the targets were no more than ten or twelve yards away. "If he's close enough for you to hold it against him when you pull the trigger, do it that way, but you should never be farther away than you are now. Simply throw up your arm and point the gun at him. Keep both eyes open and fire very fast."

She hit the target six times in the general area of the chest and belly. "Oh, my word," she said, very excited. "That wasn't bad, was it?"

As they walked back to the firing line he said, "Yes, but could you do it for real?"

"I'll only know when the time comes, won't I?" she said. "Anyway, what about you? I hear a lot of talk, but not much to justify it."

There was another Walther on the table with a round cylinder of polished black steel screwed on to the end of the barrel. "This is what's called a Carswell silencer," Martineau told her. "Specially developed for use by SOE agents."

His arm swung up. He didn't appear to take aim, firing twice, shooting out the heart of the target. The only sound had been two dull thuds, and the effect was quite terrifying.

He laid the gun down and turned, eyes blank in the white face. "I've got things to do. Dougal wants us in the library in half an hour. I'll see you then."

He walked out. There was an awkward silence. Sarah said, "He seemed angry."

"The colonel gets like that, miss. I don't think he likes what he sees in himself sometimes. Last November he killed the head of the

Gestapo at Lyons. Man called Kaufmann. A real butcher. They brought him back from over there in a puddle of blood in a Lysander. Two bullets in his left lung for starters. He's been different since then."

"In what way?"

"I don't know, miss." Kelly frowned. "Here, don't you go getting silly ideas about him. I know what you young girls can be like. I've got a daughter your age on an antiaircraft battery in London. Just remember he's got twenty-five years on you."

"You mean he's too old?" Sarah said. "Isn't that like saying you can't love someone because they're Catholic or Jewish or American or something? What's the difference?"

"Too clever for me, that kind of talk." Kelly opened a drawer and took out a cloth bundle which he unwrapped. "A little present for you, miss, in spite of what the colonel says." It was a small black automatic pistol, very light, almost swallowed up by her hand. "Belgian. Only .25, but it'll do the trick when you need it and, at that size, very easy to hide." He looked awkward. "I've known ladies to tuck them in the top of their stocking, not intending to be disrespectful, miss."

She reached up and kissed him on the cheek. "I think you're wonderful."

"You can't do that, miss, you being an officer. Against regulations."

"But I'm not an officer, Sergeant."

"I think you'll find you are, miss. Probably one of the things the brigadier wants to tell you. I'd cut off and go to the library now if I were you."

"All right and thank you."

She went out and Kelly sighed and started to clear away the weapons.

Munro, Carter and Martineau were already in the library when she went in, sitting by the fire having afternoon tea. "Ah, there you are," Munro said. "Do join us. The crumpets are delicious."

Carter poured her a cup of tea. She said, "Sergeant Kelly said something about my being an officer now. What was he talking about?"

"Yes, well, we do prefer our women operatives to hold some sort of commissioned rank. In theory it's supposed to help you if you fall into enemy hands," Munro told her.

"In practice, it doesn't do you any good at all," Martineau interrupted. "However, for good or ill, you are now a flight officer in the

WAAF," Munro said. "I trust that is satisfactory. Now, let's look at the map."

They all got up and went to the table where there were several large-scale maps, together making a patchwork that included the south of England, the Channel, and the general area of the Channel Islands and Normandy and Brittany.

"All those jolly films they make at Elstree showing you our gallant secret agents at work usually have them parachuting into France. In fact, we prefer to take people in by plane wherever possible."

"I see," she said.

"Our popular choice is the Lysander. These days the pilot usually manages on his own. That way we can take up to three passengers. They're operated by a Special Duties Squadron at Hornley Field. It's not too far from here."

"How long will the flight take?"

"No more than an hour and a half, perhaps less depending on wind conditions. You'll land not far from Granville.

The local Resistance people will be on hand to take care of you. We find the early hours of the morning best. Say four or five."

"Then what?"

"The evening of the same day you'll leave Granville by ship for Jersey. Most convoys go by night now. We have air superiority during daylight hours." He turned to Martineau. "Naturally, the question of passage is a matter for Standartenführer Max Vogel, but I doubt whether anyone is likely to do anything other than run round in circles when they see your credentials."

Martineau nodded. "We'll be in trouble if they don't."

"As regards your dealings with Mrs. de Ville and General Gallagher. Well, you have Sarah to vouch for you."

"And Kelso?"

"Entirely in your hands, dear boy. You're the officer in the field. I'll back whatever you decide to do. You know how critical the situation is."

"Fair enough."

Munro picked up the phone at his side. "Send Mrs. Moon in now." He put the phone down and said to Sarah. "We're very lucky to have Mrs. Moon. We borrow her from Denham Studios by courtesy of

Alexander Korda. There's nothing she doesn't know about makeup, dress and so on."

Hilda Moon was a large fat woman with a cockney accent. Her own appearance inspired little confidence, for her hair was dyed red and it showed, and she wore too much lipstick. A cigarette dangled from the corner of her mouth, ash spilling down on her ample bosom.

"Yes." She nodded, walking round Sarah. "Very nice. Of course I'll have to do something with the hair."

"Do you think so?" Sarah asked in alarm.

"Girls who get by the way you're supposed to in this part, dear, always carry it up front. They make a living from pleasing men, which means they have to make the best of what they've got. You trust me, I know what's best for you."

She took Sarah by the arm and led her out. As the door closed, Martineau said, "We probably won't even recognize her when we see her again."

"Of course," Munro said. "But then, I should have thought that was the general idea."

It was early evening when the phone rang at Gallagher's cottage. He was in the kitchen, working through farm accounts at the table, and answered it instantly.

"Savary here, General. The matter of the package we discussed."

"Yes."

"My contact in Granville was in touch with their head office. It seems someone will be with you by Thursday at the latest to give you the advice you need."

"You're certain of that."

"Absolutely."

The phone went dead. Gallagher sat there thinking about it, then he put on his old corduroy jacket and went up to de Ville Place. He found Helen in the kitchen with Mrs. Vibert, preparing the evening meal. The old lady didn't live on the premises, but just down the road in another farm cottage with her niece and young daughter. She was a widow herself, a good-hearted woman of sixty-five, devoted to Helen.

She dried her hands and took a coat down from behind the door. "If that's all, I'll be off now, Mrs. de Ville."

"See you in the morning," Helen told her.

As the door closed behind her, Gallagher said, "She doesn't suspect anything, does she?"

"No, and I want it to stay that way, for her own good, as much as anyone else's."

"I've just had Savary on the phone. They got through to London. Someone will be with us by Thursday."

She turned quickly. "Are you certain?"

"As much as I can be. How is the good colonel?"

"Still feverish. George saw him this afternoon. He seems satisfied. He's trying him on this penicillin stuff."

"I'm surprised Savary was in so early. They must have made the run this afternoon."

"They did," she said. "Taking advantage of the fog again. Most of the officers have turned up here within the past hour."

"Most?"

'Two dead. Bohlen and Wendel. Two of the ships were attacked by Hurricanes."

At that moment, the green baize door leading to the dining room opened and Guido Orsini came in. He was wearing his best uniform, his hair still damp from the shower, and looked rather dashing. He wore the Italian Medal for Military Valor in gold, a medal equivalent to the British Victoria Cross and very rarely awarded. On his left breast he also wore an Iron Cross First Class.

Gallagher said in English, "Still in one piece are you? Hear you had a bad time."

"It could have been worse," Guido told him. "They're all sitting in there doing their conspicuous mourning bit." He put a bag he was carrying on the table. "Dozen bottles of Sancerre there from Granville."

"You're a good boy," she said.

"So I believe. Don't you think I also look rather beautiful tonight?"

"Very possibly." He was mocking her as usual, she knew that. "Now move to one side while I dish up the food."

Guido inched open the serving hatch to the dining room and whispered to Gallagher. "Sean, come and look at this."

The hall was paneled in oak, darkly magnificent, and the long oaken table down the center could accommodate twenty-five. There were only eight in there now, all naval officers, seated at various places. In each gap, where someone was missing, a lighted candle stood at the plate. There were six such candles, each representing a member of the mess who had died in action. The atmosphere was funereal to say the least.

"They have to make everything into a Shakespearean tragedy," Orsini said. "It's really very boring. If it wasn't for Helen's cooking I'd go elsewhere. I discovered a remarkably good black-market restaurant in St. Aubin's Bay the other night. Amazing what one got and without coupons."

"Now that *is* interesting," Gallagher said. "Tell me more."

As Mrs. Moon and her two assistants worked on Sarah, the fat woman talked incessantly. "I've been everywhere. Denham, Elstree, Pinewood. I do all Miss Margaret Lockwood's makeup and Mr. James Mason. Oh, and I've worked with Mr. Coward. Now he *was* a gentleman."

When Sarah came out from under the dryer, she couldn't believe what she saw. Her dark hair was now a golden blond, and they'd marcelled it tight against her face. Now, Mrs. Moon started with the makeup, plucking hairs from the eyebrows painfully then lining them into two thin streaks.

"Plenty of rouge, dear. A little too much, if you know what I mean, and lots of lipstick. Everything just a little overdone, that's what we want. Now, what do you think?"

Sarah sat looking into the mirror. It was the face of a stranger. Who am I? she thought. Did Sarah Drayton ever exist at all?

"We'll try one of the dresses. Of course, the underwear and every individual item will be of French origin, but you only need the dress at the moment, just for the effect."

It was black satin, very tight and rather short. She helped Sarah into it and zipped it at the back. "It certainly helps your breasts along, dear. They look very good."

"I don't know about that, I can't breathe." Sarah pulled on a pair of high-heeled shoes and looked at herself in the mirror. She giggled. "I look the most awful tart."

"Well, that *is* the idea, love. Now go and see what the brigadier thinks."

Munro and Carter were still sitting by the fire when she went in, talking in low tones. Sarah said, "No one told me my name."

"Anne-Marie Latour," Carter said automatically and then looked up. "Good God!" he said.

Munro was far more positive. "I like it. Like it very much indeed." Sarah pirouetted. "Yes, they'll go for you in the German officers' club in St. Helier."

"Or in the Army and Navy in London, I should have thought," Carter said dryly.

The door opened and Martineau entered. She turned to face him, hands on hips in a deliberate challenge. "Well?" she demanded.

"Well, what?"

"Oh, damn you." She was cross enough to stamp a foot. "You're the most infuriating man I've ever met. Is there a village near here with a pub?"

"Yes."

"Will you take me for a drink?"

"Like that?"

"You mean I don't look nice enough?"

"Actually, you transcend all Mrs. Moon's efforts. You couldn't be a tart if you tried, brat. I'll see you in the hall in fifteen minutes," and he turned and went out.

There was a spring fete on in the village in aid of war charities. Stalls and sideshows on the village green and a couple of old-fashioned roundabouts. Sarah wore a coat over the dress and hung onto his arm. She was obviously enjoying herself as they moved through the noisy and good-humored crowd.

There was a tent marked *Fortunes—Gypsy Sara*. "Sara without the H," he said. "Let's give it a try."

"All right," he said, humoring her.

Surprisingly, the woman inside had dispensed with the usual gypsy trappings, the headscarf and the earrings. She was about forty with a sallow face, neat black hair and wore a smart gabardine suit. She took the girl's hand. "Just you, lady, or your gentleman as well?"

"But he isn't my gentleman," she protested.

"He'll never belong to anyone else, never know another woman."

She took a deep breath as if trying to clear her head, and Martineau said, "Now let's hear the good news."

She handed a tarot pack to Sarah, folded her own hands over Sarah's, then shuffled the pack several times and extracted three cards.

The first was Fortitude, a young woman grasping the jaws of a lion. "There is an opportunity to put an important plan into action if one will take risks," Gypsy Sara said.

The next card was the Star, a naked girl kneeling by a pool. "I see fire and water, mingling at the same time. A contradiction and yet you come through both unscathed."

Sarah turned to Martineau. "I had that last month at the Cromwell. Incendiary bombs on the nurses' quarters and water everywhere from the fire hoses."

The third card was the Hanged Man. The woman said, "He will not change however long he hangs in the tree. He cannot alter the mirror image, however much he fears it. You must journey on alone. Adversity will always be your strength. You will find love only by not seeking it, that is the lesson you must learn."

Sarah said to Martineau, "Now you."

Gypsy Sara gathered up the cards. "There is nothing I can tell the gentleman that he does not know already."

"Best thing I've heard since the Brothers Grimm." Martineau pushed a pound across the table and stood up. "Let's go."

"Are you angry?" Sarah demanded as they pushed through the crowd to the village pub.

"Why should I be?"

"It was only a bit of fun. Nothing to be taken seriously."

"Oh, but I take everything seriously," he assured her.

The bar was crowded but they managed to find a couple of seats in the corner by the fire, and he ordered her a shandy and had a scotch for himself. "Well, what do you think of it so far?" he asked.

"Rather more interesting than the wards at the Cromwell."

"In other circumstances you'd be trained for about six weeks," he said. "The Scottish Highlands to toughen you up. Courses in unarmed combat and so on. Twelve ways of killing someone with your bare hands."

"That sounds very gruesome."

"But effective. I remember one of our agents, a journalist in civilian life, who stopped going into pubs when he was home. He was afraid to get into an argument because of what he might do."

"Can you do that sort of thing?" she asked him.

"Anybody can be taught to do it. It's brains that's important in this game."

There were three soldiers in khaki battle dress at the bar, an older man who was a sergeant and a couple of privates. Hard young men who kept laughing, heads together, as they looked across at Martineau. When he went to replenish the drinks, one of them deliberately jogged his arm as he turned from the bar, spilling a little scotch.

"You want to be more careful, mate," the youth told him.

"If you say so." Martineau smiled cheerfully, and the sergeant put a hand on the youth's sleeve and muttered something.

When he sat down Sarah said, "Jack Carter tells me you knew Freud."

"Yes, I last saw him in London in nineteen thirty-nine just before he died."

"Do you agree with psychoanalysis?"

"Everything coming down to sex? God knows, old Sigmund had enough problems in that direction himself. He was once doing a lecture tour in the States with Jung and told him one day that he kept dreaming of prostitutes. Jung simply asked him why he didn't do something about it. Freud was terribly shocked. 'But I'm a married man,' he said."

She laughed helplessly. "That's marvelous."

"Talking of great minds, I used to have dealings with Bertrand Russell, who liked the ladies more than somewhat, which he justified by his strongly held personal belief that you couldn't get to know a woman properly until you'd slept with her."

"That doesn't sound very philosophical to me," she said.

"On the contrary."

She got up and excused herself. "I'll be back in a minute."

As she went out to the cloakroom the three soldiers watched her go, then glanced at Martineau, and there was a burst of laughter. As she returned, the young soldier who had bumped Martineau at the bar grabbed her arm. She struggled to pull away and Martineau was on his feet and pushing through the crowd to her side.

"That's enough."

"Who the hell are you, her father?" the boy demanded.

Martineau took him by the wrist, applying leverage in the way the instructor had shown him on the silent killing course at Arisaig in Scotland in the early days. The boy grimaced in pain. The sergeant said, "Leave off. He didn't mean any harm. Just a bit of fun."

"Yes, I can see that."

As he took her back to the table she said, "That was quick."

"When I feel, I act. I'm a very existentialist person."

"Existentialist?" She frowned. "I don't understand."

"Oh, a new perspective to things a friend of mine's come up with. A French writer called Jean-Paul Sartre. When I was on the run in Paris three years ago I holed up at his apartment for a couple of weeks. He's involved with the Resistance."

"But what does it mean?"

"Oh, lots of things. The bit I like is the suggestion that you should create values for yourself through action and by living each moment to the full."

"Is that how you've got yourself through the last four years?"

"Something like that. Sartre just put it into words for me." He helped her into her coat. "Let's go."

It was dark outside, music and merriment drifting from the direction of the fair, although most of the stands were already closed because of the blackout regulations. They started across the deserted car park to where Martineau had left the car, and there was a sound of running footsteps. He turned as the two young soldiers ran up. The sergeant emerged on the porch at the rear of the pub and stood watching.

"Now then," the young soldier who'd caused the scene at the bar said. "You and me aren't finished yet. You need to be taught a lesson."

"Is that a fact?" Martineau demanded, and as the youth moved in, swinging a punch, he caught the wrist, twisted it up and around, locking the shoulder. The soldier cried out as the muscle tore. The other soldier gave a cry of alarm and recoiled as Martineau dropped his friend on the ground and the sergeant ran forward angrily.

"You bastard!" he said.

"Not me, you for letting it happen." Martineau had his identity card out. "I think you'd better look at that."

The sergeant's face dropped. "Colonel, sir!" He sprang to attention.

"That's better. You're going to need a doctor. Tell chummy here when he's capable of listening that I hope he's learned something. Next time it could be the death of him."

As they drove away, Sarah said, "You don't hesitate at all, do you?"

"What's the point?"

"I think I understand what Jack Carter meant. You have an aptitude for killing, I think."

"Words," he said. "Games in the head. That's all I had for years. Nothing but talk, nothing but ideas. Let's have some facts. Let's stop playing games in black satin dresses with our hair blonded. You know what the first technique is that the Gestapo employ in breaking down any woman agent who falls into their hands?"

"You're obviously going to tell me."

"Multiple rape. If that doesn't do the trick, the electric shock treatment comes next. I used to have a girlfriend in Berlin. She was Jewish."

"I know. Carter told me about her as well."

"How they tortured, then murdered her in the Gestapo cellars at Prince Albrechtstrasse?" Martineau shook his head. "He doesn't know everything. He doesn't know that Kaufmann, the head of the Gestapo in Lyons who I killed last November, was the man responsible for Rosa's death in Berlin in nineteen thirty-eight."

"I see now," she said softly. "Sergeant Kelly said you were different and he was right. You hated Kaufmann for years and when you finally took your revenge, you found it meant nothing."

"All this wisdom." He laughed coldly. "Going over there and taking on the Gestapo isn't like one of those movies they make at Elstree Studios. There are fifty million people in France. You know how many we estimate are active members of the Resistance?"

"No."

"Two thousand, Sarah. Two lousy thousand." He was disgusted. "I don't know why we bother."

"Then why do you? Not just for Rosa or your grandfather." He turned briefly and she said, "Oh, yes, I know about that too."

There was a silence. He opened his cigarette case one-handed. "Do you want one of these things? A bad habit, but a great comfort in the clinches."

"All right," she said and took one.

He gave her a light. "Something I've never talked about. I was due to go to Harvard in nineteen seventeen. Then America joined in the war. I was seventeen, officially under age. Joined up on sheer impulse and ended up in the trenches in Flanders." He shook his head. "Whatever you mean by hell on earth, that was the trenches. So many dead you lost count."

"It must have been terrible," she said.

"And I loved every minute of it. Can you understand that? I lived more in one day, felt more, than in a year of ordinary living. Life became real, bloody, exciting. I couldn't get enough."

"Like a drug?"

"Exactly. I was like the man in the poem, constantly seeking Death on the battlefield. That was what I ran away from, back to Harvard and Oxford cloisters and the safe world of classrooms and books, everything in the head."

"And then the war came round again."

"And Dougal Munro yanked me out into the real world… And the rest, as they say, you know."

Later, lying in bed smoking a cigarette, listening to the rain tapping at the window, he heard the door open. She said softly through the darkness, "It's only me."

"Really?" Martineau said.

She took off her robe and got into bed beside him. She was wearing a cotton nightdress and he put an arm around her automatically. "Harry," she whispered. "Can I make a confession?"

"You obviously intend to."

"I know you probably imagine, along with everyone else that I'm a delicate little middle-class virgin, but I'm afraid I'm not."

"Is that a fact?"

"Yes, I met a Spitfire pilot at the hospital last year. He used to come in for treatment for a broken ankle."

"And true love blossomed?"

"Not really. More like mutual lust, but he was a nice chap and I don't regret it. He was shot down over the Channel three months ago."

She started to cry, for no reason that made any kind of sense, and Martineau held her tight, wordless in the dark.

8

THE FOLLOWING DAY JUST after noon at Fermanville on the Cherbourg Peninsula, Karl Hagan, the duty sergeant at the central strongpoint of the 15th Coastal Artillery Battery, was leaning on a concrete parapet idly enjoying a cigarette in the pale afternoon sunshine when he observed a black Mercedes coming up the track. No escort so it couldn't be anyone important—and then he noticed the pennant fluttering on the bonnet. Too far away to see what it was, but to an old soldier it was enough. He was inside the operations room in a flash, where Captain Reimann, the battery commander, sprawled at his desk, tunic buttons undone, reading a book.

"Someone coming, sir. Looks like top brass to me. Shock inspection perhaps."

"Right. Klaxon alarm. Get the men to fall in, just in case."

Reimann buttoned his tunic, buckled his belt and adjusted his cap to a satisfactory angle. As he went out on the redoubt, the Mercedes pulled in below. The driver got out. The first person out was an army major with staff stripes on his pants. The second was Field Marshal Erwin Rommel in leather trenchcoat, white scarf knotted carelessly at his neck, desert goggles pulled up above the peak of his cap.

Reimann had never been so shocked in his life and he grabbed at the parapet. At the same moment he heard Sergeant Hagan's voice and the battery personnel doubled out in the courtyard below. As Reimann hurried down the steps the two battery lieutenants, Scheel and Planck, took up their positions.

Reimann moved forward and remembering what he'd heard of Rommel's preferences chose the military rather than the Nazi salute. "Herr Field Marshal. You do us a great honor."

Rommel tapped the end of his field marshal's baton against the peak of his cap. "Your name?"

"Reimann, Herr Field Marshal."

"Major Hofer, my aide."

Hofer said, "The Field Marshal will see everything, including the subsidiary strongpoints. Please lead the way."

"First, Major, I'll inspect the troops," Rommel told him. "An army is only as strong as its weakest point, always remember that."

"Of course, Herr Field Marshal," Hofer said.

Rommel moved down the line, stopping here and there to talk to an individual who took his fancy. Finally he turned. "Good turnout. Highly satisfactory. Now we go."

For the next hour he tramped the clifftop from one strongpoint to another as Reimann led the way. Radio rooms, men's quarters, ammunition stores, even the urinals. Nothing escaped his attention.

"Excellent, Reimann," he told the young artillery officer. "First-rate performance. I'll endorse your field unit report personally."

Reimann almost fainted with pleasure. "Herr Field Marshal—what can I say?"

He called the honor guard to attention. Rommel tapped the baton against his cap again and got into the Mercedes. Hofer joined him on the other side, and as the driver drove away, the major checked that the glass partition was closed tight.

"Excellent," Hofer said. "Have a cigarette. I think you carried that off very well, Berger."

"Really, Herr Major?" Heini Baum said. "I get the booking then?"

"One more test, I think. Something a little bit more ambitious.

Dinner at some officers' mess, perhaps. Yes, that would be good. Then you'll be ready for Jersey."

"Anything you say." Baum leaned back, inhaling deeply on the cigarette.

"So, back to the field marshal to report," Konrad Hofer said.

When Sarah and Harry Martineau went into the library at Berkley Hall, Jack Carter was sitting at the table, the maps spread before him.

"Ah, there you are," he said. "Brigadier Munro has gone up to London to report to General Eisenhower, but he'll be back tonight. We'll both see you off from Hornley Field. Any problems?"

"None that I can think of." Martineau turned to Sarah. "What about you?"

"I don't think so."

"Your clothes have all been double-checked for Frenchness," Carter said. "So that's taken care of. Here are your papers, Sarah. French identity card with photo. German Ausweis, with different photo. Now you know why they asked you to change clothes at the photography session. Ration cards. Oh, and a tobacco ration card."

"You're supposed to have one of those even if you don't smoke," Martineau told her.

"These documents are one hundred percent," Carter said. "Right paper, same watermarks. Typewriters, ink—everything perfect. I can assure you that there is no way that even the most skilled Abwehr or Gestapo operative could find them anything but genuine." He handed her a slip of paper. "There are your personal details. Anne-Marie Latour. We've kept to your own age and birthdate. Born in Brittany naturally, to explain your accent. We've made your place of birth Paimpol on the coast. I believe you know it well?"

"Yes, my grandmother lived there. I spent many holidays with her."

"Normally you'd have some considerable length of time to get used to your new identity. In this case that just isn't possible. However, you will have Harry with you and it should be for no more than three days. Four at the most."

"I understand."

"One more thing. Your relationship with Standartenführer Vogel must at all times seem convincing. You do appreciate what that could entail?"

"Sharing a room?" The smile when she turned to Martineau was mischievous. "Is that all right with you, Colonel?"

For once, Martineau was put out and he frowned. "You little bitch!"

It was as if they were alone for a moment and she touched his face gently with her fingertips. "Oh, Harry Martineau, you are lovely when you're angry." She turned to Carter. "I think you can take it there'll be no problem, Captain."

Carter, hugely embarrassed, said hurriedly, "All right. Then read this, both of you. Regulations, Sarah."

It was a typical SOE operations order, cold, flat, precise, no-nonsense language. It laid out the task ahead of them, procedure, communication channel via the Cressons in Granville. Everything was covered, even down to a code name for the operation, JERSEYMAN. At the end of the flimsy it said: NOW DESTROY NOW DESTROY.

"All right?" Martineau asked her.

She nodded and he struck a match and touched it to the paper, dropping it into the ashtray. "That's it then," he said. "I'll go and do my packing. See you two later."

On the bed in his room, the wardrobe people had laid out a three-piece suit in light-gray tweed, shoes, some white shirts, two black ties. There was also a military overcoat in soft black leather of a kind worn by many SS officers.

The gray-green SS uniform hung behind the door. He checked it carefully. On the left sleeve was the RFSS cuff title of Himmler's personal staff, an SD patch above it. The Waffenfarben, the colored piping on the uniform and cap, was toxic green, indicating that he belonged to the SS Security Service. The oak leaves of his collar patches indicating his rank were in silver thread. There was an Iron Cross First Class on the left side of the tunic. His only other decoration was the Order of Blood, a medal struck specially for old comrades of the Führer who had served prison sentences for political crimes during the twenties.

He decided to try the uniform on and undressed quickly. Everything fit to perfection. He buttoned the tunic and fastened the belt, a rare specimen that had an eagle on the buckle with a swastika in one claw and SS runes in the other. He picked up the cap and examined the silver death's-head badge, running his sleeve across it, then reached

NIGHT OF THE FOX

inside, scratched a slight tear in the silk lining and withdrew the rigid spring so that the cap crumpled. It was an affectation of many oldtimers, although against regulations.

He put it on his head at a slight angle. From behind, Sarah said quietly, "You look as if you're enjoying yourself. I get the feeling you like uniforms."

"I like getting it right," he said. "I often think I missed my vocation. I should have been an actor. Getting it right is important, Sarah. You don't get second chances."

There was a kind of distress on her face and she moved close and gripped his arm. "I'm not sure if it's you anymore, Harry."

"It isn't, not in this uniform. Standartenführer Max Vogel, of the SD. Feared by his own side as much as the French. You'll see. This isn't a game anymore."

She shivered and put her arms around him. "I know, Harry, I know."

"Are you frightened?"

"Good God, no." She smiled up at him. "Not with Gypsy Sara in my corner."

Eisenhower sat at his desk in the study at Hayes Lodge, reading glasses perched on his nose as he worked his way through the file. He sat back, removed the glasses and looked across at Dougal Munro.

"Quite a man, Martineau. Extraordinary record, and an American."

"Yes, sir. He told me once that his great-grandmother had immigrated to Virginia in the eighteen-fifties from England. Small town in Lancashire, I believe."

"It sounds a kind of exotic name for Lancashire."

"Not unknown, General. I believe it goes back to Norman times."

He realized that Eisenhower was simply stalling for time while he thought about things. He got up and peered out the window, then turned. "Flight Officer Drayton. She's very young."

"I'm aware of that, General. However, she is in a unique position to help us."

"Of course. You really think this could work?"

"I believe we can put Colonel Martineau and Flight Officer Drayton into France with no trouble. I can't see any problem with their continuing onward to Jersey by boat. Martineau has unique authority. No one would dare question it. If you want to query the Reichsführer's personal representative, the only way you can do it is to ring the Reichsführer himself in Berlin."

"Yes, I see that," Eisenhower said.

"However, once they're in Jersey, the game is really wide open. There is no way I can give you any assurance about what happens. We'll be entirely in Martineau's hands." There was silence for a while, and then Munro added, "They should be in Jersey by Thursday. Martineau has until Sunday. That's his deadline. It's only a few days."

"And a hell of a lot of lives depending on it." Eisenhower sat down behind the desk. "Okay, Brigadier. Carry on and keep me informed at all times."

Hornley Field had been an aero club before the war. It had also been used as a temporary fighter station during the Battle of Britain. It was now used for clandestine flights to the continent only, mainly Lysanders and the occasional Liberator. The runway was grass, but long enough. There was a tower, several huts and two hangars.

The commanding officer was a Squadron Leader Barnes, an ex-fighter pilot who'd lost his left arm in the summer of 1940. The pilot of the Lysander was a flight lieutenant named Peter Green. Sarah, standing at the window, saw him now, bulky in his flying jacket and helmet, standing by the plane.

It was two-thirty in the morning, but warm enough, the stove roaring away. "Can I offer you some more coffee, Flight Officer?" Barnes asked Sarah.

She turned and smiled. "No thanks. I shouldn't imagine Westland included a toilet facility in their Lysander."

He smiled. "No, I'm afraid there wasn't the room."

Martineau stood by the stove, hands in the pockets of his leather trenchcoat. He wore the tweed suit and a dark slouch hat and smoked a cigarette. Carter sat by the stove, tapping his stick restlessly on the floor.

"We're really going to have to get moving, I'm afraid," Barnes said. "Just the right conditions at the other end if you go now. Too light if we wait."

"I can't imagine what's happened to the brigadier," Carter said.

"It doesn't matter." Martineau turned to Sarah. "Ready to go?"

She nodded and very carefully pulled on her fashionable leather gloves. She was wearing a black coat over her dress, nipped in at the waist with large shoulders, all very fashionable.

Barnes put a very large fur-lined flying jacket over her shoulders. "It might be cold up there."

"Thank you."

Martineau picked up their two suitcases and they went out and crossed to the Lysander where Green waited. "Any problems?" Martineau asked.

"Coastal fog, but only in patches. Slight headwind." He glanced at his watch. "We'll be there by four-thirty at the outside."

Sarah went first and strapped herself in. Martineau passed up the suitcases then turned and shook hands with Carter. "See you soon, Jack."

"You've got the call sign," Carter said. "All Cresson has to do is send that. No message needed. We'll have a Lysander out to the same field at ten o'clock at night of the same day to pick you up."

Martineau climbed in next to Sarah and fastened his seat belt. He didn't look at her or say anything, but he took her hand as Green climbed into the pilot's seat. The sound of the engines shattered the night. They started to taxi to the far end of the runway and turned. As they started to roll between the two lines of lights, gradually increasing speed, the Austin Princess turned in through the main gate, hesitated for the sentry's inspection then bumped across the grass to the huts. As Dougal Munro got out, the Lysander lifted over the trees at the far end of the field and was swallowed by darkness.

"Damnation!" he said. "Held up at Baker Street, Jack. Something came up. Thought I'd just make it."

"They couldn't wait, sir," Barnes told him. "Might have made things difficult at the other end."

"Of course," Munro said.

Barnes walked away and Carter said, "What did General Eisenhower have to say, sir?"

"What could he say, Jack? What can any of us say?" Munro shrugged. "The ball's in Harry Martineau's court now. All up to him."

"And Sarah Drayton, sir."

"Yes, I liked that young woman." Aware suddenly that he had spoken in the past tense, Munro shivered as if at an omen. "Come on, Jack, let's go home," he said, and he turned and got back into the Austin.

Sophia Cresson waited on the edge of a wood beside the field seven miles northwest of Granville which was the designated landing strip. She was on her own and stood beside an old Renault van smoking a cigarette in her cupped hands. The door of the van was open, and a Sten gun lay ready to hand on the passenger seat. There was also the homing beacon. She'd waited at the bar until Gerard had received the message that they had actually left Hornley. Timing was critical in these things.

She wore a woolen cap pulled down over her ears against the cold, an old fur-lined hunting coat of Gerard's, belted at the waist, and slacks. She wasn't worried about problems with any security patrol she might run across. She knew all the soldiers in the Granville area and they knew her. As for the police, they did as they were told. There wasn't one she didn't know too much about. In the back of the van were several dead chickens and a few pheasants. Out on another black-market trip, that was her cover.

She checked her watch and switched on the homing beacon. Then she took three torches from the van and ran forward into the broad meadow and arranged them in an inverted L-shape with the crossbar at the upwind end. Then she moved back to the van and waited.

The flight had been completely uneventful, mainly because Green was an old hand, with more than forty such sorties under his belt. He had never belonged to the school of thought that recommended approaching the French coast below the radar screen. The one time he had tried this tactic the Royal Navy had fired at him. So, it was at 8,000 feet that the Lysander crossed over the Cherbourg Peninsula and turned slightly south.

He spoke over the intercom. "Fifteen minutes, so be ready."

"Any chance of running into a night fighter?" Martineau asked.

"Unlikely. Maximum effort strike by Bomber Command on various towns in the Ruhr. Jerry will have scrambled every night fighter in France to go and protect the Fatherland."

"Look!" Sarah cut in. "I can see lights."

The L-shape was clearly visible below as they descended rapidly. "That's it," Green told them. "I've landed here twice before so I know my stuff. In and out very fast. You know the drill, Colonel."

And then they were drifting down over the trees into the meadow, rolling forward across the lights. Sophie Cresson ran forward, waving, the Sten gun in one hand. Martineau got the door open, threw out the suitcases and followed them. He turned to help Sarah. Behind her, Green reached for the door and slammed it shut, locking the handle. The engine note deepened to a full-throated roar as the Lysander raced across the meadow and took off.

Sophie Cresson said, "Come on, let's get out of here. Bring your suitcases while I get my lamps." They followed her to the van and she opened the rear door. "There's just enough room for both of you to sit behind the two barrels. Don't worry, I know every flic in the district. If they stop me, all they'll do is take a chicken and go home."

"Some things never change," Sarah said.

"Heh, a Breton girl?" Sophie flashed her torch on Sarah's face and grunted. "My God, now they send little girls." She shrugged. "In you get and let's be out of here."

Sarah crouched behind the barrels, her knees touching Martineau as Sophie drove away. So, this was it, she thought, the real thing. No more games now. She opened her handbag and felt for the butt of the Walther PPK inside. The little Belgian automatic Kelly had given her was in her case. Would she be able to use them if necessary? Only time would tell. Martineau lit a cigarette and passed it to her. When she inhaled, nothing had ever felt better, and she leaned back against the side of the van feeling wonderfully, marvelously alive.

It was noon before she awoke, yawning and stretching her arms. The small bedroom under the roof was plainly furnished but comfortable. She threw back the sheets and crossed to the window. The view across the walls down to the harbor was really quite special. Behind her the door opened and Sophie came in with a bowl of coffee on a tray.

"So, you're up."

"It's good to be back." Sarah took the bowl from her and sat on the window seat.

Sophie lit a cigarette. "You've been here before?"

"Many times. My mother was a de Ville. Half-Jersey, half-Breton. My grandmother was born at Paimpol. I used to come over to Granville from the island when I was a little girl. There was a fishermen's café on the quay that had the finest hot rolls in the world. The best coffee."

"Not anymore," Sophie said. "The war has changed everything. Look down there."

The harbor was crammed with shipping. Rhine barges, three coasters and a number of German naval craft. It was a scene of considerable activity as dockers unloaded the contents of a line of trucks on the quay into the barges.

"They're definitely sailing for the islands tonight?" Sarah asked.

"Oh yes. Some for Jersey, the rest on to Guernsey."

"How do you find them?"

"The Boche?" Sophie shrugged. "I'm a reasonable woman. I don't want to hate anybody. I just want them out of France."

"It's just that we hear such bad things about them in England."

"True," Sophie said. "SS and Gestapo are devils, but they frighten the hell out of the ordinary German soldier as much as they do anyone else. In any case, we've got those among our own people who are as bad as the Gestapo. Daman's *milice*. Frenchmen who work with the Nazis to betray Frenchmen."

"That's terrible," Sarah said.

"It's life, child, and what it means is you can never really trust anyone. Now get dressed and come downstairs and we'll have some lunch."

At Gavray in what had once been the country home of the count of that name, Heini Baum sat at one end of the table in the officers' mess of the 41st Panzer Grenadiers and smilingly acknowledged the cheers as the officers toasted him then applauded. When they were finished, he nodded his thanks.

The young colonel of the regiment, a veteran of the Russian Front, his black panzer uniform scattered with decorations, said, "If you could manage a few words, Herr Field Marshal. It would mean so much to my officers."

There was a worried look in Hofer's eye when Baum glanced at him, but he disregarded it and stood up, straightening his tunic. "Gentlemen, the Führer has given us a simple task. To keep the enemy off our beaches. Yes, I say our beaches. Europe, one and indivisible, is our goal. The battle will be won on those beaches. There is no possibility of our losing. The destiny of the Führer is God-given. So much is obvious to anyone with a grain of sense." His irony was lost on them as they gazed up, enraptured, drinking in every word. He raised his glass. "So, gentlemen, join me. To our beloved Führer, Adolf Hitler."

"Adolf Hitler!" they chorused.

Baum tossed his glass into the fire, and with a stirring of excitement, they all followed him. Then they applauded again, forming two lines as he walked out, followed by Hofer.

"Rather heavy on the glasses, I should have thought," Hofer said as they drove back to Cressy where Rommel had established temporary headquarters at the old castle there.

"You didn't approve?" Baum said.

"I didn't say that. Actually, the speech was rather good."

"If the Herr Major will excuse my saying so, it was heavily over the top, to use theatrical vernacular," Baum told him.

"I take your point," Hofer said. "On the other hand, it's exactly what they wanted to hear."

Crazy, Baum thought. *Am I the only sane man left alive?* But by then, they were drawing into the courtyard of the castle. He went up the steps fast, acknowledging the salutes, Hofer trailing him, all the way up to the suite on the second floor.

Rommel had locked himself in the study and only came out on Hofer's knock. "How did it go?"

"Perfect," Hofer said. "Passed with flying colors. You should have heard the speech you made."

"Excellent." Rommel nodded. "Everything progresses in the Channel Islands? You spoke to von Schmettow in Guernsey?"

"Personally, Herr Field Marshal. He's also had his orders in writing. As you were told by Naval HQ at Cherbourg, they do most of their traveling between the islands by night these days because of the enemy air superiority in the area. So they will travel from Jersey to Guernsey on Thursday night for the conference, returning on Sunday night."

"Good," Rommel said. "Which still leaves you and Berger flying in out of the dawn in a Fiesler Storch with all that RAF superiority in the area that you speak of." He turned to Baum. "What do you think about that, Berger?"

"I think it could be interesting if the Herr Major and I went down in flames into the sea. The Desert Fox is dead." He shrugged. "That could lead to some strange possibilities, you must admit, Herr Field Marshal."

Gerard Cresson sat in his wheelchair at the table in the sitting room and refilled the glasses with red wine. "No, I hate to dispel your illusions," he said to Sarah. "But out in Jersey, just as in France and every other occupied country in Europe, the real enemy is the informer. Without them the Gestapo couldn't operate."

"But I was told there weren't any Gestapo in Jersey," Sarah said.

"Officially they have a Geheime Feldpolizei setup there. That's Secret Field Police, and they're supposed to be controlled by the Abwehr. Military Intelligence. The whole thing is part of the ruling-by-kindness policy, a cosmetic exercise aimed at fooling the people. The implication is that because you're British we won't sick the Gestapo onto you."

"Which is shit," Sophie said as she came in from the kitchen with fresh coffee, "because several of the men working for the GFP in Jersey are Gestapo operatives on loan."

"Do you know where they are?" Sarah asked.

"A hotel at Havre des Pas called Silvertide. You know it?"

She nodded. "Oh yes. I used to go swimming at Havre des Pas when I was a child."

"Gestapo, Secret Field Police, SD, Abwehr. Wherever you go, whoever the man is who knocks on the door, it's the Gestapo to the poor devil being arrested."

"Exactly the same in Jersey," Gerard told him. "To the locals, they're Gestapo and that's it. Mind you, it's a Mickey Mouse operation compared to what goes on in Lyons or Paris, but watch out for a Captain Muller. He's temporarily in command, and his chief aide, an inspector called Kleist."

"Are they SS?"

"I don't know. Probably not. They've never been seen in uniform. Probably seconded from the police in some big city. Full of themselves, like all flics. Out to prove something." He shrugged. "You don't have to be in the SS to be in the Gestapo. You don't even have to be a member of the Nazi Party."

"True." Martineau said. "Anyway, how do you rate our chances of bringing Kelso over from Jersey?"

"Very difficult indeed. That's one item they are very tight on, civilian traffic. It would be impossible in a small boat at the moment."

"And if he isn't able to walk …" Sophie shrugged expressively.

"They'll be standing by at SOE for a call from you at any time this weekend," Martineau said. "The Lysander can pick up on Sunday night."

Gerard laughed suddenly. "I've just had a brilliant thought. You could always arrest Kelso. Find him and arrest him, if you follow me. Bring him over here officially, then cut out."

"That's all very well," Sarah put in, "but where would that leave Aunt Helen and the General? Wouldn't they have to be arrested too?"

Martineau nodded. "It's one of those ideas that sounds good until you think about it. Never mind. We'll think of something when we get there."

"Like a bullet in the head maybe?" Cresson suggested. "I mean, if this man is as important as they say…"

"He's entitled to a chance," Martineau said. "If there's any way I can pull him out I will, if not…" He shrugged. "Now, what's the procedure for booking passage to the island tonight?"

'There's a movement officer in the office in the green hut on the quay. He issues the passes. No difficulty in your case."

"Good," Martineau said. "That seems to be about it then."

Sophie filled four glasses with red wine. "I'm not going to wish you luck, I'm just going to tell you something."

"What's that?" Martineau inquired.

She put an arm around Sarah's shoulders. "I like the kid here very much. Whatever happens over there, you bring her back in one piece, because if you don't, and you show your face here again, I'll put a bullet in you myself." She smiled genially and toasted him.

9

THE 5TH SCHNELLBOOTE FLOTILLA, as was common with all
German Navy E-boat units, was used to living on the move. On returning to their Cherbourg base after the Slapton Sands affair, three
boats had been ordered to Guernsey for temporary duty as convoy
escorts. One of them, S92, was tied up at the quay at Granville now.

Darkness was already falling and the harbor was a scene of fren-
zied activity as the convoy got ready to leave. Chief Petty Officer Hans
Richter, checking the 40-mm Bofors gun in the stern, paused to watch
dockers working on the *Victor Hugo* which was moored next to them.
Now that her holds were crammed full, they were dumping sacks of coal
and bales of hay on her decks so that there was hardly room to move.

The *Hugo*'s antiaircraft defenses were 7.92-mm machine guns and
a Bofors gun—not too much use when the Tommies swept in from
the darkness in those damned Beau-fighters with their searchlights
on, but that's the way things were these days, and the Luftwaffe didn't
seem to be able to do much about it. Richter could see the master of
the *Hugo,* Savary, on the bridge talking to the officer in command of
the gun crew, the Italian lieutenant, Orsini. Flamboyant as usual with
the white top to his cap and the scarf at his neck. A good seaman for all

that. They said he'd sunk a British destroyer off Taranto before being seconded to the 5th Schnellboote as an E-boat commander. They were only using him on secondary duties these days because nobody trusted the Italians anymore. After all, most of them were fighting for the Allies now.

As Richter watched, Guido Orsini went down the ladder and then the gangway to the quay and walked toward the port officer's hut. Richter turned back to the gun and a voice called "Petty Officer!"

Richter looked over the rail. Standing a few feet away was an SS officer, a black leather trenchcoat over his uniform, the silver death's-head on the cap gleaming dully in the evening light. When Richter saw the oak leaf collar patches of a full colonel his heart sank.

He got his heels together quickly. "Standartenführer. What can I do for you?"

The young woman standing at the colonel's shoulder was pretty in her little black beret and belted raincoat, the hair very fair, just like his daughter's back home in Hamburg. Too young for an SS bastard like this, Richter thought.

"Your commanding officer, Kapitanleutnant Dietrich, commands the convoy, I understand?" Martineau said. "Is he on board?"

"Not at the moment."

"Where is he?"

"Port officer's hut. The green one over there, Standartenführer."

"Good. I'll have a word with him." Martineau gestured to the two suit-cases. "See these go on board. We'll be traveling with you as far as Jersey."

Which was a turnup for the book. Richter watched them walk away, then nodded to a young seaman who'd been listening with inter-est. "You heard the man. Get those cases."

"He was SD," the sailor said. "Did you notice?"

"Yes," Richter said. "As it happens I did. Now get on with it."

Erich Dietrich was thirty years of age, a young architect in Hamburg before the war who had discovered his true vocation. He had never been happier than when he was at sea and in command, especially in E-boats. He did not want the war to end. It had taken its toll, of course, on him as much as anyone. Just now, leaning over the chart table with the port officer, Lieutenant Schroeder, and Guido Orsini, he was in the best of humors.

"Winds three to four at the most with rain squalls. Could be worse." Schroeder said, "Intelligence is expecting big raids on the Ruhr again tonight, so things should be reasonably clear for us down here as regards the RAF."

"If you believe that, you'll believe anything," Orsini said.

"You're a pessimist, Guido," Erich Dietrich told him. "Expect good things and they'll always fall into your lap. That's what my old mother used to say."

The door opened behind him, Schroeder's face dropped and Guido stopped smiling. Dietrich turned and found Martineau standing there, Sarah at his shoulder.

"Kapitanleutnant Dietrich? My name is Vogel." Martineau produced his SD identity card and passed it across, then he took Himmler's letter from its envelope. "If you would be kind enough to read this also."

Sarah couldn't understand a word. He sounded like someone else, held himself like another person, the voice cold and dry. Dietrich read the letter, and Guido and Schroeder peered over his shoulder. The Italian made a face and Dietrich handed the document back.

"You noticed, of course, that the Führer himself was kind enough to countersign my orders?"

"Your credentials are without doubt the most remarkable I've ever seen, Standartenführer," Dietrich said. "In what way can we serve you?"

"I need passage for myself and Mademoiselle Latour to Jersey. As you are convoy commander I shall naturally travel with you. I've already told your petty officer to take our cases on board."

Which would have been enough to reduce Erich Dietrich to speechless rage at the best of times, but there was another factor here. The Kriegsmarine had always been notoriously the least Nazi of all the German armed forces. Dietrich personally had never cared for the Party one little bit, which hardly disposed him in Standartenführer Max Vogel's favor. There were limits, of course, to what he could do, but he still had one possible objection on his side.

"Happy to oblige, Standartenführer," he said smoothly. "There is one problem, however. Naval regulations forbid the carrying of civilians on a fighting ship at sea. I can accommodate you, but not, alas, this charming young lady."

It was difficult to argue with him because he was right. Martineau tried to handle it as a man like Vogel would have done, arrogant, demanding, determined not to be put down. "What would you suggest?"

"One of the convoy ships, perhaps. Lieutenant Orsini here is in command of the gun crew on the SS *Victor Hugo*, whose cargo is destined for the port of St. Helier on Jersey. You could go with him."

But Vogel would not have allowed himself to lose face completely. "No," he said calmly. "It is good that I should see something of your work, Kapitanleutnant. I shall travel with you. Mademoiselle Latour, on the other hand, can proceed on the *Victor Hugo* if Lieutenant Orsini has no objections."

"Certainly not," said Guido who had hardly been able to take his eyes off her. "A distinct pleasure."

"Unfortunately Mademoiselle Latour speaks no German." Martineau turned to her and carried on in French. "We must separate for the journey across, my dear. A matter of regulations. I'll keep your luggage with me, so don't worry about that. This young officer will take care of you."

"Guido Orsini, at your service, signorina," he said gallantly and saluted. "If you come with me I'll see you safely on board. We sail in thirty minutes."

She turned to Martineau. "I'll see you later then, Max."

"In Jersey." He nodded calmly.

She went out, Orsini holding the door open for her. Dietrich said, "A charming girl."

"I think so." Martineau leaned over the chart table. "Are we to enjoy an uneventful run tonight? I understand your convoys are often attacked by RAF night fighters."

"Frequently, Standartenführer," Schroeder told him. "But the RAF will be busy elsewhere tonight."

"Terror bombing the civilian population of our major cities as usual," Martineau said because it was the kind of thing they would expect a Party fanatic like him to say. "And the British Royal Navy?"

"Yes, their MTBs are often active in the area," Dietrich admitted and tapped the map. "From bases at Falmouth and Devonport."

"And this doesn't worry you?"

"Standartenführer, there are more of them these days, but our E-boats are still the fastest thing of their kind afloat, as I will certainly have the chance to show you tonight." He gathered up his charts. "Now, if you will follow me, we'll go on board."

The convoy left just after ten o'clock, eleven ships in all, including the barges. S92 led the way out of harbor, then swung hard to port. There was a light rain falling, and Dietrich stood on the bridge, probing into the darkness with his Zeiss night glasses. Martineau was at his right shoulder. Below them the wheelhouse was even more cramped with the helmsman and engine room telegraphist in there and the navigating officer at his small table behind. The wireless room was down a passage farther on.

"Not much room on these things," Martineau commented.

"All engines, that's what we say," Dietrich told him.

"And armaments?"

"The torpedoes. Bofors gun aft, twenty-millimeter cannon in the forward well deck. Eight machine guns. We manage."

"And radar, of course?"

"Yes, but that's a difficult one in these waters. Lots of reefs, rocks, small islands. It makes for a lot of clutter on the screen. When the Tommies come down here they do exactly what I do when I'm operating out of Cherbourg and hitting their convoys."

"What's that?"

"Turn off our radar so they can't find us with their location equipment and maintain radio silence."

Martineau nodded and looked astern at the other ships bulking in the dark. "What speed will the convoy maintain?"

"Six knots."

"You must feel like a racing horse pulling a cart sometimes."

Dietrich laughed. "Yes, but I've got two thousand horses under me." He slapped the rail. "Nice to know just how fast they can get up and go when I ask them to."

On the bridge of the *Victor Hugo* it was like being in a safe and enclosed world, rain and spray drifting against the glass. Savary stood beside the helmsman, and Sarah and Guido Orsini leaned over the chart table.

"This is the convoy route, what the Navy call Weg Ida, from Granville, east of the Chausey Isles."

She liked him a lot, had from the moment he'd turned to look at her in the hut on the quay. He was certainly good-looking. Too handsome, really, in a way that Latins could be sometimes, but there was strength there too, and when he smiled …

His shoulder was touching hers. He said, "Come to the saloon. I'll get you a coffee and you can use my cabin if you'd like to lie down."

Savary turned. "Not just now, Count. I want to check the engine room. You'll have to take the bridge."

He went out. Sarah said, "Count?"

"Lots of counts in Italy. Don't let it worry you."

He offered her a cigarette and they smoked in companionable silence, looking out into the night, the noise of the engines a muted throbbing. "I thought Italy capitulated last year?" she said.

"Oh, it did, except for those Fascist fanatics who decided to fight on under the Germans, especially when Otto Skorzeny hoisted Mussolini off that mountaintop and flew him to Berlin to continue the holy struggle."

"Are you a Fascist?"

He looked down into that appealing young face, aware of a tenderness that he had never experienced with any woman in his life before. It was perhaps because of that fact that he found himself speaking so frankly.

"To be honest, I'm not anything. I loathe politics. It reminds me of the senator in Rome who's supposed to have said: 'Don't tell my mother I'm in politics. She thinks I play the piano in a brothel.' "

She laughed. "I like that."

"Most of my former comrades are now working with the British and American Navies. I, on the other hand, was seconded on special duties to serve with the Fifth Schnellboote Flotilla in Cherbourg. When Italy decided to sue for peace, there wasn't a great deal I could do about it, and I didn't fancy a prison camp. Of course, they don't trust me enough to allow me to command an E-boat anymore. I suppose they think I might roar across to England."

"Would you?"

Savary returned to the bridge at that moment, and the Italian said, "Right, let's go below now and get that coffee."

She moved ahead of him. As he watched her descend the companionway he was conscious of a curious excitement. He'd known many women, and many who were more beautiful than Anne-Marie Latour with her ridiculous dyed hair. Certainly more sophisticated. And there was something about her that was not quite right. The image was one thing, but the girl herself, when he spoke to her, was something else again.

"Mother of God, Guido, what's happening to you?" he asked softly as he went down the companionway after her.

Captain Karl Muller, the officer in command of the Secret Field Police in Jersey, sat at his desk in the Silvertide Hotel at Havre des Pas and worked his way though a bulky file. It was wholly devoted to anonymous letters, the tip-offs that led to whatever success his unit enjoyed. The crimes were varied. Anything from possession of an illegal radio to helping a Russian slave worker on the run or involvement in the black market. Muller always insisted on his men tracking down the writers of anonymous letters. Once uncovered, they could be used in many ways because of his threat to expose them to friends and neighbors.

It was all very small beer, of course. Nothing like it had been at Gestapo Headquarters at Rue des Saussaies in Paris. Muller was not SS, but he was a Party member, a onetime Chief Inspector of Police in the Hamburg Criminal Investigation Department. Unfortunately, a young Frenchwoman in his hands for interrogation had died without disclosing the names of her associates. As she had been involved with the principal Resistance circuit in Paris, it had been a matter of some importance. To his superiors he'd botched things badly by being too eager. The posting to this island backwater had followed. So now, he was a man in a hurry, seeking any way he could to get back into the mainstream of things.

He stood up, a shade under six feet, with hair that was still dark brown in spite of the fact that he was in his fiftieth year. He stretched, started to the window to look out at the weather, and the phone rang.

He picked it up. "Yes."

It wasn't a local call, he could tell by the crackling. "Captain Midler? This is Schroeder, port officer at Granville."

Ten minutes later he was standing at the window, staring out into the dark, when there was a knock at the door. He turned and went to his desk and sat down.

The two men who entered were, like Muller, in civilian clothes. The GFP never wore uniform if they could help it. The one who led the way was broad and squat with a Slavic face and hard gray eyes. This was Inspector Willi Kleist, Muller's second-in-command, also seconded from the Gestapo and, like Muller, a former detective with the Hamburg police. They had known each other for years. The man with him was much younger with fair hair, blue eyes and a weak mouth. A suggestion of perverse cruelty there, but when confronted with Muller, so eager to please that it showed. This was Sergeant Ernst Greiser, who had been transferred from the Army's Field Police to the GFP six months earlier.

"An interesting development," Muller told them. "I've had Schroeder on the phone from Granville. Apparently an SD Standartenführer Vogel presented himself on the quay with a young French woman and demanded passage to Jersey. They put the woman on the *Victor Hugo*. He comes on the S92 with Dietrich."

"But why, Herr Captain?" Kleist asked. "We've had no notification. Why would he be coming?"

"The bad news," Muller said, "is that he's traveling under a special warrant from Reichsführer Himmler. According to Schroeder it's countersigned by the Führer."

"My God!" Greiser said.

"So, my friends, we must be ready for him. You were going to take care of the passenger checks when the convoy ships get into St. Helier, isn't that so, Ernst?" he inquired of Greiser.

"Yes, Herr Captain."

"Inspector Kleist and I will join you. Whatever his reason for being here, I want to be in on the action. I'll see you later."

They went out. He lit a cigarette and went to the window, more excited than he had been in months.

It was just after eleven when Helen de Ville took the tray to her room, using the back stairs that led straight up from the kitchen. None of the officers ever used it, keeping strictly to their own end of the house. In any case, she was careful. Only one cup on the tray. Everything for one. If she chose to have late supper in her room, that was her affair.

She went into the bedroom, locking the door behind her, crossed to the bookshelves, opened the secret entrance and moved inside, closing it before going up the narrow stairway. Kelso was sitting up in bed, propped against pillows, reading by the light of an oil lamp. The wooden shutters in the gable window were closed, a heavy curtain drawn across.

He looked up and smiled. "What have we got here?"

"Not much. Tea, but at least it's the real stuff, and a cheese sandwich. I make my own cheese these days, so you'd better like it. What are you reading?"

"One of the books you brought up. Eliot. *The Four Quartets*."

"Poetry and you an engineer?" She sat on the end of the bed and lit one of the Gitanes Gallagher had given her.

"I certainly wasn't interested in that kind of thing in the old days, but this war." He shrugged. "Like a lot of people I want answers, I suppose. In my end is my beginning, that's what the man says. But what comes in between? What's it all mean?"

"Well, if you find out, don't forget to let me know." She noticed the snap of his wife and daughters on the bedside locker and picked it up. "Do you think of them often?"

"All the time. They mean everything. My marriage really worked. It was as simple as that. I never wanted anything else, and then the war came along and messed things up."

"Yes, it has a bad habit of doing that."

"Still, I can't complain. Comfortable bed, decent cooking, and the oil lamp gives things a nicely old-fashioned atmosphere."

"They cut off the electricity to this part of the island at nine o'clock sharp," she said. "I know people who would be glad of that oil lamp."

"Are things really as bad as that?"

"Of course they are." There was a trace of anger in her voice. "What on earth would you expect? You're lucky to have that cup of tea. Elsewhere in the island it could be a rather inferior substitute made from parsnips or blackberry leaves. Or you could try acorn coffee. Not one of life's great experiences."

"And food?"

"You just have to get used to getting by with a lot less of it, that's all. The same with tobacco." She held up her cigarette. "This is real and very black market, but you can get anything if you have the right connections or plenty of cash. The rich here still do very well. The banks just operate in reichsmarks instead of pounds." She smiled. "Do you want to know what it's really like being occupied in Jersey?"

"It would be interesting."

"Boring." She plumped up his pillows. "I'm going to bed now."

"The big day tomorrow," he said.

"If we're to believe the message Savary brought." She picked up the tray. "Try and get some sleep."

Orsini had given Sarah his cabin. It was very small indeed, with a cupboard and washstand and a single bunk. It was hot and stuffy, the porthole blacked over, and the noise of the engine churning below gave her a headache. She lay on the bunk and closed her eyes and tried to relax. The ship seemed to stagger. An illusion, of course. She sat up and there was an explosion.

Things seemed to happen in slow motion after that. The ship fell perfectly still, as if everything waited, and then there was another violent shock. The explosion this time caused the walls to tremble. She cried out and tried to stand up, and then the floor tilted and she fell against the door. Her handbag, thrown from the locker top, was on the floor beside her. She picked it up automatically and tried the door handle, but the door stuck fast. She shook the handle desperately and then the door opened so unexpectedly that she was hurled back against the opposite wall.

Orsini stood in the entrance, his face wild. "Move!" he ordered. "Now! No time to lose."

"What is it?" she demanded as he grabbed her hand and pulled her after him.

"Torpedo attack. We've been hit twice. We've only got minutes. This old tub will go down like a stone."

They went up the companionway to the saloon which was deserted. He took off his reefer coat and held it out to her. "Get this on." She hesitated, aware suddenly that she was still clutching her handbag, then did as she was told, stuffing the bag into one of the reefer coat's ample pockets. He pulled her arms roughly through a life jacket and laced it up. Then he put one on himself as he led the way out onto the boat deck.

There was a scene of indescribable confusion as the crew tried to launch the boats and, above them, the machine-gun crews fired into the night. Fire arced toward them in return, raking the bridge above, where Savary shouted orders. He cried out in fear and jumped over the rail, bouncing off some bales of hay below. Cannon shell ripped into one of the lifeboats a few yards away, tearing great holes in it.

Orsini pushed Sarah down behind some sacks of coal. At the same moment there was another explosion, inside the ship this time, and a portion of the deck in the stern disintegrated, flames billowing into the night. The entire ship tilted sharply to port, and the deck cargo started to break free, sacks of coal, bales of hay, sliding down against the rail.

It had not been possible to launch a single boat, so rapidly had disaster struck, and men were already going over the rail, Savary leading the way. Orsini lost his balance and Sarah fell on her back, felt herself slide down the slippery deck, and then the rail dipped under and she was in the water.

The E-boat surged forward at speed within seconds of the first explosion, Dietrich scanning the darkness with his night glasses. Martineau almost lost his balance at the sudden burst of speed and hung on grimly.

"What is it?"

"I'm not sure," Dietrich said, and then flames blossomed in the night five hundred yards away and he focused on the *Victor Hugo*. A dark shape flashed across that patch of light like a shadow and then another. "British MTBs. They've hit the *Hugo*."

He pressed the button on the battle stations alarm, and the ugly sound of the klaxon rose above the roaring of the Mercedes Benz engines winding up to top speed. Already the crew were moving to their stations. The Bofors gun and the well-deck cannon started to fire, lines of tracer curving into the night.

The only thing Martineau could think of was Sarah, and he grabbed Dietrich by the sleeve. "But the people on that ship. We must help them."

"Later!" Dietrich shrugged him aside. "This is business. Now keep out of the way."

Sarah kicked desperately to get as far from the ship as possible as the *Victor Hugo* continued to tilt. There was burning oil on the water toward the stern, men swimming hard to get away from it as it advanced relentlessly. One man was overtaken. She heard his screams as he disappeared.

She moved awkwardly because of the life jacket and the reefer coat was bulky, already saturated with water. She realized now why Orsini had given it to her as the cold started to eat at her legs. Where was he? She turned trying to make sense of the oil-stained faces. An MTB spun around the stern of the *Victor Hugo*, the violence of its wash hurling some of those in the sea up out of the water. There was a burst of machine-gun fire.

A hand grabbed at her life jacket from behind, and she turned and Orsini was there. "Over here, cara. Just do as I say."

There was wreckage floating everywhere, the bales of hay from the deck cargo buoyant in the water. He towed her toward one of these and they hung onto its binding ropes.

"Who were they?" she gasped.

"MTBs."

"British?"

"Or French or Dutch. They all operate out of Falmouth."

There was another mighty rushing sound in the night and machine-gun bullets churned the water as an MTB again carved its way through men and wreckage. A tracer flashed through the darkness in a great arc and a starshell burst. A moment later, a parachute flare illuminated the scene.

Some distance away two MTBs ran for cover, and the E-boat roared after them. "Go get the bastards, Erich!" Orsini shouted.

She almost joined in. My God, she thought, what a way to go. My own people trying to kill me. She hung onto the rope and said, gasping, "Did they have to do that? Machine-gun men in the water?"

"War, cara, is a nasty business, it makes everyone crazy. Are you managing?"

"My arms are tired."

A hatch drifted by and he swam to it and towed it toward her. "Let's get you onto this."

It was a struggle, but she finally managed it. "What about you?"

"I'll be fine hanging on." He laughed. "Don't worry, I've been in the water before. My luck is good, so stick with me."

And then she remembered the spring fete and Gypsy Sara and her fire and water and she started to laugh shakily. "Are you all right?" he demanded.

"Lovely. Nothing like the Channel Islands for a holiday at this time of the year. Perfect for sea bathing," and then she realized, to her horror, that she'd spoken in English.

He floated there, staring up at her, and then said in excellent English, "Did I tell you I went to Winchester? My father felt that only an English public school could give me the backbone I needed." He laughed. "Oh, I do so like to be right, and I knew there was something different about you from the first moment, cara." He laughed again, excitedly this time. "Which means there's something unusual about the good Standartenführer Vogel."

"Please," she said desperately.

"Don't worry, cara, I fell in love with you the moment you came through the door of that hut on the quay. I like you, I don't like them— whoever they are. We Italians are a very simple people."

He coughed, rubbing oil from his face, and she reached for his hand. "You saved my life, Guido."

There was the sound of a throttled-down engine approaching.

He glanced over his shoulder and saw an armed trawler, one of the escorts, approaching. "Yes," he said. "I'm pleased to say I probably did."

A moment later, the trawler was looming above them, a net over the side. Two or three German sailors clambered down, reaching for Sarah, and pulled her up. Guido followed and collapsed on the deck beside her.

A young lieutenant came down the ladder from the bridge and hurried forward. "Guido, is that you?" he said in German.

"As ever, Bruno," Guido answered in the same language.

"And you, fraulein, are you all right? We must get you to my cabin."

"Mademoiselle Latour, Bruno, and she speaks no German," Guido told him in French. He smiled at Sarah and helped her to her feet. "Now let's take you below."

10

AS SARAH PULLED THE heavy white sweater over her head there was a knock on the door of Bruno's cabin. She opened it and a young rating said in poor French, "Lieutenant Feldt's compliments. We're entering St. Helier Harbor." He closed the door and she went to the basin and tried to do something with her hair, which was impossible. The effects of salt water had proved disastrous, and it was now a tangled straw-colored mess. She gave up and rolled the Kriegsmarine dungarees up at her ankles.

The contents of her handbag, which she had stuffed into a pocket of Orsini's reefer before leaving the *Victor Hugo,* had survived surprisingly well. Her identity card and other papers were soaked, of course. She had laid them out now on the hot-water pipes to dry with her handbag. She replaced them all and retrieved the Walther PPK from under the pillow. The Belgian pistol Sergeant Kelly had given her was in her suitcase on board the E-boat. She sat on the edge of the bunk and pulled on a pair of old tennis shoes one of the young ratings had given her.

There was a knock and Guido came in. "How are you?" he asked in French.

"Fine," she said, "except for the hair. I look like a scarecrow."

He was carrying a Kriegsmarine reefer coat. "Put this on. A damp morning out there."

As she stood her handbag fell to the floor, spilling some of the contents, including the Walther. Guido picked it up and said softly, "What a lot of gun for a little girl. Mystery piles on mystery with you."

She took it from him and returned it to her handbag. "All part of my fatal attraction."

"Very fatal if an item like that is involved."

His eyes were serious now, but she smiled lightly and, on impulse, kissed him on the cheek. Then she went out and he followed her.

A scene so familiar from her childhood. The harbor, Elizabeth Castle on her left in the bay, the Albert Pier, the sprawl of St. Helier, Fort Regent on the hill above. The same and yet not the same. Military strongpoints everywhere and the harbor more crammed with vessels than she had ever known it. The Rhine barges from the convoy were already safely in, but there was no sign of S92.

"Where's the E-boat?" Sarah asked Guido as she leaned on the bridge rail beside him and Lieutenant Feldt.

"Probably having a last look for survivors," he said as they nosed in toward the Albert Pier.

Dockers were already starting to unload the barges, and there seemed to be soldiers everywhere. Below, half-a-dozen French seamen, survivors of the crew of the *Victor Hugo* picked up by the trawler after Guido and Sarah, waited at the rail in borrowed clothes. Two had sustained facial burns and were heavily bandaged. Another man who had swallowed oil lay on a stretcher.

"No sign of Savary," Orsini said.

"Someone else may have picked him up," Bruno Feldt said. "I see the GFP are ready and waiting. Why is it that policemen always look like policemen?"

"GFP?" Sarah asked in a deliberate display of ignorance. "What's that?"

"Geheime Feldpolizei," Guido told her. "As a matter of interest, the tall one, Captain Muller, is on loan from the Gestapo. So is the thug next to him, the one built like a brick wall. That's Inspector Willi Kleist. The young one with the fair hair is Sergeant Ernst Greiser. Now he *isn't* ex-Gestapo."

"But wishes he were," Bruno Feldt put in.

The three were the first up the gangway when it went over. Greiser paused among the French seamen, and Muller came on up the ladder to the ridge followed by Kleist. Sarah was aware of Guido's hand going into the pocket of her reefer coat and fumbling inside her handbag.

She turned to glance briefly at him. As she realized it was the Walther he was seeking, it was already too late, as Muller reached the bridge.

"Herr Leutnant." He nodded to Feldt and said to Orsini, "You had quite a night of it, I hear?" He wore an old Burberry raincoat and felt hat and there was something curiously gentle about him as he turned to Sarah and said in French, "You were a passenger on the *Hugo*, mademoiselle ... ?"

"Latour," Orsini put in. "We were in the water together."

"A remarkable escape," Muller nodded. "You lost your papers?"

"No," she said. "I have them here." She took the handbag from her pocket and started to open it. Muller held out his hand. "The bag, if you please, mademoiselle."

There was a moment only as if everyone waited, then Sarah handed it to him. "Of course."

He turned to Bruno Feldt. "We'll use your cabin for a few minutes, if we may."

He seemed so reasonable, Sarah thought, so polite, when very obviously most of those standing around were frightened to death of him. Not Guido, of course, who smiled and squeezed her arm. "I'll wait for you, cara, and if the colonel doesn't arrive you can come up to my billet at de Ville Place. I have a very superior landlady. She'll look after you, I promise. All very high class. Only naval officers."

She went down the companionway and back into Lieutenant Feldt's cabin. Muller followed her in and Kleist leaned against the open door.

"So, mademoiselle." Muller sat on the bed, turned the handbag upside down and emptied it. Her papers fell out, her makeup case, powder compact and comb, and also the Walther. He made no comment. He opened her French identity card, examined it, the German Ausweis and the ration cards. He replaced them carefully in the bag and lit a cigarette. Only then did he pick up the Walther, a finger through the trigger guard. "You are, I'm sure, aware that there is only one penalty for a civilian caught in possession of any kind of firearm?"

"Yes," Sarah said.

"This is yours, I take it?"

"Certainly. It was a gift from a friend. He was concerned for my safety. These are troubled times, Captain."

"And what kind of friend would encourage you to break the law so flagrantly? Would it not make him as guilty as you?"

From behind, a cold voice said in German, "Then perhaps you should address that question to me?"

Harry Martineau stood in the doorway. Guido just behind him in the corridor. He presented a supremely menacing figure in the SS uniform and black leather trenchcoat, the silver death's-head in the crumpled cap.

Karl Muller knew the devil when he met him face-to-face and got to his feet very fast indeed. "Standartenführer."

"You are?"

"Captain Karl Muller, in charge of Geheime Feldpolizei here in Jersey. This is my second in command, Inspector Kleist."

"My name is Vogel." Martineau took out his SD pass and handed it over. Muller examined it and passed it back. Martineau produced the Himmler warrant. "Read that—both of you."

Muller did as he was told. Kleist, peering over his shoulder, was awestruck and gazed at Martineau in astonishment. Muller took it much more calmly, folded the letter and handed it back. "In what way can I serve you, Standartenführer?"

"Mademoiselle Latour travels under my protection." Martineau picked up the Walther and put it back in her handbag. "She has done me the honor of choosing my friendship. There are those among her countrymen who do not approve. I prefer that she should be in a position to defend herself should any unfortunate situation arise."

"Of course, Standartenführer."

"Good, then kindly wait for me on deck."

Muller didn't even hesitate. "Certainly, Standartenführer." He nodded to Kleist and they went out.

Martineau closed the door and turned. He smiled suddenly, turning Vogel into Harry. "You look awful. Are you all right?"

"Yes," she said. "Thanks to Guido."

"Guido is it?"

"He saved my life, Harry. It wasn't good when we went down. Burning oil, men dying." She shuddered. "And the MTBs machine-gunned us in the water. I thought it was only the Germans who were supposed to do that?"

"Only at the cinema, sweetheart." He gave her a cigarette. "In real life everybody does it."

"We've got a problem," she said. "At one point when we were in the water I spoke to Guido in English."

"Good God!"

She put up a hand defensively. "It was pretty confusing out there to put it mildly. Anyway, he speaks good English himself. It seems he went to Winchester."

"Stop!" Martineau said. "It gets worse."

"Not really. After we were saved he told the officer commanding the ship that I only spoke French. And he knows about the Walther and kept quiet about that."

"You *have* been careless."

"He's no Fascist, Harry. He's an Italian aristocrat who doesn't give a damn about politics, stuck here because he happened to be in the wrong place when the Italian government capitulated."

"I see. So why should he go to all this trouble to lay himself on the line for you?"

"He likes me?"

"Likes you? He only met you last night."

"You know what these Latins are like."

She smiled mischievously and Martineau shook his head. "Nineteen they told me. More like a hundred and nineteen."

"Another thing, Harry, Guido's billeted on Aunt Helen at de Ville Place. Apparently a number of naval officers are. He was going to take me up there if you hadn't arrived."

"Perfect," Martineau said. "As for the other business, we'll tell him your mother was English. You've kept quiet about this during the Occupation years in case it caused you problems."

"Will he believe it?"

"I don't see why not. Are you going to be all right for clothes?"

"Yes. I've got a coat, shoes, hat, everything I need in the large case. A good job it traveled with you on the E-boat."

They went up the companionway. Muller was standing on the bridge talking to Feldt and Orsini. Below, Kleist and Greiser were shepherding the French seamen ashore.

Martineau said to Orsini in French, "Anne-Marie tells me you are billeted in most congenial circumstances. Some country house called de Ville Place?"

"That's right, Colonel."

Martineau turned to Muller. "It sounds as if it would suit my needs exactly. Would there be any objection?"

Muller, eager to please, said, "None at all, Standartenführer. It has, by tradition, been allocated to officers of the Kriegsmarine, but Mrs. de Ville, the owner, is seven or eight below her complement."

"That's settled then."

Orsini said, "I'll take you up there now, if you like. I have a car parked at the end of the pier."

"Good," Martineau said. "I suggest we get moving then."

They went down the gangway to the pier, and a Kriegsmarine rating, standing by the E-boat waiting, picked up the two suitcases and followed. Orsini and Sarah walked in front, Martineau followed with Muller at his side.

"Naturally once I'm settled in, I'll return to town to pay my respects to the military commandant. Colonel Heine, isn't it?"

"That's correct, Standartenführer. I understand he's leaving for Guernsey first thing in the morning for a weekend meeting with General von Schmettow."

"I need to see him only to present my compliments," Martineau told him. "One thing I will need is a vehicle. A Kubelwagen would serve my purposes best in case I wish to use it over rough country."

The Kubelwagen was the German Army's equivalent of the jeep, a general purpose vehicle that would go virtually anywhere.

"No problem, Standartenführer. I will also be happy to provide one of my men as a driver."

"Not necessary," Martineau said. "I prefer to do things for

myself, Muller. I'll find my way about this little island of yours, believe me."

Muller said, "If I could have some idea of the purpose of your visit."

"I am here on special instruction from Reischführer Himmler himself, countersigned by the Führer. You have seen my orders," Martineau told him. "Are you querying them?"

"Certainly not."

"Good." They had reached Orsini's Morris sedan, and the sailor was stowing the suitcases. "When the time comes, you will be informed, if and when necessary. I'll possibly call in on you later today. Where are your headquarters?"

"Silvertide Hotel. Havre des Pas."

"I'll find it. In the meantime have the Kubelwagen delivered to me."

Sarah was already in the back, Orsini behind the wheel. Martineau got into the front passenger seat beside him and the Italian moved away.

As they drove along Victoria Avenue, the military railway tracks between them and the bay, Martineau wound down the window and lit one of the Gitanes he'd got from the Cressons. "You like it here?" he asked Orsini.

"There are worse places to wait out the end of a war. In the summer it's particularly beautiful."

Martineau said. "I believe there's a misunderstanding to be cleared up. Anne-Marie has a Breton father, but an English mother. She felt it sensible to keep quiet about this in case it caused problems with the occupying powers. In fact it was one of my own people who first made the discovery, a happy one for me as it brought us together. Isn't that so, my love?"

"An intriguing story, Colonel," Orsini said. "You may rely on my discretion in the matter. The last thing I would wish to do is embarrass Mademoiselle Latour in any way."

"Good," Martineau said. "I felt sure you'd understand."

Back in his office at the Silvertide, Muller sat behind his desk thinking about things. After a while, he flipped the intercom. "Have Inspector Kleist and Sergeant Greiser come in."

He went to the window and looked out. The sky was clear now, sud-

denly blue, and the tide, still advancing, blanketed the rocks on the shore
with white foam. The door opened and the two policemen entered.

"You wanted us, Herr Captain?" Kleist asked.

"Yes, Willi." Muller sat down, leaned back in his chair, lit a cigarette
and blew smoke to the ceiling.

"What is it?" the Inspector asked.

"Remember old Dieckhoff, Chief of Detectives in Hamburg?"

"How could I forget him?"

"I always recall his number-one rule when I was a young detective.
Dieckhoff's Law, he called it."

"That it doesn't matter how good an egg looks. If it smells, there's
something wrong," Kleist said.

"Exactly." Muller nodded. "And this smells, Willi." He got up and
paced around the room. "Nothing to do with evidence or appearance.
Just every instinct I have as a detective tells me things aren't as they
seem. I'd like to know more about Standartenführer Vogel."

Kleist was obviously worried. "But, Herr Captain, his background
is impeccable. You can't very well ring up Reichsführer Himmler and
ask him to fill you in on his personal envoy."

"No, of course not." Muller turned. "But there is another possibility. Your brother used to work at Gestapo headquarters at Prince
Albrechtstrasse in Berlin, Ernst?"

"Peter? Yes, Herr Captain, but now he's at Stuttgart Headquarters.
Criminal records," Greiser said.

"He must still have connections in Berlin. Book a call through to
him. Ask about Vogel. I want to know how important he is."

"Shall I telex? It would be quicker."

"I want a judicious inquiry, you fool," Muller told him wearily.
"Not a public one."

"But I would remind you, sir, that calls for Germany are routed,
as you know, via Cherbourg and Paris. They've been taking fifteen or
sixteen hours recently, even at priority level."

"Then book one now, Ernst." The young man went out, and Muller
said to Kleist, "See about a Kubelwagen. Have it delivered to de Ville
Place. Let's keep him happy for the time being."

In the kitchen, Helen was rolling out the pastry made from potato flour when Gallagher came in. "Good, you can clean the fish for me," she said.

There were some plaice on the marble slab beside the sink. Gallagher took a knife from his pocket. The handle was of yellowing ivory. When he pressed one end, a razor-sharp double-edged blade sprang into view.

"You know I loathe that thing," she said.

"When my old grandfather, Harvey Le Brocq, was twelve he made his first trip in a schooner, all the way from Jersey to the Grand Banks off Newfoundland for cod. This knife was his father's gift to him. He left it to me in his will. Knives, guns—it's how they're used that's important, Helen."

"What do you want me to do, applaud?" she asked as he started to clean the fish. At that moment there was the sound of a car drawing up outside. "Probably Guido. I wonder what kind of a run they had?"

There were steps in the passageway, a knock on the door, and Guido came in carrying two suitcases. He put them down and straightened. "A good passage?" Helen asked.

"No, the *Hugo* was torpedoed. Savary missing, three crew members dead and four of my gun crew." Sarah stepped in through the door followed by Martineau, and Orsini carried on, "This is Anne-Marie Latour. She was a passenger on the *Hugo*. We were in the water together." He nodded to Martineau. "Standartenführer Vogel."

Helen looked bewildered. "What can I do for you?"

"Put us up, Mrs. de Ville," Martineau spoke in English. "I'm in the island for a few days. We need quarters."

"Impossible," Helen told him. "This is a billet for officers of the Kriegsmarine only."

"And you are well short of your complement," Martineau told her. "However inconvenient, the matter is an accomplished fact. If you would be kind enough therefore to show us to a suitable room."

Helen was angrier than she had been in years. The ice-cold assurance of the man, the SS uniform and the silly little tart traveling with him, with the tousled hair almost swallowed up by the huge reefer coat.

Guido said hurriedly, "Right, I'm going to have a bath and catch up on a little sleep. I'll see you all later."

The door closed behind him. Gallagher still stood by the sink, the knife in hand. Helen turned, pushing him out of the way angrily, washing the potato flour from her hands under the tap. She was aware of the SS officer still at the door with the girl.

Very softly, a voice said, "Aunt Helen, don't you know me?" Helen went quite still. Gallagher was looking over her shoulder in astonishment. "Uncle Sean?" And then, as Helen turned, "It's me, Aunt Helen. It's Sarah."

Helen dropped the cloth, moved forward and grabbed her by the shoulders, gazing at her searchingly. With recognition, there were sudden tears in her eyes. She laughed unsteadily and ran her fingers through the girl's hair.

"Oh, my God, Sarah, what have they done to you?" And then they were in each other's arms.

Hugh Kelso said, "So what happens now? You two have obviously had one hell of a trip just getting to Jersey, so where do we go from here?"

"I know where Sarah goes. Straight into a hot bath," Helen de Ville said. "You three can carry on talking as long as you like."

As she moved to the door. Gallagher said, "I've been thinking. Mrs. Vibert's due this afternoon. It might be an idea to give her a few days off."

"All right," Helen told him. "You can take care of it."

They went out and Kelso said, "What *does* happen now?" There was impatience in his voice.

Martineau said, "I just got here, my friend, so give me time to catch my breath. When it's time to go, you'll be the first to know."

"Does that include a bullet in the head, Colonel?" Kelso demanded, "If that's the decision, do we get to talk about it or just do it?"

Martineau didn't bother to answer. He simply went downstairs and waited in the master bedroom for Gallagher. The Irishman closed the secret door and shrugged. "He's had a hard time and that leg gives him a lot of pain."

"We're all in pain one way or another," Martineau said.

As he was about to open the door, Gallagher put a hand on his shoulder. "Could he be right? About the bullet in the head, I mean?"

"Maybe," Martineau said. "We'll have to see, won't we? Now I think I'll have a bath as well."

In London, Dougal Munro was just finishing breakfast at his flat when Jack Carter came in. "Some mixed news, sir, about Jerseyman."

"Tell me the worst, Jack."

"We've heard from Cresson. Everything went according to plan, and Martineau and Sarah left Granville for Jersey last night."

"And?"

"We've had another message from Cresson to say the word is the convoy ran into trouble. Attacked by MTBs. They don't have any hard facts."

"Have you?"

"I've checked with Naval Intelligence. Apparently MTBs of the Royal Dutch Navy operating out of Falmouth last night did hit that convoy, and they claim one merchantman sunk. They were driven off by the escorts."

"Good God, Jack, you're not seriously suggesting that Harry and the Drayton girl were on that boat?"

"We just don't know, sir, and what's more, there's no possible way we can find out."

"Exactly, so sit down, stop worrying about it and have a cup of tea, Jack. You know what your trouble is." Munro reached for the toast. "You don't have enough faith."

Sarah had washed her hair, using some homemade soft soap Helen had provided. She still looked a mess, and when Helen came into the bathroom she said, "It's no good. You need a hairdresser."

"Are there still such things?"

"Oh, yes, if you go into St. Helier. The general run of shops still function. The opening hours are shorter. Two hours in the mornings and two in the afternoon for most places."

She tried combing the girl's hair into some semblance of a style and Sarah said, "What's it been like?"

"Not good, but not too bad if you behave yourself. Plenty of people think the Germans are all right and a lot of the time they are, but step out of line and see what happens. You have to do as you're told, you see. They even made the Jersey States pass anti-Semitic laws. A lot of people try to excuse it by saying all the Jews had left, but I know two living in St. Brelade now."

"What happens if the German authorities discover them?"

"God knows. We've had people sent off to those concentration camps we hear about for keeping Russian slave workers who were on the run. I have a friend, a teacher at Jersey College for Girls, whose father kept an illegal radio. She used to spread the BBC news around to her friends until an anonymous letter brought the Gestapo to the house. They sent her to prison in France for a year."

"An anonymous letter? You mean from a local person? But that's terrible."

"You get bad apples in every barrel, Sarah. Jersey is no different from anywhere else in that respect. And we've got the other kind as well. The postmen at the sorting office who try to lose as many of the letters addressed to Gestapo Headquarters as possible." She finished combing. "There, that's the best I can do."

Sarah sat down, pulled on silk stockings and fastened them. "My God!" Helen said. "I haven't seen anything like that for four years. And that dress." She helped Sarah pull it over her head and zipped it up. "You and Martineau. What's the situation there? He's old enough to be your father."

"My father he very definitely is not." Sarah smiled as she pulled on her shoes. "He's probably the most infuriating man I've ever met and the most fascinating."

"And you sleep with him?"

"I *am* supposed to be Vogel's tart, Aunt Helen."

"And to think that the last time I saw you, you had pigtails," Helen said.

In the kitchen, she put two spoonfuls of her precious China tea into the pot, but Gallagher made his excuses. "I'll go and put Mrs. Vibert off," he said. "It'll only complicate things having her around. Always the chance she might recognize you, Sarah. She knew you well enough, God knows."

He went out and Helen, Sarah and Martineau sat around the table drinking tea and smoking. There was a knock at the door. When Helen opened it, Willi Kleist stood there.

Martineau got up. "You want me?"

"We've brought your Kubelwagen, Standartenführer," Kleist told him.

Martineau went out to have a look at it. The canvas top was up and the body was camouflaged. He looked inside and said, "That seems satisfactory."

Ernst Greiser was sitting behind the wheel of a black Citroën. Kleist said, "If there's anything else we can do ..."

"I don't think so."

"By the way, Captain Muller wanted me to tell you he's spoken to Colonel Heine, the military commandant. Apparently he'll be at the Town Hall this afternoon if you'd care to call in and see him."

"Thank you, I will."

They drove away and Martineau went back inside. "Transport problems taken care of. I'll go into town this afternoon, call on the military commandant, then Muller and his friends at this Silvertide place."

"You'd better go in with him and get your hair done," Helen told Sarah. "There's a good hairdresser at Charing Cross. You can tell her I sent you." She turned to Martineau. "Very convenient. It's close to the Town Hall."

"Fine," he said, "except for one thing. She mustn't say you sent her. In the circumstances that would be quite wrong." He got up. "I feel like a breath of air. How about showing me round the estate, Sarah?"

"A good idea," Helen said. "I've got things to do. I already had eight to cook for tonight so I've got my work cut out. I'll see you later."

After leaving de Ville Place, Kleist and Greiser started down the road, but after about a quarter of a mile, the inspector touched the young man on the arm. "Let's pull in here, Ernst. Stick the car in that track over there. We'll take a walk back through the woods."

"Any particular reason?"

"I'd just like to have a look around, that's all."

The cart track was heavily overgrown. Greiser drove along it until they were out of sight of the road, and they got out and left the Citroën there, taking a field path across the woods of the de Ville estate. It was very quiet and really rather pleasant, only the sound of the birds, and then a young woman carrying a basket appeared unexpectedly from beyond the high granite wall at the end of the field. It was impossible to see her face. For one thing, she was wearing a headscarf, but the old cotton frock was tight enough to reveal, even at a distance, a body that was full and ripe. She didn't notice them and followed the path into the wood.

Kleist said, "Now that's interesting." He turned to Greiser and smiled. "Would you say we should investigate, Sergeant?"

"Very definitely, Herr Inspector," the younger man said eagerly and they quickened their pace.

The young woman was in fact Mrs. Vibert's daughter, Mary. After Sean Gallagher's visit to tell her to take the weekend off, the old woman had remembered the eggs she had promised Helen de Ville for the evening meal. It was these that the girl was taking to the house now.

She was only sixteen and already blossoming into womanhood, but not very bright, with a simple, kindly face. She loved the countryside, the flowers, the birds, was never happier than when walking alone in the woods. Some little way in, there was an old granite barn long disused, the roof gaping, the doors hanging crazily. It always made her feel uneasy, and yet drawn to it by a strange fascination, she paused, then walked across the grass between crumbled walls to peer inside.

A harsh voice called, "Now then. What do you think you're doing?"

She turned quickly and saw Kleist and Greiser advancing toward her.

After leaving Mrs. Vibert's, Sean Gallagher walked down to the south meadow where he had three cows grazing, tethered to long chains in the Jersey manner. They were a precious commodity in these hard times and he stayed with them there in the sunshine for a while then started back to his cottage.

When he was still two fields away he saw the Germans walking toward the wood, saw and recognized Mary. He paused, shading his eyes against the sun, saw the girl disappear into the trees, the Germans following. Suddenly uneasy, he started to hurry. It was when he was halfway across the field that he heard the first scream. He cursed softly and broke into a run.

The weather was the best of spring, delightfully warm as Sarah and Martineau followed the track from the house through the pine trees.

There were daffodils everywhere, crocuses and snowdrops in profusion, camellias blooming. Beyond, through the trees, the waters of the bay were blue merging into green in places. Birds sang everywhere.

Sarah held his arm as they strolled along. "God, that wonderful marvelous smell. Straight back to childhood and those long hot summers. Did they ever exist, I wonder, or was it all an impossible dream?"

"No," he said. "They were the only true reality. It's the past four years that have been the nightmare."

"I love this place," she said. "It's an old race, the Norman stock here, and the de Villes are as old as any of them. We go back a long way. Robert de Ville fought at the Battle of Hastings with Duke William of Normandy."

"Good old William the Conqueror?"

"That's right. He ruled Jersey before he became king of England, so it's we who colonized the English, if you like, not the other way about."

"There's arrogance for you."

"These are my roots." she said. "Here I belong. This is home. Where do you belong, Harry?"

"Stateless person, that's me." he said lightly. "For years an American living and working in Europe. No family left worth speaking of."

"Citizen of the world?"

"Not really." He was upset and it showed in a sudden angry unease. "I just don't belong. Don't belong anywhere. Could be I should have died in those trenches back in nineteen eighteen. Maybe the man upstairs made a mistake. Perhaps I shouldn't be here at all."

She pulled him around, angry. "That's a terrible thing to say. I'm beginning to get rather tired of the cynical and sardonic bit, Harry Martineau. Can't you drop your guard just occasionally? Even with me?"

Before he could reply there was a sudden scream. They turned and looked down to the barn in the clearing through trees and saw Mary struggling in Kleist's arms, Greiser standing to one side laughing.

"For God's sake, Harry, do something," Sarah said.

"I will, only you stay out of it."

He started down the slope as Sean Gallagher ran out of the trees.

Kleist was excited, the supple young body squirming against him. "Shut up!" he told her. "Just be a good girl and I won't hurt you."

Greiser's eyes were shining, the mouth loose. "Don't forget, Inspector, fair shares for all, that's my motto." Gallagher arrived on the run, shouldering the sergeant out of the way like a rugby forward. As he reached Kleist, he stamped hard behind the German's left knee, causing the leg to buckle and punched him hard in the kidneys. Kleist grunted and went down, releasing the terrified girl.

Gallagher picked up Mary's basket and gave it to her and patted her face. "It's all right now, love," he said. "You run on up to the house to Mrs. de Ville. Nobody's going to harm you this day."

She ran like a frightened rabbit. As Gallagher turned, Greiser took a Mauser from his pocket, his eyes wild. Kleist called, "No, Ernst, and that's an order. He's mine." He got up, easing his back, and took off his raincoat. "Like all the Irish you're cracked in the head. Now I shall teach you a lesson. I shall break both your arms."

"Half-Irish, so only half-cracked, let's get it right." Sean Gallagher took off his jacket and tossed it to one side. "Didn't I ever tell you about my grandfather, old Harvey le Brocq? He was sailing in cod schooners at the age of twelve, bosun on windjammers on the grain run from Australia. Twelve times round the Horn by the age of twenty-three."

"Talk away," Kleist said circling him. "It won't do you any good."

He rushed in and swung a tremendous punch which Gallagher avoided with ease. "In those days a bosun was only as good as his fists, and he was good. Very good." He ducked in and landed a punch under the German's left eye. "When I used to come over from Ireland as a kid to stay with him, the village lads would work me over because I talked funny. When I went home crying, he took me out in the orchard and gave me the first of many lessons. Science, timing, punching, that's what counts, not size. God, as he often reminded me, and he was a lay preacher, had never intended the brutes to rule on earth."

Every punch the German threw was sidestepped, and in return, Gallagher seemed to be able to hit him wherever he wanted. On the hillside a few yards away, Sarah, Martineau and the Vibert girl watched as the Irishman drove the inspector back across the grass.

And then there was a sudden moment of disaster, for as Gallagher moved in, his right foot slipped on the grass and he went down. Kleist seized his chance, lifting a knee into his forehead and kicking him in the side as he went down. Gallagher rolled away with surprising speed and came up on one knee.

"God save us, you can't even kick straight."

As he came up, Kleist rushed at him, arms reaching to destroy. Gallagher slipped to one side, tripping the German so that he went headfirst into the wall of the bam. The Irishman gave him a left and a right in the kidneys. Kleist cried out sharply and Gallagher swung him around. He grabbed him by the lapels and smashed his forehead against the bridge of the German's nose, breaking it. Then he stepped back. Kleist swayed and fell.

"Bastard!" Greiser called.

Gallagher swung around to find the sergeant confronting him with the Mauser, but in the same moment a shot rang out, kicking up dirt at Greiser's feet. They turned as Martineau walked down the slope, Walther in hand.

"Put it away!" he ordered.

Greiser stood there, staring at him, and it was Kleist, getting to his feet, who said hoarsely, "Do as he says, Ernst."

Greiser obeyed and Martineau said, "Good. You are, of course, a disgrace to everything the Reich stands for. This I shall discuss with your commanding officer later. Now leave."

Greiser tried to give Kleist his arm. The big man shoved him away and walked off through the trees. Gallagher turned and shouted to Mary Vibert, "Go on girl, go up to the house."

She turned and ran. Sarah took out a handkerchief and wiped blood from Gallagher's mouth. "I never realized what a deadly combination Jersey was with the Irish."

"A fine day for it, thanks be to God." Gallagher squinted up at the sun through the trees. "Better times coming." He grinned and turned to Martineau. "You wouldn't happen to have a cigarette on you? I seem to have left mine at home."

11

MARTINEAU AND SARAH DROVE down through St. Aubin and along toward Bel Royal, passing a number of fortifications and gun positions on the way. The sky was very blue, the sun bright, and yet on the horizon, beyond Fort Elizabeth, there was a dark curtain.

"Rain," she said. "Typical Jersey spring weather. Wonderful sunshine and then the squalls sweep in across the bay, sometimes only for a few minutes."

"It's warmer than I'd expected," he said. "Quite Mediterranean." He nodded at the gardens as they passed. "Especially with all those palm trees. I didn't expect those."

She leaned back and closed her eyes. 'This island has a special smell to it in the spring. Nothing quite like it anywhere else in the world." She opened her eyes again and smiled. "That's the de Ville side of me speaking. Hopelessly prejudiced. Tell me something. Why have you taken off your uniform?"

He was wearing the leather military trenchcoat, but underneath was a gray tweed suit with a waistcoat and white shirt with a black tie. The slouch hat was also in black, the brim down at the front and back.

"Tactics," he said. "Everybody who is anybody will know I'm here, will know who I am, thanks to Muller. I don't need to appear in uniform if I don't want to. SD officers wear civilian clothes most of the time. It emphasizes our power. It's more frightening."

"You said *our* power."

"Did I?"

"Yes. You frighten me sometimes, Harry."

He pulled the Kubelwagen in at the side of the road and switched off. "Let's take a walk."

He helped her out and they paused as one of the military trains approached and moved past, then they crossed the track to the seawall. There was a café there, all closed up, probably from before the war, a huge bunker not too far away.

A new unlooked-for delight was music, two young soldiers on the seawall, a portable radio between them. Below, on the sands, children played, their mothers sitting against the wall, faces turned to the sun. A number of German soldiers swam in the sea, two or three young women among them.

Martineau and Sarah leaned on the wall. "Unexpectedly domestic, isn't it?" He gave her a cigarette.

The soldiers glanced at them, attracted by the girl, but turned from his dark stare. "Yes," she said. "Not what I expected."

"If you look closely you'll see that most of the soldiers on the beach are boys. Twenty at the most. Difficult to hate. When someone's a Nazi, then it's explicit. You know where you stand. But the average twenty-year-old German in uniform"—he shrugged—"is just a twenty-year-old in uniform."

"What do you believe in, Harry? Where are you going?" Her face was strained, intense.

"As I once told you, I'm a very existentialist person. 'Action this day'—Churchill's favorite phrase. And that means defeating the Nazis because they must be destroyed totally. Hitler's personal philosophy is unacceptable in terms of any kind of common humanity."

"And afterward, when it's all over? What happens to you?"

He stared out to sea, eyes very dark, leaning on the wall. "When I was young I used to love railway stations, especially at night. The smell of the steam, the dying fall of a train whistle in the distance, the platforms in those great deserted Victorian palaces at night, waiting to go somewhere, anywhere. I loved it and yet I also used to get a feeling of tremendous unease. Something to do with getting on the wrong train." He turned to her. "And once the train's on its way, you see, you can't get off."

"The station is ominous at midnight," she said softly. "Hope is a dead letter."

He stared at her. "Where did you hear that?"

"One of your bad poems," she said. "That first day I met you at the cottage the brigadier was reading it. You took it from him, crumpled it up and threw it into the fireplace."

"And you retrieved it?"

"Yes."

For a moment she thought he would be angry. Instead he smiled. "Wait here." He left her and crossed the line to the Kubelwagen and opened the door. When he returned he was carrying a small Kodak camera. "Helen gave me this. As the film is four years old she can't guarantee the results."

He walked up to the soldiers. There was a brief exchange in which they put their heads together for a moment, standing stiffly to attention. Martineau gave one of them the camera and returned to her.

"Don't forget to smile." He lit a cigarette and turned, hands in the pockets of the trenchcoat.

Sarah took his arm. "What's this for?"

"Something to remember me by."

It made her feel uneasy and she held his arm even more tightly. The young soldier took the photo. "Another," Martineau called in German, "just to make sure."

The boy returned the camera, smiling shyly, then saluted and walked away. "Did you tell him who you were?" she asked.

"Of course I did." He took her arm. "Let's get going. I've got things to do." They crossed the railway track and returned to the Kubelwagen.

Karl Muller prided himself on his control, his remarkable lack of emotion in all situations. He thought of it as his greatest asset, and yet, standing by the window in his office at the Silvertide Hotel, it almost deserted him for the first time.

"You what?" he demanded.

Kleist's face was in a dreadful state, flesh around the eyes purple and dark, the broken nose swollen. "A misunderstanding, Herr Captain."

Muller turned to Greiser. "And that's your version also? A misunderstanding?"

"We were only questioning the girl, Herr Captain. She panicked, then Gallagher arrived. He placed entirely the wrong construction on the affair."

"As your face proves, Willi," Muller said. "And Vogel was involved."

"He arrived on the scene at an unfortunate moment," Greiser told him.

"And *he* also placed entirely the wrong construction on things." Muller was furious. "Leaving me to get you off the hook when he turns up here this afternoon. Go on, get out of my sight!"

He turned to the window and slammed his palm against the wall.

Following Sarah's instructions, Martineau drove along Gloucester Street past the prison. "One thing," he said. "When we're together in the town speak French. You never know who's listening, understand?"

"Of course."

They could hear music now and turned into the Parade to find a German military band playing on the grass between the statue of General Don, a previous governor of the island, and the Cenotaph. There was quite a crowd standing listening, mainly civilians with a few soldiers.

"Just like *Workers' Playtime* on the BBC back in the UK," Martineau said. "Supposed to make people feel better about being occupied."

"Pull in here," she said. "The Town Hall is just at the end."

He parked at the curb and they got out, people turning to stare curiously, attracted by the sight of the military vehicle. Many seemed indifferent, but there were those unable to hide their anger when they looked at Sarah, especially the older women.

Someone muttered "Gerrybag!" as they walked past. It was an ugly word meant to express the contempt most people felt for a girl who consorted with the enemy. Martineau swung around, Vogel to the life, and confronted the gray-haired woman who had spoken.

"You said something, madam?" he asked in English.

She was immediately terrified. "No—not me. You're mistaken." She turned and hurried away in a panic.

Sarah took his arm and said softly, "There are times when I hate you myself, Harry Martineau."

They passed the entrance of the Town Hall with the Nazi flag flying above and a Luftwaffe sentry on the steps with a rifle. They crossed to the other side of York Street and came to Charing Cross. Some of the shop windows were still taped to avoid flying glass, probably from the first year of the war. The Luftwaffe had bombed St. Helier once in 1940. It was obviously the last thing the RAF intended to do, which probably explained why a lot of shopkeepers had cleaned the tape off.

They paused at a doorway between two shops. The sign indicated that the hairdresser was upstairs. Sarah said, "I remember this place."

"Would you be recognized?"

"I shouldn't think so. The last time I was in here was to have my hair cut when I was ten years old."

She led the way up the stairs, pushed open a door with a frosted glass pane and Martineau followed her in. It was only a small salon with two washbasins and a couple of hairdriers. The woman who sat in the corner reading a magazine was about forty with a round, pleasant face. She glanced up smiling, and then the smile was wiped clear away.

"Yes?" she said.

"I need my hair fixed rather badly," Sarah said in French.

"I don't speak French," the woman replied.

Martineau said in English, "The young lady was a passenger on the *Victor Hugo* from Granville last night. As I am sure you are aware of the fate of that unhappy vessel, you will appreciate that she was in the water for some time. As she has no English I must speak for her. Her hair, as you can see, requires attention."

"I can't help. I'm booked up."

Martineau looked around the empty salon. "So I see. Your identity card, if you please."

"Why should I? I've done nothing."

"Would you rather continue this conversation at Silvertide?"

There was fear in her eyes. Sarah had never felt so wretched in her life and waited as the unfortunate woman found her handbag and produced the identity card. It was in the name of Mrs. Emily Johnson. Martineau examined it and handed it back.

"My name is Vogel—Standartenführer Max Vogel. I have an appointment at the Town Hall with Colonel Heine, the commandant. I'll be gone for an hour, perhaps a little longer. While I am away you will do whatever is necessary to the young lady's hair. When I return, I am sure it will look quite delightful." He opened the door. "If it doesn't, I'll close this establishment so fast you won't know what's hit you."

They listened to him descend the stairs. Mrs. Johnson took a robe down from behind the door and turned to Sarah with a delightful smile. "All right, you dirty little French tart. Let's make you look pretty for that butcher," she said in English. Her smile became even more charming. "And I can only hope you get what you deserve."

Sarah felt like cheering her out loud. Instead she stayed in control and replied in French, "Ah, the coat."

She took it off, handed it to her, put on the robe and went to the nearest chair.

As Martineau crossed to the Town Hall he saw a policeman in traditional British bobby's uniform and helmet standing on the steps talking to the sentry. They stopped talking, watching him warily as he approached.

"Standartenführer Vogel for the commandant."

The sentry jumped to attention and the police constable faded away discreetly. "The commandant arrived twenty minutes ago, Standartenführer."

Martineau moved into the hall and found a table at the bottom of the stairs, an army sergeant sitting there. He glanced up and Martineau said, "My name is Vogel. I believe Colonel Heine is expecting me."

The sergeant leaped to his feet and picked up the phone. "Standartenführer Vogel is here, Herr Major." He replaced the receiver. "Major Necker will be down directly, sir."

"Thank you." Martineau walked away and looked out through the open door. Within moments there was the sound of boots on the stairs. He turned to find a young man hurrying down, an infantry major, no more than thirty from the look of him.

He was all cordiality, but then he would be, pausing briefly to click his heels before putting out a hand. "Felix Necker, Standartenführer."

He'd seen action, that was plain enough from the shrapnel scar running into the right eye. As well as the Iron Cross First Class he wore the Wounded Badge in silver, which meant he'd been a casualty at least three times, the infantry Assault Badge and a Close Combat Clasp in gilt. It was recognition and familiarity with such items that kept Martineau alive. What they told him about people was important. What they said about this man was that he was a war hero.

"A pleasure to meet you, Herr Major," he said. "You've been in Jersey long?"

"Only a couple of months," Necker told him. "I'm not with the 319th Division normally. Only on loan."

They went upstairs, he knocked and opened a door, stood to one side and Martineau went in first. It was a pleasant enough room, obviously originally the office of some official. The officer who stood up and came around the desk to meet him was a type he recognized instantly. A little stiff in manner, rather old-fashioned regular army and very definitely no Nazi. An officer and a gentleman.

"Standartenführer. A pleasure to see you." The handshake was firm, friendly enough, but the eyes said something else. Only surface courtesy here.

"Colonel Heine." Martineau opened his coat and produced his SD card.

Heine examined it and handed it back. "Please sit down. In what way can we serve you? You've met Felix Necker, of course. He's only on loan from Paris. Temporarily my second in command. A holiday for him. Just out of hospital. He was on the Russian Front."

"Indeed?" Martineau said. He took out the Himmler letter and passed it across.

Heine read it slowly, his face grave, then passed it to Necker. "If I could know the purpose of your visit?"

"Not at this stage." Martineau took the letter as Necker handed it back to him. "All I need is assurance of total cooperation as and when required."

"That goes without saying," Heine hesitated. "As for billeting arrangements, I understand you are staying at de Ville Place."

"Yes, I spoke to Captain Muller of the GFP on the pier when we arrived. He was most cooperative. He has already supplied me with a suitable vehicle, so for the moment, there is really nothing else I require. It would be useful if you informed all unit commanders of my presence."

"Of course. There is one thing," Heine added. "I have to go to Guernsey and so does the civil affairs commander. A weekend conference with General von Schmettow."

Martineau turned to Necker. "Presumably you will be in command?"

"That is correct."

"Then I can see no problem." He got to his feet and picked up his hat.

Heine said, "I'll see you when I get back then?"

"Possibly." Martineau shook hands. "A pleasure, Herr Colonel. I'll let you get on with it now. Don't bother to see me out, Major."

The door closed behind him. Heine's whole demeanor changed. "My flesh always crawls when these SS security people appear. What in the hell does he want, Felix?"

"God alone knows, Herr Colonel, but his credentials …" Necker shrugged. "Not only signed by Himmler, but by the Führer himself."

"I know." Heine put up a hand defensively. "Just watch him, that's all. I'll see what von Schmettow thinks when I get to Guernsey. But at all costs keep him sweet. Trouble with Himmler is the last thing we need."

"Of course, Herr Colonel."

"Good. Now show in these good citizens from the Food Control Committee and let's get on with it."

Martineau had time in hand so he walked through the town. There were plenty of people about, more civilians than soldiers. Most people looked underweight, but that was to be expected, and clothes looked old and well-worn. There were few children about, they'd be at school. The ones he did see were in better shape than he had expected, but then, people always did put their children first.

So, people managed. He knew, because Helen de Ville had told them, of the communal kitchens and bakeries to conserve fuel. It occurred to him that people in the town obviously had a more difficult time of it than those in the country. At that moment, as he moved into Queen Street, he saw a crowd overflowing the pavement ahead, all staring into a shop window.

It contained an amazing display of food of every description. Canned goods, sacks of potatoes and flour, hams, bottles of red wine and champagne. People said nothing, just looked. A notice in the window said: *Black market goods. The enemy may be your own neighbor. Help defeat him.* It was signed by Muller. The pain in the faces of ordinary people deprived too long was unbearable. Martineau turned and went back to Charing Cross.

When he went upstairs to the salon, Sarah was just adjusting her hat in the mirror. Her hair looked excellent. He helped her on with her coat.

Emily Johnson said, "Satisfied?"

"Very much so." He opened his wallet and took out a ten-mark note.

"No!" Her anger overflowed. "I don't want your money. You told me to do her hair and I've done it." There were tears of frustration in her eyes. "Just go."

Martineau pushed Sarah out of the door. When he turned, his voice, to Emily Johnson's astonishment, was quite gentle. It was as if, for a moment, he had stepped out of the role of brutal SS officer that he had played so well. "I salute you, Mrs. Johnson. You are a brave woman."

The door closed behind him. She sat down, head in hands, and started to cry.

Martineau parked the Kubelwagen outside the Silvertide Hotel at Havre des Pas beside several other cars. "I shan't be long."

She smiled. "Don't worry about me I'll just take a walk along the seawall. I used to come to swim in the pool here when I was a kid."

"As you please. Just try not to talk to any strange men."

Muller had seen him arrive from the window of his office. When Martineau went inside, a young military policeman in plain clothes was waiting to greet him. "Standartenführer Vogel? This way please."

He ushered Martineau into Muller's office and closed the door. The captain stood up behind the desk. "A great pleasure."

"I wish I could say the same," Martineau said. "You've spoken to Kleist and Greiser?"

"About this misunderstanding at de Ville Place? Yes, they did explain ..."

"Misunderstanding?" Martineau said coldly. "You will have them in here now, Herr Captain, if you please, and quickly. My time is limited." He turned away and stood at the window, hands behind his back, as Muller asked for Kleist and Greiser over the intercom. They came in only a few moments. Martineau didn't bother to turn around, but looked out across the road to the seawall where Sarah was standing.

He said softly, "Inspector Kleist, I understand you have put this morning's events at de Ville Place down to a misunderstanding?"

"Well, yes, Standartenführer."

"Liar!" Martineau's voice was low and dangerous. "Both of you liars." He turned to face them. "As I walked through the wood with Mademoiselle Latour we heard a girl scream. A child, Captain, barely sixteen, being dragged toward a barn by this animal here while the other stood and laughed. I was about to interfere when General Gallagher came on the scene and gave a bully the thrashing he deserved."

"I see," Muller said.

"Just to make things worse, I was obliged to draw my own pistol and fire a warning shot to prevent this idiot shooting Gallagher in the back. God in heaven, what kind of an imbecile are you, Greiser?" He spoke slowly as if to a child. "The man is Irish, which means he is a neutral, and the Führer's declared policy is good relations with Ireland. On top of that he is a famous man back there in the old country. A hero of their revolution. A general. We don't shoot people like that in the back. Understand?"

"Yes, Standartenführer."

Now he turned his attention to Kleist. "And as the Führer's declared policy toward the inhabitants of Jersey has been one of reconciliation, we do not attempt to rape sixteen-year-old girls." He turned to Muller. "The actions of these men are an affront to every ideal the Reich holds dear and to German honor."

He was thoroughly enjoying himself, especially when Kleist's anger overflowed. "I'm not a child to be lectured like this."

"Kleist!" Martineau said. "As a member of the Gestapo you took an oath to our Führer. A holy oath. As I recall it runs: I vow to you and the superiors you appoint, obedience unto death. Is it not so?"

"Yes," Kleist answered.

"Then remember from now on that you are here to obey orders. If I ask a question you answer, '*Jawohl, Standartenführer.*' If I give you an order it's '*Zu befehl, Standartenführer.*' Do you follow?"

There was a pause before Kleist said in a low voice, "*Jawohl, Standartenführer.*"

Martineau turned on Muller. "And you wonder why Reichsführer Himmler thought it worthwhile sending me here?"

He walked out without another word, went through the foyer and crossed the road to the Kubelwagen. Sarah was sitting on the bonnet. "How did it go?" she asked.

"Oh, I think you could say I put the fear of God in them all rather satisfactorily." He opened the door for her. "Now you can take me on a Cook's tour of this island of yours."

Muller started to laugh. "I wish you could see yourself standing there in front of the desk, Willi. All you need is short pants."

"I swear to God I'll…"

"You'll do nothing, Willi, just like the rest of us. You'll just do as you're told." He went to a cupboard, opened it and found a glass and a bottle of cognac. "I must say he sounded just like the Reichsführer on a bad day. All that German purity nonsense. All those platitudes."

"Do you still want me to speak to my brother, Herr Captain?" Greiser asked. "I've got a call booked through to Stuttgart for ten o'clock tonight."

"Why not?" Muller poured some cognac into his glass and said impatiently, "For God's sake, go down to the hospital and get that nose seen to, Willi. Go on, get out of my sight, both of you."

Rommel was staying at a villa near Bayeux, in a place deep in the countryside and quite remote. It had been used as a weekend retreat by the commanding general of the area who had been happy to offer it to the field marshal when he'd expressed a desire for a quiet weekend. The Bernards, who ran the house, were extremely discreet. The wife was an excellent cook, the husband acted as butler.

Baum drove to the house ahead of the field marshal that afternoon in a Kubelwagen wearing his own Fallschirmjäger uniform. He also affected a heavy black patch over the right eye on Rommel's insistence. To Baum, he did not resemble the field marshal until he put on the clothes, changed his appearance with a few artful touches of makeup, the rubber cheekpads that made the face squarer. But the real change was in himself—the change that started inside. He thought Rommel, so he became Rommel. That was his unique talent as a performer.

Rommel and Hofer arrived later in the afternoon in the Mercedes driven by an engineer sergeant named Dreschler, an Afrika Korps veteran whom Hofer had specially selected. Madame Bernard provided the field marshal with a late luncheon in the drawing room. Afterward, Hofer brought Baum in to join them.

"Right, let's go over things," Rommel said.

"According to my information the people from Jersey will leave for Guernsey at around two in the morning. Berger and I will leave here in the Kubelwagen at nine. There is an empty cottage on the estate a kilometer from here where we stop for him to change."

"And afterward?"

"To a Luftwaffe reserve airstrip only ten kilometers from here. There is a pilot, an Oberleutnant Sorsa, waiting there under your personal order with a Fiesler Storch."

"Sorsa? Isn't that a Finnish name?" Rommel asked.

"That's right."

"Then what's he doing with the Luftwaffe? Why isn't he on the Eastern Front shooting down Russians with his own people?"

"Sorsa is hot stuff, a real ace. One of the greatest night fighter pilots in the business. These days he's of more use flying over the Reich knocking down Lancaster bombers. He's an excellent choice for this venture. He doesn't fit into the usual Luftwaffe command structure. An outsider."

"They don't like us very much, the Finns," Rommel said. "I've never trusted them." He lit a cigarette. "Still, carry on."

"Sorsa won't know his destination until we join the plane. I estimate we will land in Jersey around eleven o'clock. I've given orders for Headquarters of Army Group B to notify Berlin at noon that you've flown to Jersey. The reason for not letting them know earlier being the need to consider your safety when in flight."

"And what happens here?"

"Generals Stulpnagel and Falkenhausen arrive later in the day. Stay overnight and leave on Saturday morning."

"And you return in the evening?"

"Of course. This couple here at the house, the Bernards, will know you are here, but then they won't know you're also in Jersey. Neither will Sergeant Dreschler. He worships you anyway. An old desert hand. If there is any problem with him later, I can handle it."

Rommel turned to Baum. "And you, my friend, can you handle it?"

"Yes, Herr Field Marshal. I really think I can," Baum told him.

"Good." Rommel took the bottle of Dom Perignon from the ice bucket that Monsieur Bernard had brought in earlier and uncorked it. He filled three glasses and gave them one each. "So, my friends, to the Jersey enterprise."

Sarah and Martineau had spent an enlightening afternoon, driving to Gorey where she had intended to show him Mont Orgeuil, one of the most magnificent castles in Europe, only to find that it was now a heavily defended enemy strongpoint.

At Fliquet Bay, they had come across a party of slave workers cutting a new road through to a coastal artillery battery. They were the most ragged, filthy, undernourished creatures even Martineau had seen. He had made himself known to the sergeant in charge of the detail who told him they were Russians. It was particularly ironic, therefore, to discover a battalion of the Russian Liberation Army staffed mainly by Ukrainians, guarding the north coast around Bonne Nuit Bay.

They carried on to Grosnez with the few stones remaining of its medieval castle and spectacular views of Sark, Herm and Jethou, all reaching toward Guernsey. The interesting thing was that not once were they stopped or challenged, even when they drove along the Five Mile Road following the curve of St. Ouen's Bay, which looked to Martineau like the most heavily defended stretch they'd seen.

It was evening when they stopped at the church at the end of St. Brelade's Bay. Sarah got out and he followed her. They stood in the archway and peered inside. There was an entire section devoted to the military, rows of crosses, each one at the end of a neat grave.

"I don't know what Christ would have made of those crosses," Martineau said. "There's a swastika in the center of each one."

She shivered. "I used to attend this church. I had my first communion here."

Martineau walked idly between the rows of German crosses. "There're a couple of Italians here and a Russian." He carried on, moving into the older section of the cemetery, passing between granite headstones and tombs. "Strange," he said. "I feel quite at home."

"That's a morbid thought," Sarah told him.

"Not really. I just find it extraordinarily peaceful and the view of the bay is sensational. Still I suppose we should be getting back now."

They got in the Kubelwagen and drove past the bay along Mont Sohier. Sarah said, "So, now you've had the guided tour. What do you think?"

"A tight little island."

"And how do we get Hugh Kelso off it?"

"To tell you the truth, I haven't the slightest idea, so if you can think of anything, let me know."

He carried on driving, whistling tunelessly between his teeth.

Dinner was a strange affair. Martineau and Sarah joined the officers in the main dining room. Guido Orsini, Bruno Feldt, Kapitanleutnant Erich Dietrich and several others. There was a fresh lighted candle at each empty place which Sarah found rather macabre, but the young officers were polite and considerate, would obviously have put themselves out even more if it had not been for Martineau's presence. He was wearing his uniform in deference to the formality of the meal, and its effect on the others had been definitely depressing. Helen de Ville passed in and out with the plates, and Sarah, bored with the stilted conversation, insisted on helping her to clear the table and joined her in the kitchen, where Sean Gallagher sat at the table eating the leftovers.

"Terrible in there. Harry's like a specter at the feast," she said.

Helen had just prepared a tray for Kelso. "I'll just take this up while they're all still in the dining room."

She went up the back stairs and opened the door to the master bedroom at the same moment that Guido Orsini passed the end of the corridor. He saw her, noted the tray in astonishment and moved cautiously along the corridor. He hesitated, then tried the door of her bedroom. Helen, for once, had omitted to turn the key. He peered inside, saw the secret door ajar and tiptoed across. There was a murmur of voices from upstairs. He listened for a moment, then turned and went out again, closing the door.

Sarah and Gallagher were talking in low voices when Guido went into the kitchen. "Ah, there you are," he said. "They're into politics now. Can I take you for a walk on the terrace?"

"Is he to be trusted?" she asked Gallagher.

"No more than most men I know, especially around a darling like you."

"I'll have to take a chance then. If Colonel Vogel comes looking for me, tell him I'll be back soon," she added formally.

There was a half-moon, the sky bright with stars, a luminosity to everything, palm trees etched against the sky. Everywhere there was the smell of flowers, drenched from the rain earlier.

"Azaleas." She breathed deeply. "One of my favorites."

"You are a remarkable girl," he said in English. "You don't mind if we use English, do you? There's no one about and it helps me keep my hand in."

"All right," she said reluctantly, "but not for long."

"You've never been to Jersey before?"

"No. I was raised by my grandmother in Paimpol after my mother died."

"I see. And it was your mother who was English?"

"That's right."

She was wary at this questioning and sat on a low granite wall, the moon behind her. He gave her a cigarette. "You smoke Gitanes, don't you?"

She was used to cigarettes by now and nodded. "On the other hand, one has to be content with whatever is available these days."

He gave her a light. "Yes, it's really quite remarkable. You speak French with a very Breton accent."

"What's strange about that? My grandmother was Breton."

"I know. It's your English that's so interesting. Very upper class. I went to Winchester, remember, so I can tell."

"Really? I'm a lucky girl, then." She stood up. "I'd better get back now, Guido. Max can get rather restless if I'm out of his sight too long with another man."

"Of course." She took his arm and they strolled back through the azaleas. "I like you, Anne-Marie Latour. I like you a lot. I want you to remember that."

"Only like?" she said. "I thought you said you loved me." A dangerous game she was playing here. She knew that and yet could not resist taking it as far as it would go.

"All right," he said. "I love you," and he pulled her into his arms and kissed her passionately. "Now do you understand?"

"Yes, Guido," she said softly. "I think I do."

Martineau appeared on the terrace in the moonlight "Anne-Marie, are you there?" he shouted in French.

"Coming!" she called back and reached to touch the Italian's face. "I'll see you tomorrow, Guido," and she ran up the steps to the terrace.

They were all in the private sitting room at the back of the house overlooking the terrace, Gallagher, Martineau, Helen and Sarah. Gallagher poured Burgundy into four glasses while Helen opened the French window a little. It was very close. She breathed in the perfumed air for a few moments, then drew the heavy curtains across.

"So, what happens now?" Sean Gallagher asked.

"He certainly can't walk at the moment," Helen de Ville said. "George Hamilton saw him this afternoon. A real chance he could lose the leg if he disturbs things."

"At least he's safe for the time being upstairs," Sarah said.

"He can't sit out the war there," Martineau pointed out. "We need to get him to Granville. Once there, Cresson can radio London and have a Lysander over any night we want."

"But how to get him there, that's the thing," Gallagher said. "They've really got the small boat traffic closed up tight here. Observation posts all along the coast as you saw for yourself today. You wouldn't get far without being spotted. Any fishing boat that leaves harbor, even the lifeboat, has to have German guards on board when they put to sea."

"So what *is* the solution?" Sarah demanded. "We must do something."

There was a movement at the window; the curtains parted. Martineau turned, drawing his Walther, and Guido Orsini stepped into the room. "Perhaps I can help," he said in English.

12

THE FOLLOWING MORNING MARTINEAU was on the upper level of the Albert Pier as Colonel Heine, the civil administration commander, and the bailiff and his party left for Guernsey on the E-boat with Dietrich. He watched them go as he leaned on the seawall, waiting for Orsini, who had gone to Kriegsmarine Headquarters at the Pomme d'Or Hotel.

The Italian's entry through the curtains the night before had certainly been as dramatic as it was unexpected. But his offer to throw in his lot with them made sense. Even if Orsini had been a thoroughgoing Fascist, it was reasonably certain who was going to win this war, and in Italy many of Mussolini's most fervent followers had transferred their allegiance to the winning side without a moment's hesitation. In any case, Orsini was not one of those. So Helen and Gallagher had assured him and so had Sarah, most fervently of all.

The young Italian came up the steps, saluted a couple of Kriegsmarine ratings and joined Martineau. "Let's walk to the end of the pier."

"What did you find out?" Martineau asked as they strolled along.

"A possible break. There's a small convoy due in from Guernsey early Sunday morning. The master of one of the ships, a Dutch coaster called the *Jan Kruger,* was taken ill yesterday. The bosun is handling her as far as Jersey."

"And then?"

"Our old friend Robert Savary takes command for the run to Granville."

"That certainly is interesting," Martineau said. "When can you speak to him?"

"There's the snag. He was picked up after the *Victor Hugo* went down by one of the search and rescue craft from St. Malo. He's due over from Granville early evening tomorrow on a fast patrol craft. What we call the dispatch boat."

"And you think he might be willing to smuggle Kelso over?"

Orsini shrugged. "From what you have told me of his part in this business already, I should imagine him an eminently suitable candidate for applied pressure. After what he's already done, I fail to see how he can say no."

"True," Martineau said. "And he knows that if he puts a foot wrong the Cressons and their friends will arrange his funeral, priest included, free of charge." He smiled. "You know something, Count? I think you may well prove to be an asset to the corporation."

"Fine," said Guido. "Only let us understand each other."

"Go on."

"I've had my bellyful of death and destruction. I'm tired of killing and sick of politics. The Allies are going to win this war, that is inevitable, so Jersey was the perfect billet for a sensible man to sit out the last few months in comfort. And don't let's pretend that anything that happens here will make the slightest difference. If the Germans got their hands on Kelso, Eisenhower's invasion plans would, at the most, be seriously inconvenienced. He'd still win in the end. We're engaged in a rather interesting game here. It's true that it's also a dangerous one, but still only a game."

"Then why throw your hat in the ring?" Martineau asked.

"I think you know why," Guido told him as they went down the steps to where his car was parked. He smiled amiably. "Be warned, my friend. There is nothing more dangerous than the libertine who suddenly finds he has fallen in love with a good woman."

When the phone rang in his office at command headquarters Felix Necker was just about to leave to go riding on the beach at St. Aubin. He picked up the receiver and listened and a look of horror appeared on his face. "My God! What's his estimated time of arrival? All right. Arrange a guard of honor. I'll be there as soon as I can."

He slammed down the receiver and sat there for a moment thinking about things, then he picked it up again and dialed GFP Headquarters at the Silvertide.

"Herr Major," Muller said when he was put through. "What can I do for you?"

"Rommel is due in at the airport in forty-five minutes."

"Who did you say?" Muller demanded.

"Field Marshal Erwin Rommel, you idiot. He's arriving with his aide, a Major Hofer, from Normandy in a Fiesler Storch."

"But why?" Muller demanded. "I don't understand."

"Well I do," Necker told him. "It all makes perfect sense. First of all his orders for Heine and the others to join General von Schmettow in Guernsey for the weekend, getting them all nicely out of the way so that he can fly in out of the blue and take the place apart. I know how Rommel operates, Muller. He'll go everywhere. Check every machine-gun post."

"At least one mystery is solved," Muller said.

"What's that?"

"The reason for Vogel being here. The whole thing ties in now."

"Yes, I suppose you're right." Necker said. "Anyway, never mind that now. I'll see you at the airport."

He put down the receiver, hesitated, then picked it up again and told the operator to connect him with de Ville Place. Martineau and Orsini had just returned, and it was Helen who answered the phone in the kitchen.

"It's for you," she said to Martineau. "Major Necker."

He took the receiver from her. "Vogel here."

"Good morning," Necker greeted him. "I'm sure it will come as no surprise to you to know that Field Marshal Rommel arrives at the airport in just over half-an-hour."

Martineau, concealing his astonishment, said, "I see."

"Naturally, you'll wish to greet him. I'll see you at the airport."
Martineau put the phone down slowly as Sarah and Gallagher
came in from the garden. "What is it, Harry?" Sarah demanded. "You
look awful."

"I should," he said. "I think the roof just fell in on me."

At the Silvertide, Muller was hurriedly changing into uniform in the
bathroom next to his office. He heard the outside door open and Kleist
called, "Are you there, Herr Captain? You wanted us."

"Yes, come in," Muller called.

He went into the office buttoning his tunic, picked up his belt with
the holstered Mauser and fastened it quickly.

"Something up?" Kleist asked. He looked terrible. The bruising
around the eyes had deepened, and the plaster they had taped across
his nose at the hospital didn't improve things.

"You could say that. I've just heard Rommel's flying in on what
looks like a snap inspection. I'll have to get up to the airport now. You
can drive me, Ernst," he told Greiser.

"What about me?" Kleist asked.

"With a face like that? I don't want you within a mile of Rommel.
Better take a couple of days off, Willi. Just keep out of the way." He
turned to Greiser. "Let's get moving."

After they had gone, Kleist went to the cupboard where the captain
kept his drink, took out a bottle of cognac and poured a large one into
a glass. He swallowed it in one quick gulp and went into the bathroom
and examined himself in the mirror. He looked awful and his face
hurt. It was all that damned Irishman's fault.

He poured himself another cognac and said softly, "My turn will
come, you swine, and when it does..." He toasted himself in the mirror and emptied his glass.

As the Citroën moved past the harbor and turned along the espla-
nade, Greiser said, "By the way, that call I had booked to my brother
in Stuttgart last night."

"What did he have to say?"

"He didn't. He was on leave. Due back today on the night shift. I'll
speak to him then."

"Not that it matters all that much now," Muller said. "Nothing very mysterious about friend Vogel any longer. He obviously came here in advance of the field marshal, that's all."

"But what does Rommel want?" Greiser asked.

"If you consider the beach fortifications, strongpoints and batteries for the entire French coast south from Dieppe, exactly half are in these islands alone," Muller told him. "Perhaps, with the invasion coming, he thought it was time to see what he was getting for his money." He glanced at his watch. "But never mind that now. Just put your foot down hard. We've only got about ten minutes."

At the airport, Martineau paused briefly to have his pass checked by the sentry. As he was in uniform, it was the merest formality. Several cars were parked outside the main entrance, drivers standing by them, obviously the official party. The big black Austin limousine in front carried the military commander's pennant.

Martineau parked the Kubelwagen behind Muller's Citroën. Greiser was at the wheel, the only driver in civilian clothes. Martineau ignored him and went inside the airport building. There were uniforms everywhere, mainly Luftwaffe. He felt a sense of detachment as he walked on through, no fear at all. He would have to do the best he could with the cards fate had dealt him.

Necker and a party of officers, Muller among them, were waiting on the apron outside, a Luftwaffe guard drawn up. The major came across, a slightly nervous smile on his face, followed by Muller. "They'll be here in a few minutes." He offered a cigarette from a silver case. "A tremendous shock for us all, the field marshal coming in out of the blue like this, but not to you, I think."

Martineau saw it all then. They thought there was some connection between his own unexplained presence in the island and Rommel's unexpected visit. "Really? I can't imagine what you mean, my dear Necker."

Necker glanced at Muller in exasperation. It was obvious that neither of them believed him, which was fine and suited his situation perfectly. He walked a few yards away and stood, hands behind his back, examining the airport. There were seven blister hangars, obviously constructed by the Luftwaffe. The doors to one of them stood open revealing the three engines and distinctive corrugated metal fuselage of a JU52, the Junkers transport plane that was the workhorse of the German Army. There was no sign of any other aircraft.

"He still persists in playing the man of mystery," Necker said to Muller out of the side of his mouth.

Martineau rejoined them. "The Luftwaffe doesn't seem to have much to offer."

"Unfortunately not. The enemy has an overwhelming superiority in the air in this region."

Martineau nodded toward the far blister hangar. "What's the JU52 doing there?"

"That's the mail plane. He makes the run once a week, just the pilot and a crewman. Always under cover of darkness. They came in last night."

"And fly out again?"

"Tomorrow night."

There was the sound of an airplane engine in the distance. As they turned, the Storch came in across St. Ouen's Bay and made a perfect landing. Konrad Hofer put a hand on Baum's for a moment in reassurance as the pilot, Oberleutnant Sorsa, taxied toward the waiting officers. Baum turned to nod briefly at Hofer, then adjusted the brim of his cap and tightened his gloves. Showtime, Heini, he told himself, so let's give a performance.

Sorsa lifted the door and Hofer got out, then turned to help Baum, who unbuttoned his old leather coat revealing the Blue Max and the Knight's Cross at his throat. Felix Necker advanced to meet him and gave him a punctilious military salute, one soldier to another. "Field Marshal. A great honor."

Baum negligently touched the peak of his cap with his field marshal's baton. "You are?"

"Felix Necker, sir. I'm temporarily in command. Colonel Heine has gone to Guernsey for the weekend. A conference with General von Schmettow."

"Yes, I know about that."

"If only we'd been aware that you were coming," Necker went on.

"Well, you weren't. Konrad Hofer, my aide. Now then, who have we here?"

Necker introduced the officers, starting with Martineau. "Standartenführer Vogel, who I think you may know."

"No," Martineau said. "I have never had the pleasure of meeting the field marshal before."

Rommel's dislike was plain for everyone to see. He passed on, greeting Midler and the other officers and then inspecting the guard of honor. Afterward, he simply took off, walking toward the nearest flak gun, everyone trailing after him. He spoke to the gun crew, then cut across the grass to a hangar where Luftwaffe ground crew waited rigidly at attention.

Finally he turned and walked back toward the airport buildings, looking up at the sky. "Fine weather. Will it stay like this?"

'The forecast is good, Herr Field Marshal," Necker told him.

"Excellent. I want to see everything. You understand? I'll be returning tomorrow, probably in the evening, so we'll need a suitable billet for tonight. However, that can wait until later."

"The officers of the Luftwaffe mess have had a light luncheon prepared, Herr Field Marshal. It would be a great honor If you would consent to join them."

"Certainly, Major, but afterward, work. I've a lot to see. So, where do we go?"

The officers' mess was upstairs in what had been the restaurant before the war. There was a buffet of salad, roast chicken and tinned ham, served rather self-consciously by young Luftwaffe boys in white coats acting as waiters. The officers hung eagerly on the field marshal's every word, conscious of their proximity to greatness. Baum, a glass of champagne in his hand, was more than enjoying himself. It was as if he were somewhere else looking in, observing. One thing was certain. He was good.

"We were surprised that you chose to fly in during daylight hours, Herr Field Marshal," Necker said.

"And with no fighter escort," Muller added.

"I've always believed in doing the unexpected thing," Baum told them. "And you must remember we had Oberleutnant Sorsa as pilot, one of our gallant Finnish comrades. He normally flies a JU88S night fighter and has thirty-eight Lancasters to his credit, which explains his Knight's Cross." Sorsa, a small, vital man of twenty-five with very fair hair, looked suitably modest, and Baum carried on, "I must also tell you that we flew across the sea so low that we were in more danger from the waves than anything the RAF might have come up with."

There was a general laugh and he excused himself and went off to the toilet followed by Hofer.

Martineau had been standing against the wall, observing everything and drinking very little. Muller approached. "A remarkable man."

"Oh, yes." Martineau nodded. "One of the few real heroes of the war. And how is your Inspector Kleist?"

"A stupid man," Martineau observed. "But then, I think you know that. More champagne?"

In the toilet, Baum checked himself in the mirror and said to Hofer, "How am I doing?"

"Superbly." Hofer was exhilarated. "There are times when I really think it's the old man himself talking."

"Good." Baum combed his hair and adjusted the cheek pads. "What about the SS colonel: I didn't expect that."

"Vogel?" Hofer was serious for a moment. "I was talking to Necker about him. He just turned up in the island yesterday, backed by a special pass signed by Himmler and the Führer himself. So far he's given no information as to why he's here."

"I don't know," Baum said. 'Those bastards always make me feel funny. You're certain his presence here has nothing to do with us?"

"How could it be? Army Group B Headquarters only released the news that you were in Jersey an hour ago. So, no need to panic, and back to the fray."

Necker said, "If you wouldn't mind coming into the CO's office, Field Marshal. General von Schmettow is on the line from Guernsey." Baum sat carelessly on the edge of the desk and took the receiver offered to him. "My dear von Schmettow, it's been a long time."

General von Schmettow said, "An unexpected honor for my entire command. Heine is quite shocked and wishes to return at once."

"Tell him if he does, it's the firing squad for him," Baum said good-humoredly. "Young Necker can show me around just as well. A fine officer. No, this suits me perfectly."

"Do you intend to visit Guernsey?"

"Not this time. I return to France tomorrow."

"May we expect you at some future date?" The line was crackling now.

"Of course, and before long, I promise you. Best wishes." Baum put down the receiver and turned to Necker. "To work. Coastal defenses, that's what I wish to see, so let's get started."

In the garden at de Ville Place Sarah sat on the wall looking out over the bay and Guido leaned beside her, smoking a cigarette. "Sarah," he said in English. "It's as if I have to get to know you all over again." He shook his head. "Whoever told you that you could pass yourself off as a French tart was gravely mistaken. I knew there was something wrong with you from the start."

"And Harry? Did you think there was something wrong about him?"

"No. He worries me, that one. He plays Vogel too well."

"I know." She shivered. "I wonder how he's getting on?"

"He'll be fine. The last person I'd ever worry about. You like him, don't you?"

"Yes," she said. "You could put it that way." Before they could take the conversation any further, Helen and Gallagher crossed the grass to join them.

"What are you two up to?" Helen demanded.

"Nothing much." Sarah told her. "We were wondering how Harry was getting on."

"The devil looks after his own," Gallagher said. "He can take care of himself, that one. More important at the moment is a decision on what to do with Kelso. I think we should move him from the chamber to my cottage."

Guido nodded. "That makes sense. Much easier to take him from there down to the harbor once I get Savary sorted out."

"Do you really think it has a chance of working?" Sarah demanded.

"Fake papers as a French seaman. The General and I can fix that up between us," Guido told her.

"We'll bandage his face. Say he was in the water after the attack on the convoy and sustained burns," Gallagher said. "We'll move Kelso late tonight." He smiled reassuringly and put an arm around Sarah. "It's going to work. Believe me."

Martineau joined on the end of the cavalcade of cars as it left the airport and took the road through St. Peter's. Rommel fascinated him, so did the idea of being so close to one of the greatest soldiers the war had produced, the commander of the Westwall himself. The man dedicated to smashing the Allies on the beaches where they landed.

He was certainly energetic. They visited Meadowbank in the Parish of St. Lawrence where for two years military engineers and slave workers had labored on tunnels designed to be an artillery depot. Now it was in process of being converted into a military hospital.

Afterward they saw the Russians in Defense Sector North and the strongpoints at Greve de Lecq, Plemont and Les Landes. It all took time. The field marshal seemed to want to look in every foxhole personally, visit every gun post.

He asked to see the war cemetery at St. Brelade and inspected the church while he was there. The Soldatenheim, the Soldiers' Home, was just along the road in a requisitioned hotel overlooking the bay. He insisted on calling in there, much to the delight of the matron in charge, and discovered a proxy wedding taking place. It was a system devised by the Nazi government to take care of the fact that it was increasingly difficult for soldiers on active duty to get married in the normal way any longer, as they seldom got furloughs back home in Germany. The groom was a burly sergeant and a Red Cross nursing sister stood in for his bride, who was in Berlin.

It was very much a Nazi marriage, totally without any religious significance at all. The insistence on the lack of Jewish blood in either the bride or bridegroom was something Baum found especially ironic, but he toasted the sergeant's good health with a glass of schnapps and moved on.

By the time they reached St. Aubin it was evening, and most of the party were beginning to flag. Baum, examining the map Necker had provided, noticed the artillery positions on Mont de la Rocque and asked to be taken up there.

Martineau followed, still on the tail of the line of cars climbing the steep hill of the Mont until they came to a narrow turning that led out on top where there were a number of flat-roofed houses.

"A gun platoon only now, Field Marshal," Necker assured Baum as he got out.

The house at the very end with a courtyard behind a wall was called Septembertide. The one next to it had a French name, Hinguette. In its garden, a narrow entrance gave access to a series of underground bunkers and machine-gun posts which ran along the crest of the hill under the gardens. There were no civilians living in any of the houses, only troops, who were overwhelmed to have the Desert Fox in proximity to them, none more so than the commanding officer, a Captain Heider.

It transpired that his personal billet was Septembertide. When the field marshal expressed an interest in it, he eagerly led the way. They all trooped down into the garden. The views across the bay, St. Aubin on the right and St. Helier on the left, were breathtaking. The garden was edged with a low concrete wall, and the ground fell almost vertically down through trees and heavy undergrowth to the road far below.

Baum said, "You'd need the Alpine Corps to get up here, gentlemen." He looked up at the house. There was a large terrace in front of the sitting room and another above running the full length at bedroom level. "Nice." He turned to Heider. "I need somewhere to lay my head tonight. Will you lend it to me?"

Heider was beside himself with joy. "An honor, Herr Field Marshal. I can move into Hinguette for the night with my second in command."

"I'm sure you can find us a decent cook among your men."

"No problem, Field Marshal."

Baum turned to Necker. "You see, my dear Necker, all taken care of. This will suit me very well indeed. Impregnable on this side and Captain Heider and his boys guarding the front. What more could one ask for?"

"It was hoped you might join us for dinner at the officers' club at Bagatelle," Necker said diffidently.

"Another time. It's been a long day and frankly, I'd welcome an early night. Call for me in the morning. Not too early. Let's say at ten, and we can do the other side of the island."

"At your orders, Herr Field Marshal."

They all went around to the front of the house where there was a general leavetaking. Heider took Baum and Hofer inside and showed them around. The living room was large and reasonably well furnished.

"It was like this when we moved in," Heider said. "If you'll excuse me, I'll get my things out of the bedroom, Field Marshal, then I'll arrange a cook."

He went upstairs. Baum turned to Hofer. "Did I do well?"

"Superb," Hofer said, "And this place is perfect. Just the right amount of isolation. You're a genius, Berger."

The evening meal had already started at de Ville Place when Martineau got back. He peered in at the window and saw Sarah sitting with Guido and half-a-dozen other naval officers at the table. He decided not to go in and, instead, went round to the back door and let himself into the kitchen. Helen was washing dishes at the sink and Gallagher was drying for her.

"How did things go?" the Irishman demanded.

"Well enough. Absolutely no problems, if that's what you mean."

"Did you see the great man?"

"As close as I am to you, but he made it clear the SS is not exactly his favorite organization."

Helen poured him a cup of tea, and Gallagher said, "We've been making decisions while you've been away."

He told him how they'd decided to move Kelso. When he was finished, Martineau nodded. "That makes sense to me. We'll make it later though. Say around eleven."

"Should be safe enough then," Gallagher said.

Martineau went upstairs and lay on the bed of the room he shared with Sarah. Although they slept in the same bed he had not made love to her again since that first night. There was no particular reason. There just didn't seem to be the need. But no. He wasn't being honest. It wasn't Sarah, it was him, something inside, some old wound of the spirit that made him afraid to give himself fully. A morose fear that it would all prove to be just another disappointment or perhaps simply the fear that this strange, enchanting, tough young woman was forcing him back into the real world again. Bringing him back to life.

He lay on the bed smoking a cigarette, staring at the ceiling, strangely restless, thinking of Rommel and the energy of the man—and what a target he was. He got up and put on his belt with the holstered PPK, then he opened his suitcase, found the Carswell silencer and put it in his pocket.

When he went downstairs, they were still eating in the great hall. He went back to the kitchen. Helen looked up in surprise. "You're going out again?"

"Things to do." He turned to Gallagher. "Tell Sarah I'll be back soon."

The Irishman frowned. "Are you all right? Is something wrong?"

"Not in the whole wide world," Martineau assured him. "I'll see you later," and he went out.

There was a half moon again and in its light, he saw the line of white houses high overhead on the ridge above the trees. He turned the Kubelwagen into La Haule Hill and parked in a track where it joined with Mont de la Rocque. For a while, he sat there thinking about it, and then he got out and started up through the trees.

It was nonsense, of course. Shoot Rommel and they'd have the island sewn up tight within an hour. Nowhere to go. On top of that they'd probably take hostages until the assassin gave himself up. They'd done that in other countries. No reason to think Jersey would be any different. But in spite of all reason and logic, the thought titillated, would not go away. He kept on climbing.

13

MULLER WAS WORKING IN his office at the Silvertide, trying to catch up on his paperwork when there was a knock on the door and Greiser looked in. "Working late tonight, Herr Captain."

"The field marshal accounted for most of my time today, and he's likely to take up more tomorrow," Muller said. "I've at least twelve case reports to work through for court appearances next week. I thought I'd try to get rid of them tonight." He stretched and yawned. "Anyway, what are you doing here?"

"The phone call I booked to my brother in Stuttgart. I've just been talking to him."

Muller was immediately interested. "What did he have to say about Vogel?"

"Well, he certainly never came across him at Gestapo Headquarters in Berlin. But he does point out that the SD are housed in a building at the other end of Prince Albrechtstrasse. He simply wasn't familiar with who was who, except for the big noises like Heydrich before they murdered him and Walter Schellenberg. However, it was an open secret during his time in Berlin, that the Reichsführer uses mystery men like Vogel with special powers and so on. He says nobody was all that sure who they were."

"Which is exactly the point of the whole exercise," Muller observed.

"Anyway, he says people like that operate out of the SD unit attached to the Reichsführer's office at the Reich Chancellery. As it happens, he knows someone on the staff there rather well."

"Who?"

"An SS auxiliary named Lotto Neumann. She was his mistress during his Berlin period. She's secretary to one of the Reichsführer's aides."

"And he's going to speak to her?"

"He has a call booked through to Berlin in the morning. He'll get back to me as soon as he can. At least it will tell us just how important Vogel is. She's bound to know something about him."

"Excellent." Muller nodded. "Have you seen Willi tonight?"

"Yes," Greiser admitted reluctantly. "At the club. Then he insisted on going to a bar in some back street in St. Helier."

"He's drinking?" Greiser hesitated and Muller said, "Come on, man, tell me the worst."

"Yes, Herr Captain, heavily. I couldn't keep up. As you know I drink very little. I stayed with him for a while, but then he grew morose and angry as he does. He told me to clear off. Became rather violent."

"Damnation!" Muller sighed. "Nothing to be done now. He's probably ended up with some woman. You'd better get off to bed. I'll need you again in the morning. Ten o'clock at Septembertide."

"Very well, Herr Captain."

He went out, and Muller opened another file and picked up his pen.

Kleist was at that moment parking his car on a track on the edge of the de Ville estate very close to Gallagher's cottage. He was dangerously drunk, way beyond any consideration of common sense. He had half a bottle of schnapps with him. He took a pull at it, put it in his pocket, got out of the car and walked unsteadily along the track toward the cottage.

There was a chink of light at the drawn curtains covering one of the sitting room windows. He kicked on the front door vigorously. There was no response. He kicked again, then tried the handle and the door opened. He peered into the sitting room. There was an oil lamp on the table, the embers of a fire on the hearth, but no other sign of life. The kitchen was also empty.

He stood at the bottom of the stairs. "Gallagher, where are you?"

There was no reply. He got the oil lamp and went upstairs to see for himself, but both bedrooms were empty. He descended the stairs again, slowly and with some difficulty, went into the sitting room and put the lamp on the table.

He turned it down, leaving the room in darkness except for a dull glow from the embers of the fire. He pulled back the curtain at the window and sat there in a wing chair, looking at the yard outside, clear in the moonlight. "Right, you bastard. You've got to come home sometime."

He took a Mauser from his right-hand pocket and sat there nursing it in his lap as he waited.

At Septembertide, Baum and Hofer had enjoyed a surprisingly excellent meal. Cold roast chicken, Jersey new potatoes and a salad, washed down with a bottle of excellent Sancerre provided by Captain Heider. The half moon gave a wonderful view of St. Aubin's Bay, and they went out onto the terrace to finish their wine.

After a while, the corporal who had cooked the meal appeared. "All is in order, Herr Major," he told Hofer, "the kitchen is clear again. I've left coffee and milk on the side. Will there be anything else?"

"Not tonight," Hofer told him. "We'll have breakfast at nine sharp in the morning. Eggs, ham, anything you can lay your hands on. You can return to your billet now."

The corporal clicked his heels and withdrew. Baum said, "What a night."

"My dear Berger, what a day," Hofer told him. "The most remarkable of my life."

"And the second act still to come." Baum yawned. "Speaking of tomorrow, I could do with some sleep," and he went back inside.

Hofer said, "You, of course, in deference to your superior rank, will take the large bedroom above this, which has its own bathroom. I'll take the small room at the end of the corridor. It overlooks the front of the house so I'll be more aware of what's going on there."

They went upstairs, Baum still carrying his glass of wine. "What time?" he said.

"If you're not already up I'll wake you at seven-thirty," Hofer told him.

"Rommel would be up at five, but one can take playacting too far." Baum smiled. He closed the outer door to the bedroom suite, walked through the dressing area into the bedroom itself. It was plainly furnished with two wardrobes, a dressing table and a double bed, presumably left by the owners from whom the house had been requisitioned. The corporal had drawn the curtains at the windows. They were large and heavy, made of red velvet and touched the floor. When he parted them, he found a steel and glass door, which he opened and stepped out onto the upper terrace.

The view was even better at this height, and he could see down into St. Aubin's Harbor in the distance on his right. It was very still, the only sound a dog barking a couple of fields away. The blackout in St. Helier was anything but complete, lights dotted here and there. The sea was calm, a white line of surf down there on the beach, the sky luminous with stars in the moonlight. A night to thank God for.

He raised his glass. "L'chayim," he said softly and he turned, parted the curtains and went back inside, leaving the door open.

It took Martineau twenty minutes to make his way up through the trees. The undergrowth was thick in places and the going was rough, but he'd expected that and there was no barbed wire on the final approach to the garden, he'd noticed that earlier. He still had no idea what he intended and pulled himself up over the concrete block wall cautiously, aware of voices. He stood in the shadow of a palm tree, and looked up to see Hofer and Rommel on the terrace in the moonlight.

"What a night," the field marshal said.

"My dear Berger, what a day," Hofer told him.

"And the second act still to come."

Martineau stayed in the shadow of the palm tree, astonished at this amazing exchange. It didn't make sense. After they had gone inside, he advanced cautiously across the lawn and paused by the covered way, A moment later, the field marshal appeared on the upper terrace and stood at the rail looking out over the bay.

He raised his glass. "L'chayim," he said softly, turned and went back inside.

L'chayim, which meant "to life," the most ancient of Hebrew toasts.

It was enough. Martineau stood on the low wall, reached for the railings on the first terrace and pulled himself over.

Heini Baum took the Blue Max and the Knight's Cross with Oak Leaves, Swords and Diamonds from around his neck and laid them on the dressing table. He removed his cheek pads and examined his face in the mirror, running his fingers through his hair.

"Not bad, Heini. Not bad. I wonder what the great man would say if he knew he was being taken off by a Jew boy?"

He started to unbutton his tunic and Martineau, who had been standing on the other side of the curtain screwing the Carswell silencer on the barrel of the Walther, stepped inside. Baum saw him instantly in the mirror, and old soldier that he was, reached at once for the Mauser pistol in its holster on his belt which lay on the dressing table.

"I wouldn't," Martineau told him. "They've really done wonders with this new model silencer. If I fired it behind your back you wouldn't even know about it. Now, hands on head and sit on the stool."

"Is this some plot of the SS to get rid of me?" Baum asked, playing his role to the hilt. "I'm aware that Reichsführer Himmler never liked me, but I didn't realize how much."

Martineau sat on the edge of the bed, took out a packet of Gitanes one-handed and shook one up. As he lit it he said, "I heard you and Hofer talking on the terrace. He called you Berger."

"You've been busy."

"And I was outside a couple of minutes ago when you were talking to yourself, so let's get down to facts. Number one, you aren't Rommel."

"If you say so."

"All right," Martineau said, "let's try again. If I am part of an SS plot to kill you on Himmler's orders, there wouldn't be much point if you aren't really Rommel. Of course, if you are ..."

He raised the PPK and Baum took a deep breath. "Very clever."

"So you aren't Rommel?"

"I should have thought that was sufficiently obvious by now."

"What are you, an actor?"

"Turned soldier, turned actor again."

"Marvelous," Martineau said. "I saw him in Paris last year and you fooled me. Does he know you're Jewish?"

"No." Baum frowned. "Listen, what kind of an SS man are you anyway?"

"I'm not," Martineau laid the PPK down on the bed beside him. "I'm a colonel in the British Army."

"I don't believe you," Baum said in astonishment.

"A pity you don't speak English and I could prove it," Martineau said.

"But I do." Baum broke into very good English indeed. "I played the Moss Empire circuit in London, Leeds and Manchester in nineteen thirty-five and six."

"And you went back to Germany?" Martineau said. "You must have been crazy."

"My parents." Baum shrugged. "Like most of the old folk, they didn't believe it would happen. I hid in the army using the identity of a man killed in an air raid in Kiel. My real name is Heini Baum. To Rommel, I'm Corporal Erich Berger, 21st Parachute Regiment."

"Harry Martineau."

Baum hesitated then shook hands. "Your German is excellent."

"My mother was German," Martineau explained. "Tell me, where is Rommel?"

"In Normandy."

"And what's the purpose of the masquerade or don't you know?"

"I'm not supposed to, but I can listen at doors as well as anybody." Baum took a cigarette from the field marshal's silver case, fitted it into the ivory holder Rommel had given him and lit it. "He's having a quiet get-together with Generals von Stulpnagel and Falkenhausen. A highly illegal business as far as I can make out. Apparently they and a number of other generals, realizing they've lost the war, want to get rid of Hitler and salvage something from the mess while there's still a chance."

"Possible," Martineau said. "There have been attempts on Hitler's life before."

"Fools, all of them," Baum told him.

"You don't approve? That surprises me."

"They've lost the war anyway. It's only a question of time so there's no point in their scheming. By the time that mad bastard Himmler's finished with them, they'll be hanging on hooks, not that it would worry me. Most of them helped Hitler to power in the first place."

"That's true."

"On the other hand, I'm a German as well as a Jew. I've got to know Rommel pretty well in the past few days. He's a good man. He's on the wrong side, that's all. Now you know all about me. What about you? What are you doing here?"

Martineau told him briefly about Kelso, although omitting, for the moment, any mention of the Operation Overlord connection. When he was finished, Baum said, "I wish you luck. From the sound of it, it's going to be tricky trying to get him out by boat. At least I fly out tomorrow night. A nice fast exit."

Martineau saw it then, the perfect answer to the whole situation. Sheer genius. "Tell me," he said. "Once back, you'll be returned to your regiment?"

"I should imagine so."

"Which means you'll have every chance of having your head blown off during the next few months because the invasion's coming and your paratroopers will be in the thick of it."

"I expect so."

"How would you like to go to England instead?"

"You've got to be joking," Baum said in astonishment "How could such a thing be?"

"Just think about it." Martineau got up and paced around the room. "What's the most useful thing about being Field Marshal Erwin Rommel?"

"You tell me."

"The fact that everyone does what you tell them to do. For example, tomorrow evening you go to the airport to return to France in the little Storch you came in."

"So what."

"There's a JU52 transport up there, the mail plane, due to leave for France around the same time. What do you think would happen if Field Marshal Rommel turned up just before takeoff with an SS Standartenführer, a wounded man on a stretcher, a young Frenchwoman, and commandeered the plane? What do you think they'd say?"

Baum smiled. "Not very much, I imagine."

"Once in the air," Martineau said, "and the nearest point on the English coast would be no more than half an hour's flying time in that mail plane."

"My God!" Baum said in awe. "You really mean it."

"Do you want to go to England or don't you?" Martineau asked. "Make up your mind. Of course, if you hadn't met me you'd have gone back to France to rejoin the field marshal, and who knows what would happen. Another mad plot to kill the Führer fails, which would mean an unpleasant end for Erwin Rommel. I suspect that might also apply to anyone connected with him and, let's face it—the Gestapo and Himmler would find you very suspect indeed."

"You really do have a way with the words," Baum told him.

Martineau lit a cigarette. "Even if you survive, my friend, Berlin will resemble a brickyard before long. The Russians want blood, and I think you'll find that the Allies will stand back and let them get on with it." He peered out through the curtains. "No, I really do think my alternative is the only option that would make sense to an intelligent man."

"You could make an excellent living selling insurance," Baum told him. "As it happens, I used to have a cousin in Leeds which is in the north of England. Yorkshire, to be precise. My only relative, if he's still alive. I need someone to say kaddish for me. That's prayers for the dead, by the way."

"I know what it is," Martineau said patiently. "Do we have a deal?"

"Berlin a brickyard." Baum shook his head and smiled. "I like that."

"That's settled then." Martineau unscrewed the silencer and put the PPK back in its holster.

"So what about Hofer?"

"What about him?"

"He's not so bad. No different from the rest of us. I wouldn't like to have to hurt him."

"I'll think of something. I'll discuss it with my friends. I'll join your tour of the east of the island tomorrow morning. Be more friendly toward me. At a suitable point when Necker is there, ask me where I'm staying. I'll tell you de Ville Place—all about it. Its magical location, wonderful grounds, and so on. You tell Necker you like the sound of it. That you'd like to have lunch there. Insist on it. I'll finalize things with you then."

"The third act, rewritten at so late a date we don't get any chance to rehearse," Baum said wryly.

"You know what they say," Martineau told him. "That's show business," and he slipped out through the curtain.

It was just after midnight when Sean Gallagher and Guido took Hugh Kelso down the narrow stairway to Helen's bedroom. Sarah waited by the partially open door for Helen's signal from the other end of the corridor. It came and she opened the door quickly.

"Now," she said.

Gallagher and Guido linked arms again and hurried out, Hugh Kelso between them. The back stairs were wider and easier to negotiate, and they were in the kitchen within a couple of minutes. They sat Kelso down and Helen closed the door to the stairs, turning the key.

"So far so good," Gallagher said. "Are you all right, Colonel?"

The American looked strained, but nodded eagerly. "I'm feeling great just to be moving again."

"Fine. We'll take the path through the woods to my place. Ten minutes, that's all."

Helen motioned him to silence. "I think I hear a car."

They waited and Sarah hurriedly turned down the lamp, went to the window and drew the curtains as a vehicle entered the yard outside. "It's Harry," she said.

Helen turned up the lamp again and Sarah unbolted the back door for him. He slipped in and closed the door behind him. After events at Mont de la Rocque he was on a high, full of energy, and the excitement was plain to see on the pale face shadowed by the SS cap.

"What is it, Harry?" Sarah demanded. "Has something happened?"

"I think you could definitely say that, but it can wait until later. Ready to go, are we?"

"As ever was," Kelso said.

"Let's get it done then."

"Sarah and I will go on ahead to make sure everything's ready for you," Helen said as she took a couple of old macs down from a peg, gave one to the girl and put the other one on herself.

She turned the lamp down again, opened the door and she and Sarah hurried across the yard. Gallagher and Guido linked hands and Kelso put his arms around their necks.

"Right," Martineau said. "Here we go. I'll lead the way. If anyone wants a rest, just say so."

He stood to one side to let them go out, closed the door behind him and they started across the courtyard.

The pale moonlight filtered through the trees, and the track was clear before them, the night perfumed with the scent of flowers again. Sarah took Helen's arm. For a moment, there was an intimacy between them, and she was very aware of that warm, safe feeling she had known in the time following her mother's death when Helen had been not only a strong right arm but the breath of life to her.

"What happens afterward?" Helen said. "When you get back?"

"Assuming that we do."

"Don't be silly. It's going to work. If ever I met a man who knows what he's doing it's Harry Martineau. So, what happens on your return? Back to nursing?"

"God knows," Sarah told her. "Nursing was always only a stopgap. It was medicine I was interested in."

"I remember."

"But after this, who knows?" Sarah said. "The whole thing's been like a mad dream. I've never known a man like Harry, never known such excitement."

"Temporary madness, Sarah, just like the war. Not real life. Neither is Harry Martineau. He's not for you, Sarah. God help him, he's not even for himself."

They paused on the edge of the clearing, the cottage a few yards away, bathed in the moonlight. "It's nothing to do with me," Sarah said. "It never was. I had no control over what happened. It's beyond reason."

In the cottage, sitting at the window, Kleist had seen them the moment they had emerged from the wood, and it was the intimacy that struck him at once. There was something wrong here, and he got up, moved to the door and opened it a little. It was then, of course, as they approached, that he realized they were speaking together in English.

Helen said, "Loving someone is different from being in love, darling. Being in love is a state of heat and that passes, believe me. Still, let's get inside. The others will be here in a moment." She put a hand to the door and it moved. "It seems to be open."

And then the door swung, a hand had her by the front of her coat, and Kleist tapped the muzzle of the Mauser against her cheek. "Inside, Frau de Ville," he said roughly. "And let us discuss the curious fact that this little French bitch not only speaks the most excellent English, but would appear to be a friend of yours."

For a moment, Helen was frozen, aware only of a terrible fear as the Mauser tapped again against her face. Kleist reached and got Sarah by the hair.

"And you are expecting others, I gather. I wonder who?" He walked backward, pulling Sarah by the hair, the gun still probing into Helen's flesh. "No stupidities or I pull the trigger." He released Sarah suddenly. "Go and draw the curtains." She did as she was told. "Good, now turn up the lamp. Let's have everything as it should be." She could see the sweat on his face, now, the terror and pain on Helen's. "Now come back here."

His fingers tightened in her hair again. The pain was dreadful. She wanted to cry a warning, but was aware of Helen's head back, the Mauser under her chin. Kleist stank of drink, was shaking with excitement as they waited, listening to the voices approaching across the yard. Only at the very last moment, as the door swung open and Gallagher and Guido backed in, Kelso between them, did he push the women away.

"Harry, look out!" Sarah cried as Martineau slipped in after them, but by then, her anguished cry was too late to help anyone.

Kelso lay on the floor and Helen, Sarah and the three men leaned against the wall in a row, arms outstretched. Kleist relieved Martineau of his PPK and slipped it into his pocket. "The SS must be doing its recruiting in some strange places these days."

Martineau said nothing, waiting, coldly, for his chance and Kleist moved on to Guido Orsini, running his hands over him expertly. "I never liked you, pretty boy," he said contemptuously. "All you sodding Italians have ever done is give us trouble. The Führer should have sorted you lot out first."

"Amazing." Guido turned his head and said amiably to Gallagher, "It can actually talk."

Kleist kicked his feet from under him and put a boot in his side, then he turned to Gallagher, running a hand over him quickly, feeling for a gun. He found nothing and stood back. "Now then, you bastard, I've been waiting for this."

He smashed his right fist into the base of the Irishman's spine. Gallagher cried out and went down. Kleist booted him in the side and Helen screamed. "Stop it!"

Kleist smiled at her. "I haven't even started." He stirred Gallagher with his boot. "Get up and put your hands on your head." Gallagher stayed on his hands and knees for a moment and Kleist prodded him with a toe. "Come on, move it, you thick piece of Irish dung."

Gallagher got to his feet and stood there, a half-smile on his face, arms at his sides. "Half-Irish," he said, "and half-Jersey. As I told you before, a bad combination."

Kleist struck him backhanded across the face. "I told you to get your hands on your head."

"Anything you say."

The gutting knife was ready in Gallagher's left hand, had been for several minutes, skillfully palmed. His arm swung, there was a click as he pressed the button, the blade flickered in the lamplight, catching Kleist in the soft flesh under the chin. Kleist discharged the Mauser once into the wall, then dropped it and fell back against the table, wrenching the knife from Gallagher's grasp. He tried to get up, one hand tearing at the handle protruding from beneath his chin, then fell sideways to the floor, kicked convulsively and was still.

"Oh, my God!" Helen said and turned and stumbled into the kitchen, where she was immediately violently sick.

Martineau said to Sarah, "Go and help her."

The girl went out and he crouched down and took his Walther from the dead man's pocket. He looked up at Gallagher. "They teach that trick in the SOE silent killing course. Where did you learn it?"

"Another legacy from my old grandfather," Gallagher said.

"He must have been a remarkable man."

He and Guido got Kelso onto the couch while Gallagher retrieved his knife. It took all his strength to pull it free. He wiped it on the dead man's coat. "Do you think this was an official visit?"

"I shouldn't imagine so." Martineau picked up the empty bottle of schnapps. "He'd been drinking and he had blood in his eye. He wanted revenge, came up here looking for you, and when you weren't here, he waited." He shook his head. "Poor sod, he almost got lucky for once. It would have been the coup of his career."

"But what happens now?" Kelso demanded. "This could ruin everything. I mean, a Gestapo man doesn't turn up for work, they start looking."

"No need to panic." Martineau picked up a rug and covered Kleist. "There's always a way out. First, we find his car. It's bound to be parked nearby." He nodded to Guido and Gallagher and led the way out.

It was Guido who found the Renault within ten minutes and whistled up the others. Martineau and Gallagher joined him. "Now what?" Guido asked.

"Kelso's right. If Kleist doesn't turn up for work in the morning, Muller will turn this island inside out," Gallagher said. "So what do we do?"

"Give him to them," Martineau said crisply. "He was drunk and ran off the road in his car, it's as simple as that."

"Preferably over a cliff," Guido put in.

"Exactly." Martineau turned to Gallagher. "Have you anywhere suitable to suggest? Not too far, but far enough for there to be no obvious connection with here."

"Yes," Gallagher said. "I think I've got just the place."

"Good. You lead the way in the Renault, and I'll follow in the Kubelwagen."

"Shall I come?" Guido asked.

"No," Martineau said. "You hold the fort here. I'll go up to the house and get the Kubelwagen. You two take the Renault back to the cottage and put Kleist in the boot."

He turned and hurried away through the wood.

When Martineau arrived back at the cottage they already had Kleist's body in the boot of the car, and Gallagher was ready to go. Martineau asked, "How long will it take us to get to this place?"

"The far side of La Moye Point." Gallagher unfolded an old pocket touring map of the island. "About fifteen or twenty minutes at this time in the morning."

"Are we likely to run into anybody?"

"We have an honorary police system out here in the parishes, and they don't turn out to work for the enemy unless they have to."

"And the Germans?"

"The odd military police patrol, no more than that. We've every chance of driving to La Moye without seeing a soul."

"Right, then let's get moving." Martineau turned to Guido and the two women standing in the doorway. "Wait for us here. There are things to discuss," and he drove away.

Gallagher was right. Their run from Noirmont to Woodbine Corner and along the main road to Red Houses passed without incident, no sign of another vehicle all the way along La Route Orange and moving toward Corbiere Point. Finally, Gallagher turned into a narrow lane. He stopped the Renault and got out.

"There's a strongpoint down there on our right at Corbiere, an artillery battery on the left toward La Moye Point. The area up ahead is clear, and the road turns along the edge of the cliffs about two hundred yards from here. It's always been a hazard. No protecting wall."

"All right," Martineau said. "We'll leave the Kubelwagen here."

He got a can of petrol and stood on the running board of the Renault as Gallagher drove along the bumpy road between high hedges. They came out on the edge of the cliffs, going down into a small valley, a defile on the left running down to rocks and surf below.

"This will do." Martineau hammered on the roof.

Gallagher braked to a halt, got out and went around to the boot. He and Martineau got Kleist out between them, carried him to the front and put him behind the wheel. Gallagher had left the engine running. As he shut the door the dead man slumped forward.

"All right?" Gallagher demanded in a low voice.

"In a minute." Martineau opened the can and poured petrol over the front seat and the dead man's clothes. "Okay, let him go."

Gallagher released the handbrake, leaving the engine in neutral and turned the wheel. He started to push and the Renault left the track, moving across the grass.

"Watch yourself!" Martineau called and struck a match and dropped it through the open passenger window.

For a moment, he thought it had gone out and then, as the Renault bumped over the edge, orange and yellow flame blossomed. They turned and ran back along the lane, and behind them, there was a grinding crash and then a brief explosion.

When they reached the Kubelwagen, Martineau said, "You get down in the back, just in case."

It was too good to last, of course, and five minutes later, as he turned from the Corbiere Road into Route du Sud, he found two military police motorcycles parked at the side of the road. One of them stepped out, hand raised in the moonlight. Martineau slowed at once. "Military police," he whispered to Gallagher. "Stay low." He opened the door and got out. "Is there a problem?" At the sight of the uniform, the two policemen jumped to attention. One of them still had a lighted cigarette between the fingers of his left hand. "Ah, now I see, what we might term a smoke break," Martineau said.

"Standartenführer, what can I say?" the man replied.

"Personally, I always find it better to say nothing." There was something supremely menacing in the way he delivered the words. "Now, what did you want?"

"Nothing, Standartenführer. It's just that we don't often see a vehicle at this time in the morning in this sector."

"And you were quite properly doing your duty." Martineau produced his papers. "My SD card. Come on, man, hurry up!" He raised his voice and it was harsh and ugly. The policeman barely glanced at it, hands shaking as he handed it back. "All is in order."

"Good, you can return to your duties then." Martineau got back in the car. "As for smoking, be a little more discreet, that's my advice."

He drove away. Gallagher said, voice slightly muffled, "How in the hell do you manage to sound such a convincing Nazi?"

"Practice, Sean, that's what it takes. Lots of practice," Martineau told him, and he turned into La Route Orange and moved toward Red Houses.

When they got back to the cottage, Sarah opened the door instantly to them. "Everything all right?"

"Perfect," Gallagher told her as he followed Martineau inside. "We put the car over a cliff near La Moye and made sure it burned."

"Was that necessary?" Helen shivered, clasping her arms around herself.

"We want him to be found," Martineau said. "And if the sentries at the coastal strongpoints in the area are even half-awake they'll have noticed the flames. On the other hand, we don't want him in too good a condition, because if he was, there would be that knife wound to explain."

Kelso said, "So, you had no trouble at all?"

"A military police patrol stopped us on the way back," Gallagher said. "I was well out of sight and Harry did his Nazi bit. No problem."

"So, all that remains now is for Guido to contact Savary in the morning," Sarah said.

"No," Martineau said. "Actually, there's been a rather significant change of plan."

There was general astonishment. Gallagher said, "Sweet Jesus, what have you been up to now?"

Martineau lit a cigarette, stood with his back to the fire and said calmly, "If you'll all sit down, I'll tell you."

14

AT NINE THE FOLLOWING morning Gallagher drove down to St. Helier, two more sacks of potatoes in the van. He didn't call at the central market, but went straight to the troop supply depot in the old garage in Wesley Street. The first trucks went out with military supplies to various units around the island at eight-thirty, which was why he had chosen his time carefully. Feldwebel Klinger was up in his glass office eating his breakfast. Sausage, eggs, bacon, all very English. The coffee was real, Gallagher could smell that as he went up the stairs.

"Good morning, Herr General, what have you got for me today?"

"A couple of sacks of potatoes if you're interested. I'll take canned food in exchange, whatever you've got, and coffee." He helped himself to a piece of bacon from Klinger's plate. "Whenever I see you, you're eating."

"And why not? The only pleasure left to me in this lousy life. Here, join me in a coffee." Klinger poured it out. "Why are human beings so stupid? I had a nice restaurant in Hamburg before the war. All the best people came. My wife does her best, but more bomb damage last week and no compensation."

"And worse to come, Hans," Gallagher told him. "They'll be on the beaches soon, all those Tommies and Yanks, and heading for the

Fatherland and the Russians coming the other way. You'll be lucky to have a business at all. Those Reichsmarks you keep hoarding won't be worth the paper they're printed on."

Klinger wiped a hand across his mouth. "Don't, you'll give me indigestion with talk like that so early in the morning."

"Of course, this kind of money never loses its value." Gallagher took a coin from his pocket, flicked it in the air, caught it and put it down on the table.

Klinger picked it up and there was awe on his face. "An English sovereign."

"Exactly," Gallagher said. "A gold sovereign."

Klinger tried it with his teeth. "The real thing."

"Would I offer you anything less?" Gallagher took a small linen bag from his pocket and held it up tantalizingly. "Another forty-nine in there."

He placed the bag on the table and Klinger spilled the coins out and touched them with his fingers. "All right, what do you want?"

"A sailor's uniform. Kriegsmarine," Gallagher told him. "No big deal, as our American friends say. You've got stacks of them in store here."

"Impossible," Klinger said. "Absolutely."

"I'd also expect boots, reefer coat and cap. We're doing a play at the Parish Hall at St. Brelade. Very good part for a German sailor in it. He falls in love with this Jersey girl and her parents …"

"Stop this nonsense," Klinger said. "Play? What play is this?"

"All right." Gallagher shrugged. "If you're not interested."

He started to pick up the coins and Klinger put a hand on his arm. "You know the GFP at Silvertide would be very interested to know what you wanted with a German uniform, Herr General."

"Of course they would, only we're not going to tell them, are we? I mean, you don't want them nosing around in here, Hans. All that booze and cigarettes in the cellar and the canned goods. And then there's the coffee and the champagne."

"Stop it!"

"I know it's spring now," Gallagher carried on relentlessly. "But it still can't be too healthy on the Russian Front serving with a penal battalion."

The threat was plain in his voice and the prospect too horrible to contemplate. Klinger was trapped, angry that he'd ever got involved with the Irishman. Too late to cry about that now. Better to give him what he wanted and hope for the best.

"All right, I hear you." Klinger scooped up the sovereigns, put them in one of his tunic pockets. "I've always loved the theater. It would be a privilege to assist."

"I knew I could rely on you," Gallagher told him. "Here are the sizes," and he pushed a piece of paper across the desk.

At ten o'clock the cavalcade left Septembertide and drove to Beaumont and Bel Royal and then along Victoria Avenue to St. Helier. The first stop was Elizabeth Castle. The tide was out and they parked the cars opposite the Grand Hotel and clambered on board an armored personnel carrier which followed the line of the causeway across the beach, its half-tracks churning sand.

"When the tide is in, the causeway is under water, Herr Field Marshal," Necker told him.

Baum was in his element, filled with excitement at the turn events had taken. He could see Martineau seated at the other end of the truck talking to a couple of young officers and Muller and for a wild moment wondered whether he might have dreamed the events of the previous night. Martineau certainly played a most convincing Nazi. On the other hand, he didn't do too bad a job on field marshals himself.

The carrier drove up from the causeway through the old castle gate and stopped. They all got out and Necker said, "The English fortified this place to keep out the French in Napoleon's time. Some of the original guns are still here."

"Now we fortify it further to keep out the English," Baum said. "There's irony for you."

As he led the way along the road to the moat and the entrance to the inner court, Martineau moved to his shoulder. "As a matter of interest, Herr Field Marshal, Sir Walter Raleigh was governor here in the time of Queen Elizabeth Tudor."

"Really?" Baum said. "An extraordinary man. Soldier, sailor, musician, poet, historian."

"Who also found time to introduce tobacco to the Western world," Martineau reminded him.

"For that alone he should have a statue in every major city," Baum said. "I remember the Italian campaign in nineteen seventeen. A terrible time. I think the only thing that got us through the trench warfare was the cigarettes."

He strode on ahead, Martineau at his shoulder, talking animatedly, and Hofer trailed anxiously behind with Necker. An hour later, after a thorough inspection of every gun and strongpoint Baum could find, they returned to the personnel carrier and were taken back across the beach to the cars.

On the cliffs near La Moye Point a group of field engineers hauled on a line, helping the corporal on the other end walk up the steep slope. He came over the edge and unhooked himself. The sergeant in charge of the detail gave him a cigarette. "You don't look too good."

"Neither would you. He's like a piece of badly cooked meat, the driver down there."

"Any papers?"

"Burned along with most of his clothes. The car is a Renault and I've got the number."

The sergeant wrote it down. "The police can handle it now." He turned to the other men. "All right, back to the post, you lot."

Mont Orgueil at Gorey on the east coast of Jersey is probably one of the most spectacular castles in Europe. The Germans had garrisoned it with coastal artillery batteries. In fact there were two regimental headquarters situated in the castle. Baum visited both of them, as well as conducting his usual energetic survey. In the observation post which had been constructed on the highest point of the castle, he stood with a pair of fieldglasses and looked across at the French coast, which was clearly visible. He was for the moment slightly apart from the others and Hofer moved to his shoulder.

"Is everything all right?" Baum asked, the glasses still to his eyes.

"Vogel seems to be pressing his attentions," Hofer said softly.

"He wanted to talk, so I let him," Baum replied. "I'm keeping him happy, Major. I'm trying to keep them all happy. Isn't that what you want?"

"Of course," Hofer told him. "Don't take it the wrong way. You're doing fine. Just be careful, that's all."

Necker moved up to join them, and Baum said, "Fantastic, this place. Now I would like to see something in the country. The sort of strongpoint one might find in a village area."

"Of course, Herr Field Marshal."

"And then some lunch."

"Arrangements have been made. The officers' mess at Battle HQ were hoping to entertain you."

"No, Necker, something different, I think. I'd like to see the other side of island life. Vogel tells me he's billeted at some manor house called de Ville Place. You know it?"

"Yes, Herr Field Marshal. The owner, Mrs. Helen de Ville, is married to the Seigneur who is an officer in the British Army. A most charming woman."

"And a delightful house according to Vogel. I think we'll have lunch there. I'm sure Mrs. de Ville won't object, especially if you provide the food and wine." He looked up at the cloudless blue sky. "A beautiful day for a picnic."

"As you say, Herr Field Marshal. If you'll excuse me I'll go and give the orders."

Ten minutes later, as the cavalcade of officers moved out through the main entrance to where the cars waited, a military police motorcyclist drove up. He pulled in beside Greiser, who sat behind the wheel of Muller's Citroën. Greiser read the message the man handed him, then got out of the car and hurried across to Muller, who was talking to a couple of officers. Martineau, standing nearby, heard everything.

"The bloody fool," Muller said softly and crumpled the message up in his hand. "All right, we'd better get moving."

He went to Necker, spoke briefly to him and then got into the Citroën. It moved away quickly, and Martineau walked over to Necker. "Muller seemed agitated."

"Yes," Necker said. "It would seem one of his men has been killed in a car accident."

"How unfortunate." Martineau offered him a cigarette. "Allow me to compliment you on the way you've handled things at such short notice."

"We do what we can. It's not every day a Rommel comes visiting."

"On the other hand, I expect you'll heave a sigh of relief when that Storch of his takes off tonight. Is he leaving before or after the mail plane?"

"In my opinion he should make the flight under cover of darkness. The mail plane usually leaves at eight for the same reason."

"Don't worry, Major." Martineau smiled. "I'm sure he'll see sense. I'll speak to him personally about it."

On a wooded slope in the parish of St. Peter with distant views of St. Ouen's Bay, the field marshal visited a complex of machine-gun nests, talking to gun crews, accepting a cigarette here and there. With the men, he was a sensational success, Necker had to admit that, although God alone knew where all the energy came from.

They had visited every part of the defense complex, were circling back through the wood, when an extraordinary incident took place. They came out of the trees, Baum in the lead. Below them, a gang of slave laborers worked on the track. They were the most wretched creatures Baum had ever seen in his life, dressed for the most part, in rags.

"What have we here?" he demanded.

"Russians, Herr Field Marshal, plus a few Poles and Spanish Reds."

No one below was aware of their presence, especially the guard who sat on a tree trunk and smoked a cigarette, his rifle across his knees. A cart emerged from the lower wood pulled by a rather thin horse, a young woman in a headscarf and overalls leading it. There was a little girl of five or six in the back of the cart. As they passed the road gang, she tossed them several turnips.

The German guard shouted angrily and ran along the track after the cart. He grabbed the horse by the bridle and brought it to a halt. He said something to the woman and then walked to the back of the cart, reached up and pulled the child down roughly. He slapped her face and, when the young woman ran to help her, knocked the woman to the ground.

Baum did not say a word, but went down the hillside like a strong wind. As he reached the track, the guard's hand rose to strike the child again. Baum caught him by the wrist, twisting it up and around. The guard turned, the anger on his face quickly replaced by astonishment, and Baum punched him in the mouth. The guard bounced off the side of the cart and fell on his hands and knees.

"Major Necker," the field marshal said. "You will oblige me by arresting this animal." He ignored them all, turning to the young woman and the child clutching her. "Your name, Fraulein?" he asked in English.

"Jean le Couteur."

"And this is?" Baum picked the child up.

"My sister Agnes."

"So?" He nodded. "You are a very brave girl, Agnes le Couteur." He put her up in the cart again, turned and saluted the young woman courteously. "My deepest regrets."

She gazed at him, bewildered, then grabbed the bridle and led the horse away along the track. Just before they disappeared from view into the trees, the child raised an arm and waved.

There was general laughter from all the officers present. Baum turned and said to Necker, "Honor being satisfied, I suggest we adjourn to the de Ville Place for lunch."

Muller stood on the edge of the cliff with Greiser and looked down at the wreck of the Renault. "There was a fire," Greiser told him. "From what the engineer sergeant I spoke to says, he's pretty unrecognizable."

"I can imagine." Muller nodded. "All right, make arrangements with them to get the body up sometime this afternoon. We'll need a postmortem, but discreetly handled. We must keep the drunkenness factor out of it."

He turned away and Greiser said, "But what was he doing out here? That's what I can't understand."

"So far the only thing we do know is that he was drinking heavily last night. Check with military police for this area, just in case some-one saw his car," Muller told him. "I'll have to get back to the official party now so I'll take the Citroën. You'll have to commandeer something from the military police. The moment you have any information at all, let me know."

The mess sergeant and his men who had descended on de Ville Place from the officers' club at Bagatelle brought ample supplies of food and wine. They simply took over, carrying tables and chairs from the house, covering them with the white linen tablecloths they had brought with them, working very fast. The mess sergeant was polite but made it clear to Helen that as the field marshal was due at any time, he would appreciate it if she did not get in the way.

She went up to her bedroom, searched through the wardrobe and found a summer dress in pale green organdy from happier days. As she was pulling it over her head, there was a tap on the door and Sarah came in.

"Getting ready to play hostess?"

"I don't have much choice, do I?" Helen told her. "Even if he was the real thing."

She brushed back her hair and fitted ivory side combs. Sarah said, "You look very nice."

"And so do you." Sarah was wearing a dark coat and tiny black hat, the hair swept up.

"We do our best. I'll be glad when it's all over."

"Not long now, love." Helen put her arms around her and held her for a moment, then turned and smoothed her dress.

"You haven't changed your mind, you and Sean? You won't come with us?"

"Good heavens no. Can you imagine what would happen to de Ville Place if I wasn't here? Nothing for Ralph to come home to, and remember that Sean, as he keeps telling us, is a neutral." She applied a little lipstick. "I certainly have nothing to worry about. You and Standartenführer Vogel were uninvited guests here. Anyway, there's always Guido in the background to back me up."

"You're really quite a remarkable woman," Sarah said.

"All women are remarkable, my darling. They have to be to get by. It's a man's world." She moved to the window. "Yes, I thought so. They're here." She turned, smiled. "Don't forget that down there among all those officers you and I are formally polite. French only."

"I'll remember."

"Good. Into battle then. I'll go first. Give me a few minutes," and she went out.

When Sarah went into the Great Hall she found Guido, Bruno Feldt and three other young naval officers, all hovering uncertainly around the front door, peering outside. "Ah, Mademoiselle Latour," Guido said in French. "You look ravishing as usual. The field marshal has just arrived."

They moved out onto the steps. Baum was being introduced to Helen by Necker, and Sarah saw Harry standing at the back of the group of officers. Someone took the field marshal's leather coat, baton and gloves. He turned back to Helen, smoothing his tunic, and spoke in English.

"This is most kind of you, Frau de Ville. A gross imposition, but I felt I wanted to see for myself one of your famous Jersey manor houses. De Ville Place comes highly recommended."

"Quite modest compared to some, Herr Field Marshal. St. Ouen's Manor, for example, is much more spectacular."

"But this is delightful. Truly delightful. The gardens, the flowers and palm trees and the sea down there. What a fantastic color." He offered her his arm gallantly. "And now, if you would do me the honor. A little lobster? Some champagne? Perhaps we can forget the war for a while?"

"Difficult, Herr Field Marshal, but I'll try." She took his arm and they walked across the grass to the tables.

The afternoon started off well. Guido Orsini asked permission to take photos which the Field Marshal graciously agreed to, posing with the assembled officers, Martineau standing next to him. The whole affair was obviously a huge success.

Necker, on his fourth glass of champagne, was standing by the drinks table with Hofer and Martineau. "I think he's enjoying himself."

Hofer nodded. "Most definitely. A marvelous place and a most charming hostess."

"However reluctant," Martineau commented acidly. "But too well bred to show it. The English upper classes are always the same."

"Perhaps," Necker said coldly. "And understandably so. Her husband, after all, is a major in the British Army."

"And therefore an enemy of the Reich, but then I hardly need remind you of that."

Martineau picked up another glass of champagne and walked away. Sarah was surrounded by the naval officers and Guido was taking a photo. She waved and Martineau joined them.

"Please, Max," she said. "We must have a photo together."

He laughed lightly and handed his glass to Bruno. "Why not?"

The others moved to one side and he and Sarah stood there together in the sunshine. She felt strange, remembering what Helen had said, her hand tightening on his arm as if trying desperately to hold on.

Guido smiled. "That's fine."

"Good." Martineau retrieved his champagne from Bruno. "And now I must speak to the field marshal. You'll look after Anne-Marie for me, Lieutenant?" he said to Guido and walked away.

He'd noticed Muller arrive, rather later than everyone else. He was standing talking to Necker, and behind him, a military police motorcycle drove up with Greiser in the saddle. Martineau paused, watching. Greiser got off, pushed the motorcycle up on its stand and approached Muller, who made his excuses to Necker and moved away, listening to what the sergeant had to say. After a while, he looked around as if searching for someone. When he found Martineau, he crossed the grass toward him.

"I wonder if I might have a few words in private, Standartenführer?"

"Of course," Martineau said, and they moved away from the others, walking toward the trees. "What can I do for you?"

"My man Kleist was killed last night. A messy business. His car went over a cliff at La Moye."

"Not good," Martineau said. "Had he been drinking?"

"Perhaps," Muller replied cautiously. "The thing is we can't think of any convincing reason for him having been there. It's a remote sort of place."

"A woman perhaps?" Martineau suggested.

"No sign of another body."

"A mystery then, but what has it to do with me?" Martineau knew, of course, what was to come.

"We ran a routine check with the military police patrols in that sector in case they'd noticed his car."

"And had they?"

"No, but we have got a report that you were stopped in your Kubelwagen on Route du Sud at approximately two o'clock this morning."

"Correct," Martineau told him calmly. "But what has that to do with the matter in hand?"

"To get to the area of La Moye where Kleist met with his unfortunate accident it would be necessary to drive along Route du Sud, then take the Corbiere road."

"Do get to the point, Muller, the field marshal is expecting me."

"Very well, Standartenführer. I was wondering what you were doing there at two o'clock in the morning."

"It's quite simple," Martineau said. "I was about my business, under direct orders of the Reichsführer, as you well know. When I return to Berlin he will expect a report on what I found here in Jersey. I'm sorry to say it will not be favorable."

Muller frowned. "Perhaps you could explain, Standartenführer."

"Security for one thing," Martineau told him. "Or the lack of it. Yes, Muller, I was stopped by a military police patrol on Route du Sud this morning. I left de Ville Place at midnight, drove through St. Peter's Valley, up to the village and along to Greve de Lecq. Just after one o'clock I reached L'Etacq at the north end of St. Ouen's Bay, having taken a back lane around Les Landes. A defense area, am I right?"

"Yes, Standartenführer."

"And the places all have important military installations?"

"True."

"I'm glad you agree. I then drove along the bay to Corbiere lighthouse and was eventually stopped in Route du Sud by two military policemen who appeared to be having a smoke at the side of the road. You do get the point, don't you, Muller?" His face was hard and dangerous. "I drove around this island in the early hours of the morning close to some of our most sensitive installations and only got stopped once." He allowed his voice to rise so that officers nearby turned curiously. "Would you say that was satisfactory?"

"No, Standartenführer."

"Then I suggest you do something about it." Martineau put his glass down on a nearby table. "And now I think I've kept the field marshal waiting long enough."

As he walked away, Greiser joined Muller. "What happened?"

"Nothing very much. He says he was on a tour of inspection. Says that in two hours of touring the west of the island, he was only stopped once—on Route du Sud."

"Do you believe him, Herr Captain?"

"Oh, it fits well enough," Muller said. "Unfortunately we're back with that policeman's nose of mine. He was in the area, that's a fact, and I hate coincidences."

"So what shall I do?"

"When they get poor old Willi's body up, get it straight in for a postmortem. If he was awash with schnapps when he died, at least it will show and we'll know where we are."

"All right, Herr Captain, I'll see to it." Greiser went back to his motorcycle, mounted and rode away quickly.

Baum, talking to Helen and a couple of officers, turned as Martineau approached. "Ah, there you are, Vogel. I'm in your debt for suggesting my visit to such a delightful spot"

"A pleasure, Herr Field Marshal."

"Come, we'll walk awhile and you can tell me how things are in Berlin these days." He took Helen's hand and kissed it. "You'll excuse us, Frau de Ville?"

"Of course, Herr Field Marshal."

Martineau and Baum turned away and strolled across the grass toward the trees, taking the path that led to the rampart walk with its view of the bay. "This whole thing becomes more like a bad play by the minute," Baum said.

"Yes, well we don't have time right now to discuss what Brecht might have made of it. This is what happens. The mail plane leaves at eight. They expect you to fly out in the Storch at about the same time."

"So?"

"I'll turn up at Septembertide at seven. I'll have Sarah with me, also Kelso in Kriegsmarine uniform and heavily bandaged."

"And how does Hofer react?"

"He does exactly as he's told. I've got a syringe and a strong sedative, courtesy of the doctor who's been treating Kelso. An armful of that and he'll be out for hours. We'll lock him in his bedroom."

"When does this happen?"

"I'd say the best time would be at the end of your tour when you return to Septembertide. Probably around five o'clock. Get rid of Necker and the others, but ask me to stay for a drink."

"But how do I explain his absence at the airport?"

"Simple. Necker will be there with his staff to bid you a fond farewell. It's at that point you announce you intend to fly out in the mail plane. You can't arrange it earlier because Hofer would want to know what you were up to. You tell Necker that the chief medical officer at the hospital has made representations on behalf of this sailor, badly wounded in the convoy attack the other night and in urgent need of specialist treatment on the mainland. As you're using the bigger plane, you're giving me and Sarah a lift."

"And Hofer?"

"Tell Necker that Hofer is following behind. That he's going to fly out in the Storch on his own."

"And you think all this will work?"

"Yes," Martineau said, "because it's actually rather simple. I could have tried something like it without you, using my letter from the Reichsführer, but perhaps the Luftwaffe commanding officer here would have insisted on getting permission from Luftwaffe HQ in Normandy." He smiled. "But to Erwin Rommel, nobody says no."

Baum sighed, took the cigarette Martineau offered and fitted it into the holder. "I'll never get a role as good as this again. Never."

15

ON THE SLAB IN the postmortem room at the general hospital, Willi Kleist's corpse looked even more appalling. Major Speer stood waiting while the two medical corporals who were assisting him carefully cut away the burned clothing. Greiser, standing by the door, watched in fascinated horror.

Speer turned to look at him. "If you feel like being sick, the bucket is over there. Nothing to be ashamed of."

"Thank you, Herr Major. Captain Muller asked me to tell you how much he appreciates your attending to him personally."

"I understand, Sergeant. Discretion, in a case like this, is of the utmost importance. So, we are ready?"

The last vestiges of clothing were stripped away, and one of the corporals washed the body down with a fine spray, while the other wheeled across a trolley on which a selection of surgical instruments had been laid out.

"I'd normally start with taking out the brain," Speer said cheerfully. "But in this case, speed being of the essence, or so you inform me, we'll have the organs out first so the lab technicians can get on with their side of things."

The scalpel in his right hand didn't seem particularly large, but when he ran it down from just below the throat to the belly, the flesh parted instantly. The smell was terrible, but Greiser hung on, a handkerchief to his mouth. Speer worked at speed, removing the heart, the liver, the kidneys, all being taken away in enamel basins to the laboratory next door.

Speer seemed to have forgotten about Greiser. One of the corporals passed him a small electric saw which plugged into a floor socket. When he started on the skull, Greiser could take no more and removed himself hurriedly to the lavatory where he was violently sick.

Afterward, he sat outside in the corridor and smoked. A young nurse with an Irish accent came up and put a hand on his shoulder. "You look awful."

"I've just been watching them do a postmortem," Greiser told her.

"Yes, well it gets you like that the first time. I'll bring you a coffee."

She meant well, but it was not the real thing: acorn coffee, a taste Greiser found particularly loathsome. He lit another cigarette and walked down to the main entrance and phoned through to Muller at the Silvertide from the porter's desk.

"It's Greiser, Herr Captain."

"How are things going?" Muller asked.

"Well, it's hardly one of life's great experiences, but Major Speer obviously knows his stuff. I'm waiting for his conclusions now. They're doing lab tests."

"You might as well hang on until they're ready. An interesting development. I've had your brother on the phone from Stuttgart. He's heard from this Neumann woman in Berlin. The one who works in the Reichsführer's office at the Chancellery."

"And?"

"She's never heard of Vogel. She's kept her inquiries discreet for the moment. Of course, as your brother points out, these special envoys of Himmler are mystery men to everyone else."

"Yes, but you'd think someone like Lotte Neumann would have at least heard of him," Greiser said. "What are you going to do?"

"Think about it. As soon as Speer's ready with those results, give me a ring and I'll come around myself to see what he has to say."

It was just before five when the cavalcade of cars returned to September-tide. Baum and Hofer got out and Necker joined them with one or two officers. Martineau stood at the back of the group and waited. "A memorable day, Major," Baum said. "I'm truly grateful."

"I'm pleased everything has gone so well, Herr Field Marshal."

"How long does it take to the airport from here?"

"No more than ten minutes."

"Good. We'll see you up there sometime between seven-thirty and eight."

Necker saluted, turned and got back into his car. As the officers dispersed, Baum and Hofer turned to the front door and Martineau stepped forward. "Might I have a word. Herr Field Marshal?"

Hofer was immediately wary, but Baum said cheerfully, "Of course, Standartenführer. Come in."

At that moment Heider, the platoon commander, appeared in the gateway and saluted. "Is there anything I can do for you, Herr Field Marshal?"

"What about the cook we had last night?"

"I'll send him over."

"Not for half an hour, Heider."

He went inside followed by Hofer and Martineau. They went into the living room. Baum took off his leather coat and his cap and opened the glass door to the terrace. "A drink, Standartenführer?"

"That would be very acceptable."

"Konrad." Baum nodded to Hofer. "Cognac, I think. You'll join us?"

He fitted a cigarette to his holder, and Martineau gave him a light as Hofer poured the drinks. "What an extraordinary view," Baum said, looking down at St. Aubin's Bay. "In peacetime, with the lights on at night down there, it must resemble Monte Carlo. Wouldn't you think so, Konrad?"

"Perhaps, Herr Field Marshal." Hofer was nervous and trying not to show it, wondering what Vogel wanted.

"To us, gentlemen." Baum raised his glass. "To soldiers everywhere who always bear the burden of man's stupidity." He emptied his glass, smiled and said in English, "All right, Harry, let's get on with it."

Hofer looked totally bewildered and Martineau produced the Walther with the Carswell silencer from his trenchcoat pocket. "It would be stupid to make me shoot you. Nobody would hear a thing." He removed the Mauser from Hofer's holster. "Sit down."

"Who are you?" Hofer demanded.

"Well I'm certainly not Standartenführer Max Vogel any more than Heini here is the Desert Fox."

"Heini?" Hofer looked even more bewildered.

"That's me," Baum said. "Heini Baum. Erich Berger was killed in an air raid on Kiel. I took his papers and joined the paratroops."

"But why?"

"Well, you see, Herr Captain, I happen to be Jewish, and what better place for a Jew to hide?"

"My God!" Hofer said hoarsely.

"Yes, I thought you'd like that. A Jew impersonating Germany's greatest war hero. A nice touch of irony there."

Hofer turned to Martineau. "And you?"

"My name is Martineau. Lieutenant Colonel Harry Martineau. I work for SOE. I'm sure you've heard of us."

"Yes." Hofer reached for his glass and finished the rest of his brandy. "I think you can say that."

"Your boss is a lucky man. I was close to putting a bullet in him last night after you'd gone to bed. Happily for our friend here, he likes to talk to himself and I discovered all was not as it seemed."

"So what do you intend to do?" Hofer asked.

"Simple. Field Marshal Rommel flies out in the mail plane tonight, not the Storch, which means I can leave with him, along with a couple of friends. Destination England."

"The young lady?" Hofer managed a smile. "I liked her. I presume she also is not what she seems."

"One more thing," Martineau said, "but it's important. You might wonder why I don't shoot you. Well, Heini having a bad habit of listening at doors, I know where Rommel has been this weekend and what he's been up to. The assassination of Hitler at this stage of the war would suit the Allied cause very well. In the circumstances, when we get back to England and I tell my people about this business, I think you'll find they keep very quiet. We wouldn't want to make things too difficult for Field Marshal Rommel, if you follow me. More power to his arm. I want you to live so you can tell him that."

"And how does he explain to the Führer what happened here?"

"I should have thought that rather simple. There's been more than one plot against Rommel's life already by French Resistance and Allied agents. The British nearly got him in North Africa, remember. To use Berger to impersonate him on occasion made good sense, and what happened here in Jersey proved it. If he'd come himself, he'd have died here. The fact that Berger has decided to change sides is regrettable, but hardly your fault."

"Now you say Berger again."

"I think he means you might overcomplicate things if you introduce the Jewish bit," Heini told him.

"Something like that." Martineau stood up. "All right, let's have you upstairs."

Hofer did as he was told, because he didn't have any choice in the matter, and they followed him up and along the corridor to the small bedroom he had been using.

Through the half-drawn curtains he could see into the courtyard and over the wall to where Heider stood beside one of the armored personnel carriers.

"Obviously you don't intend to kill me," he said.

"Of course not. I need you to tell all to Rommel, don't I?" Martineau replied. "Just keep still and don't make a fuss and you'll be fine."

There was a burning pain in Hofer's right arm and almost instantaneous darkness. Baum emptied the contents of the syringe before pulling it out, and Martineau eased the major down onto the bed, arranged his limbs in a comfortable position and covered him with a blanket.

They went down to the hall. Martineau said, "Seven o'clock."

As he opened the front door, the cook corporal from the night before walked across the courtyard. Baum said, "I'll see you later then, Standartenführer."

He turned and walked back inside to the living room and the corporal followed. "At your orders, Herr Field Marshal."

"Something simple," Baum said. "Scrambled eggs, toast and coffee,

I think. Just for me. Major Hofer isn't feeling too well. He's having a rest before we leave."

In Gallagher's cottage, he and Martineau eased Kelso into the Kriegsmarine uniform while Sarah stayed discreetly out of the way in the kitchen. Gallagher cut the right trouser leg so that it would fit over the cast.

"How's that?" he asked.

"Not bad." Kelso hesitated then said awkwardly, "There's a lot of people putting themselves on the line because of me."

"Oh, I see," Martineau said. "You mean you deliberately got yourself blown over the rail of that LST in Lyme Bay?"

"No, of course not."

"Then stop agonizing," Martineau told him and called to Sarah: "You can come in now."

She entered from the kitchen with two large bandage rolls and surgical tape. She went to work on Kelso's face and head, leaving only one eye and the mouth visible.

"That's really very professional," Gallagher said.

"I am a professional, you fool," she told him.

He grinned amiably. "Jesus, girl, I bet you look great in that nurse's uniform."

Martineau glanced at his watch. It was almost six o'clock. "We'll go up to the house now, General. You keep an eye on him. I'll be back with the Kubelwagen in an hour."

He and Sarah left, and Gallagher went into the hall and came back with a pair of crutches. "Present for you." He propped them against the table. "See how you get on."

Kelso pushed himself up on one leg, got first one crutch under an arm and then the other. He took one hesitant step forward, paused, then moved on with increasing confidence, until he reached the other side of the room.

"Brilliant!" Gallagher told him. "Long John Silver to the life. Now try again."

"Are you certain?" Muller asked.

"Oh, it's quite definite," Speer said. "I'll show you." The brain slopped about in the enamel basin and he turned it over in gloved hands. "See the pink discoloration at the base? That's blood, and that's what gave me the clue. Something sharp sheared right up through the roof of the mouth into the brain."

"Is it likely such an injury would be explained by the kind of accident he was in?"

"Oh, no," Speer said. "Whatever did this was as razor sharp as a scalpel. The external flesh of the face and neck is badly burned and I can't be certain, but if you want my opinion, he was stabbed under the chin. Does that make any kind of sense?"

"Yes," Muller said. "I think it does. Thanks very much." He nodded to Greiser. "Let's go."

As he reached the door and opened it, Speer said, "Oh, one more thing."

"What's that?"

"You were quite right. He had been drinking heavily. I'd say, from the tests, about a bottle and a half of spirits."

On the steps outside the main entrance of the hospital, Muller paused to light a cigarette. "What do you think, Herr Captain?" Greiser asked.

"That another word with Standartenführer Vogel is indicated, Ernst, so let's get moving."

He got into the passenger seat of the Citroën. Greiser slid behind the wheel and drove away.

In the kitchen at de Ville Place, Sarah, Helen and Martineau sat round the table. The door opened and Guido came in with a bottle. "Warm champagne," he said. "The best I can do."

"Are you certain the place is empty?" Sarah asked.

"Oh, yes. Bruno was the last to leave. They're all on tonight's convoy to Granville. Kriegsmarine Headquarters haven't come up with a new assignment for me yet."

He pulled the cork and poured champagne into the four kitchen glasses Helen provided. She raised hers. "What shall we drink to?"

"Better days," Sarah said.

"And life, liberty and the pursuit of happiness," Guido added, "not forgetting love."

"You wouldn't." Sarah kissed his cheek and turned to Martineau. "And you, Harry, what do you wish?"

"One day at a time is all I can manage." He finished the champagne. "My God, that tastes awful." He put down the glass. "I'll go and get Kelso now. Be ready to leave when I get back, Sarah."

He went out, got into the Kubelwagen and drove away, taking the track down through the wood. At the same time, two hundred yards to the right, the Citroën carrying Muller and Greiser moved along the road to de Ville Place and turned into the courtyard.

In the bedroom, Sarah put on her hat and coat, turning to check in the mirror that her stocking seams were straight. She freshened her mouth with lipstick and made a face at herself in the mirror. "Good-bye, little French tart, it's been nice knowing you."

At that moment she heard a car outside and glanced out of the window and saw Muller get out of the Citroën. It was trouble, she knew that instantly. She opened her handbag. The PPK was in there but also the little Belgian automatic Kelly had given her. She lifted her skirt and slipped the smaller gun into the top of her right stocking. It fit surprisingly snugly. She smoothed down her coat and left the room.

Muller was in the hall talking to Helen, Greiser over by the entrance. Guido was standing by the green baize door leading to the kitchen. As Sarah came down the stairs, Muller looked up and saw her.

"Ah, there you are, mademoiselle," Helen said in French. "Captain Muller was looking for the Standartenführer. Do you know where he is?"

"I've no idea," Sarah said continuing on down. "Is there a problem?"

"Perhaps." Muller took her handbag from her quite gently, opened it and removed the PPK which he put in his pocket. He handed the bag back to her. "You've no idea when he'll be back?"

"None at all," Sarah said.

"But you are dressed to go out?"

"Mademoiselle Latour was going to take a walk in the grounds with me," Guido put in.

Muller nodded. "Very well, if the Standartenführer isn't available, I'll have to make do with you." He said to Greiser. "Take her out to the car."

"But I protest," Sarah started to say.

Greiser smiled, his fingers hooking painfully into her arm. "You protest all you like, sweetheart. I like it," and he hustled her through the door.

Muller turned to Helen who managed to stay calm with difficulty. "Perhaps you would be good enough to tell Standartenführer Vogel on his return that if he wishes to see Mademoiselle Latour, he must come to the Silvertide," and he turned and walked out.

Kelso was doing quite well with the crutches. He made it to the Kubelwagen under his own steam, and Gallagher helped him into the rear seat. "Nice going, me old son."

Martineau got behind the wheel and Guido emerged from the trees on the run. He leaned against the car, gasping.

"What is it, man?" Gallagher demanded.

"Muller and Greiser turned up. They were looking for you, Harry."

"And?" Martineau's face was very pale.

"They've taken Sarah. Muller says if you want to see her, you'll have to go to the Silvertide. What are we going to do?"

"Get in!" Martineau said and drove away as the Italian and Gallagher scrambled aboard.

He braked to a halt in the courtyard where Helen waited anxiously on the steps. She hurried down and leaned in the Kubelwagen. "What are we going to do, Harry?"

"I'll take Kelso up to Septembertide to connect with Baum. If worse comes to worst, they can fly off into the blue together. Baum knows what to do."

"But we can't leave Sarah," Kelso protested.

"I can't," Martineau said, "but you can, so don't give me a lot of false sentimentality. You're what brought us here in the first place. The reason for everything."

Helen clutched his arm. "Harry!"

"Don't worry. I'll think of something."

"Such as?" Gallagher demanded.

"I don't know," Martineau said. "But you keep out of it, that's essential. We'll have to go."

The Kubelwagen moved away across the yard, and the noise of the engine faded. Gallagher turned to Guido. "Get the Morris out and you and I'll take a run down to the Silvertide."

"What do you have in mind?" Guido asked.

"God knows. I never could stand just sitting around and waiting, that's all."

Martineau drove into the courtyard at Septembertide and braked to a halt. He helped Kelso out and the American followed him, swinging between his crutches. The door was opened by the corporal. As they went in, Baum appeared from the sitting room.

"Ah, there you are, Vogel! And this is the young man you told me about?" He turned to the corporal. "Dismissed. I'll call you when I want you."

Baum stood back and Kelso moved past him into the sitting room. Martineau said, "There's been a change of plan. Muller came looking for me at de Ville Place. As it happens, I wasn't around at the right moment, but Sarah was. They've taken her to the Silvertide."

"Don't tell me, let me guess," Baum said. "You're going to go to the rescue."

"Something like that."

"And what about us?"

Martineau glanced at his watch. It was just after seven. "You and Kelso keep to your schedule. Getting him out of here is what's important."

"Now look here," Kelso began, but Martineau had already walked out.

The Kubelwagen roared out of the courtyard. Kelso turned and found Baum pouring cognac into a glass. He drank it slowly. "That's really very good."

"What goes on here?" the American demanded.

"I was thinking of Martineau," Baum said. "I might have known that under all that surface cynicism he was the kind of man who'd go back for the girl. I was at Stalingrad, did you know that? I've had enough of heroes to last me for a lifetime."

He pulled on his leather trenchcoat and gloves, twisted the white scarf around his neck, adjusted the angle of the cap and picked up his baton.

"What are you going to do?" Kelso demanded.

"Martineau told me that the important thing about being Field Marshal Erwin Rommel was that everyone would do what I told them to do. Now we'll see if he's right. You stay here."

He strode through the courtyard into the road and the men leaning beside the personnel carrier sprang to attention. "One of you get Captain Heider."

Baum took out a cigarette and fitted it in his holder. A sergeant sprang forward with a light. A second later Heider hurried out. "Herr Field Marshal?"

"Get through to the airport. A message for Major Necker. I shall be a little later than I thought. Tell him also that I shall leave for France, not in my Storch, but in the mail plane. I expect it waiting and ready to go when I arrive, and I'd like my personal pilot to fly it."

"Very well, Herr Field Marshal."

"Excellent. I need them all, fully armed and ready to go in five minutes. You'll find a wounded sailor in Septembertide. Have a couple of men help him out and put him in the personnel carrier. And they can bring the corporal you loaned me with them, too. No sense in leaving him hanging around the kitchen."

"But Herr Field Marshal, I don't understand," the captain said.

"You will, Heider," the field marshal told him. "You will. Now send that message to the airport."

Muller had drawn the curtains in his office and Sarah sat on a chair in front of his desk, hands folded in her lap, knees together. They'd made her take off her coat and Greiser was searching the lining while Muller went through the handbag.

He said, "So you are from Paimpol?"

"That's right."

"Sophisticated clothes for a Breton girl from a fishing village."

"Oh, but she's been around this one, haven't you?" Greiser ran his fingers up and down her neck, making her flesh crawl.

Muller said, "Where did you and Standartenführer Vogel meet?"

"Paris," she said.

"But there is no visa for Paris among your papers."

"I had one. It ran out."

"Have you ever heard of the Cherche Midi or the women's prison at Troyes? Bad places for a young woman like you to be."

"I don't know what you're talking about. I've done nothing," she said. Her stomach contracted with fear, her throat was dry.

Oh, God, Harry, she thought, fly away. Just fly away. And then the door opened and Martineau walked into the office.

There were tears in her eyes and she had never known such emotion as Greiser stood back and Harry put an arm around her gently.

The emotion she felt was so overwhelming that she committed the greatest blunder of all then. "Oh, you bloody fool," she said in English. "Why didn't you go?"

Muller smiled gently and picked up the Mauser that lay on his desk. "So, you speak English also, mademoiselle. This whole business becomes even more intriguing. I think you'd better relieve the Standartenführer of his Walther, Ernst."

Greiser did as he was told, and Martineau said in German, "Do you know what you're doing, Muller? There's a perfectly good reason for Mademoiselle Latour to speak English. Her mother was English. The facts are on file at SD headquarters in Paris. You can check."

"You have an answer for everything," Muller said. "What if I told you that a postmortem has indicated that Willi Kleist was murdered last night? The medical examiner indicates the time of death as being between midnight and two o'clock. I need hardly remind you that it was two o'clock when you were stopped on Route du Sud, no more than a mile from where the body was discovered. What do you have to say to that?"

"I can only imagine you've been grossly overworking. Your career's on the line here, Muller, you realize that. When the Reichsführer hears the full facts he'll..."

For the first time Muller almost lost his temper. "Enough of this. I've been a policeman all my life—a good policeman and I detest violence. However, there are those with a different attitude. Greiser here, for instance. A strange thing about Greiser. He doesn't like women. He would actually find it pleasurable to discuss this whole affair in private with Mademoiselle Latour, but I doubt that she would."

"Oh, I don't know." Greiser put an arm around Sarah and slipped a hand inside her dress, fondling a breast. "I think she might get to like it after I've taught her her manners."

Sarah's left hand clawed down his face, drawing blood, only feeling rage now, more powerful than she had ever known. As Greiser staggered back, her hand went up her skirt, pulling the tiny automatic from her stocking. Her arm swung up and she fired at point-blank range, shooting Muller between the eyes. The Mauser dropped from his nerveless hand to the desk; he staggered back against the wall and fell to the floor. Greiser tried to get his own gun from his pocket, too late as Martineau picked up the Mauser from the desk.

Gallagher and Guido were sitting in the Morris on the other side of the road from the Silvertide when they heard the sound of approaching vehicles. They turned to see a military column approaching. The lead vehicle was a Kubelwagen with the top down and Field Marshal Erwin Rommel standing in the passenger seat for the whole world to see. The Kubelwagen braked to a halt, he got out as the soldiers, carried by the other vehicles in the column, jumped down and ran forward in obedience to Heider's shouted orders.

"Right, follow me!" Baum called and marched straight in through the entrance of the Silvertide. A moment after Sarah fired the shot that killed Muller, the door crashed open and Baum appeared. He advanced into the room, Heider and a dozen armed men behind him. He peered over the desk at Muller's body.

Greiser said, "Herr Field Marshal, this woman has murdered Captain Muller."

Baum ignored him and said to Heider, "Put this man in a cell."

"Yes, Herr Field Marshal." Heider nodded and three of his men grabbed the protesting Greiser. Heider followed them out.

"Back in your vehicles," Baum shouted to the others and held Sarah's coat for her. "Can we go now?"

Gallagher and Guido saw them come out of the entrance to the hotel and get into the Kubelwagen, Martineau and Sarah in the back, Baum standing up in front. He waved his arm, the Kubelwagen led off, the whole column following.

"Now what do we do?" Guido asked.

"Jesus, is there no poetry in you at all?" Gallagher demanded. "We follow them, of course. I wouldn't miss the last act for anything."

At Septembertide, on the bed in the small room, Konrad Hofer groaned and moved restlessly. The sedative the doctor had given Martineau was, like most of his drugs, of prewar vintage, and Hofer was no longer completely unconscious. He opened his eyes, mouth dry, and stared at the ceiling, trying to work out where he was. It was like awaking from a bad dream, something you knew had been terrible and yet already forgotten. And then he remembered, tried to sit up and rolled off the bed to the floor. He pulled himself up, head swimming, and reached for the door handle. It refused to budge and he turned and lurched across to the window. He fumbled with the catch and then gave up the struggle and slammed his elbow through the pane.

The sound of breaking glass brought the two soldiers Captain Heider had left on sentry duty at Hinguette next door running into the courtyard. They stared up, machine pistols at the ready, a young private and an older man, a corporal.

"Up here!" Hofer called. "Get me out. I'm locked in."

He sat on the bed, his head in his hands, and tried to breathe deeply, aware of the sound of their boots clattering up the stairs and along the corridor. He could hear voices, saw the handle turn.

"There's no key, Herr Hofer," one of them called.

"Then break it down, you fool!" he replied.

A moment later, the door burst open, crashing against the wall, and they stood staring at him.

"Get Captain Heider," Hofer said.

"He's gone, Herr Major."

"Gone?" Hofer still had difficulty thinking clearly.

"With the field marshal, Herr Major. The whole unit went with them. We're the only two here."

The effects of the drug made Hofer feel as if he were underwater and he shook his head vigorously. "Did they leave any vehicles?"

"There's a Kubelwagen, Herr Major," the corporal told him.

"Can you drive?"

"Of course, sir. Where does the Herr Major wish to go?"

"The airport," Hofer said. "And there's no time to lose, so help me downstairs and let's get moving."

16

AT THE AIRPORT, THE Luftwaffe honor guard waited patiently as darkness fell. The same group of officers who had greeted the field marshal on his arrival now presented themselves to say goodbye. The Storch was parked on the far side of the JU52, which awaited its illustrious passenger some fifty yards from the terminal building. Necker paced up and down anxiously, wondering what on earth was going on. First of all that extraordinary message from Heider at Mont de la Rocque about the mail plane and now this. Twenty minutes past eight and still no sign.

There was the sudden roar of engines, the rattle of a half-track on concrete. He turned in time to witness the extraordinary sight of the armored column coming around the corner of the main airport building, the field marshal standing up in the Kubelwagen at the front, hands braced on the edge of the windshield.

The column made straight for the Junkers. Necker saw the field marshal wave to Sorsa in the cockpit, who was looking out of the side window. The center engine of the plane coughed into life, and Rommel was turning and waving, barking orders. Soldiers leaped from the trucks, rifles ready. Necker recognized Heider and then saw a bandaged sailor being taken from the personnel carrier by two soldiers who led him to the Junkers and helped him inside.

The whole thing had happened in seconds. As Necker started forward, the field marshal came to meet him. It was noisy now as the Junkers' wing engines also started to turn. To Necker's further astonishment he saw, beyond the field marshal, Standartenführer Vogel and the French girl dismount from the personnel carrier and go up the short ladder into the plane.

Baum was enjoying himself. The ride up from the Silvertide had been truly exhilarating, and he smiled and put a hand on Necker's shoulder. "My deepest apologies, Necker, but I had things to do. Young Heider was good enough to assist me with his men. A promising officer."

Necker was truly bewildered. "But, Herr Field Marshal ..." he began.

Baum carried on. "The chief medical officer at the hospital told me of this young sailor wounded in some convoy attack the other night and badly in need of treatment at the burns unit in Rennes. He asked me if I'd take him with me. Of course, in the state he's in we'd never have got him into the Storch. That's why I need the mail plane."

"And Standartenführer Vogel?"

"He was going back tomorrow anyway, so I might as well give him and the young woman a lift." He clapped Necker on the shoulder again. "But we must be off now. Again, my thanks for all you've done. I shall, of course, be in touch with General von Schmettow to express my entire satisfaction with the way things are in Jersey."

He saluted and turned to go up the ladder into the plane. Necker called, "But, Herr Field Marshal, what about Major Hofer?"

"He should be arriving any minute," Baum told him. "He'll leave in the Storch as arranged. The mail plane pilot can fly him across."

He scrambled inside the plane; the crewman pulled up the ladder and closed the door. The Junkers taxied away to the east end of the runway and turned. There was a deepening roar from the three engines as it moved faster and faster, a silhouette only in the gathering gloom, and then it lifted, drifting out over St. Ouen's Bay, still climbing.

~

Guido had parked the Morris a couple of hundred yards along the airport road. Standing there beside it, they saw the Junkers lift into the evening sky and fly west to where the horizon was tipped with fire.

The noise of the engines faded into the distance and Guido said softly, "My God, they actually pulled it off."

Gallagher nodded. "So now we can go home and get our stories straight for when all the questioning starts."

"No problem," Guido said. "Not if we stick together. I am, after all, an authentic war hero, which always helps."

"That's what I love about you, Guido. Your engaging modesty," Gallagher told him. "Now let's move. Helen will be getting worried."

They got into the Morris and Guido drove away quickly, a Kubelwagen passing them a moment later coming the other way, driving so fast that they failed to see Hofer sitting in the rear seat.

At the airport, most of the officers had dispersed, but Necker was standing by his car talking to Captain Adler, the Luftwaffe duty control officer, when the Kubelwagen came around the corner of the main airport building and braked to a halt. They turned to see Hofer being helped out of the rear seat by the two soldiers.

Necker knew trouble when he saw it. "Hofer? What is it?"

Hofer slumped against the Kubelwagen. "Have they gone?"

"Less than five minutes ago. The field marshal took the mail plane. He said you'd follow in the Storch. He took his own pilot."

"No!" Hofer said. "Not the field marshal."

Necker's stomach contracted. So many things that had worried him and yet... He took a deep breath. "What are you saying?"

"That the man you thought was Field Marshal Rommel is his double, a damn traitor called Berger who's thrown in his lot with the enemy. You'll also be happy to know that Standartenführer Max Vogel is an agent of the British Special Operations Executive: So is the girl, by the way. The wounded sailor is an American colonel."

But Necker, by now, was totally bewildered. "I don't understand any of this."

"It's really quite simple," Hofer told him. "They're flying to England in the mail plane." His head was suddenly clearer and he stood up. "Naturally, they must be stopped." He turned to Adler. "Get on the radio to Cher-bourg. Scramble a night fighter squadron. Now let's get moving. There's no time to lose." He turned and led the way to the operations building.

The Junkers was a workhorse and not built for comfort. Most of the interior was crammed with mail sacks and Kelso sat on the floor propped against them, legs outstretched. Sarah was on a bench on one side of the plane, Baum and Martineau on the other.

The crewman came out of the cockpit and joined them. "My name is Braun, Herr Field Marshal. Sergeant observer. If there is anything I can get you. We have a thermos flask of coffee and ..."

"Nothing, thank you." Baum took out his cigarette case and offered Martineau one.

"And Oberleutnant Sorsa would take it as an honor if you would care to come up front."

"You don't have a full crew? Just the two of you?" Martineau inquired.

"All that's necessary on these mail runs, Standartenführer."

"Tell Oberleutnant Sorsa I'll be happy to take him up on his offer a little later. I'll just finish my cigarette," Baum said.

"Certainly, Herr Field Marshal."

Braun opened the door and went back into the cockpit. Baum turned to Martineau and smiled. "Five minutes?"

"That should be about right." Martineau moved across to sit beside Sarah. He gave her his lighted cigarette. "Are you all right?"

"Absolutely."

"You're sure?"

"You mean am I going through hell because I just killed a man?" Her face was very calm. "Not at all. My one regret is that it was Muller instead of Greiser. He was from under a stone. Muller was just a police-man on the wrong side."

"From our point of view."

"No, Harry," she said. "Most wars are a stupidity. This one isn't. We're right and the Nazis are wrong. They're wrong for Germany and they're wrong for everyone else. It's as simple as that."

"Good for you," Kelso said. "A lady who stands up to be counted. I like that."

"I know," Martineau said. "It's wonderful to be young." He tapped Baum on the knee. "Ready?"

"I think so."

Martineau took his Walther from its holster and gave it to Sarah. "Action stations. You'll need that to take care of the observer. Here we go." He opened the cabin door and he and Baum squeezed into the cockpit behind the pilot and the observer. Oberleutnant Sorsa turned. "Everything to your satisfaction, Field Marshal?"

"I think you could say that," Baum told him.

"If there is anything we can do for you?"

"There is actually. You can haul this thing round and fly forty miles due west until we are completely clear of all Channel Islands traffic."

"But I don't understand."

Baum took the Mauser from his holster and touched it against the back of Sorsa's neck. "Perhaps this will help you."

"Later on when I call you, you'll turn north," Martineau said, "and make for England."

"England?" young Braun said in horror.

"Yes," Martineau told him. "As they say, for you, the war is over. Frankly, the way it's shaping up, you're well out of it."

"This is crazy," Sorsa said.

"If it helps you to believe that the field marshal is proceeding to England as a special envoy of the Führer, why not?" Martineau said. "Now change course like a good boy."

Sorsa did as he was told and the Junkers plowed on through the darkness. Martineau leaned over Braun. "Right, now for the radio. Show me the frequency selection procedure." Braun did as he was told. "Good. Now go and sit down in the cabin and don't do anything stupid. The lady has a gun."

The boy squeezed past him, and Martineau got into the copilot's seat and started to transmit on the frequency reserved by SOE for emergency procedure.

In the control room in the tower at Jersey Airport, Hofer and Necker waited anxiously while Adler spoke on the radio. A Luftwaffe corporal came up and spoke to him briefly.

Adler turned to the two officers. "We've still got them on radar, but they appear to be moving due west out to sea."

"My God!" Necker said.

Adler talked into the microphone for a moment, then turned to Hofer. "All night fighters in the Brittany area were scrambled an hour ago for operations over the Reich. Heavy bombing raids expected over the Ruhr."

"There must be something, for God's sake," Hofer said.

Adler waved him to silence, listening, then put down the mike and turned, smiling. "There is. One JU88S night fighter. Its port engine needed a check and it wasn't finished in time to leave with the rest of the squadron."

"But is it now?" Necker demanded eagerly.

"Oh, yes." Adler was enjoying himself. "He's just taken off from Cherbourg."

"But can he catch them?" Necker asked.

"Herr Major, that old crate they're flying in can do a hundred and eighty flat out. The JU88S with the new engine boosting system does better than four hundred. He'll be with them before they know it."

Necker turned in triumph to Hofer. "They'll have to turn back, otherwise he'll blow them out of the sky."

But Hofer had been thinking about that, among other things. If the mail plane returned, it would mean only one thing. Martineau and the others would be flown to Berlin, and few people survived interrogation in the cellars of Gestapo Headquarters at Prince Albrechtstrasse. That couldn't be allowed to happen. Berger knew about Rommel's connection with the generals' plot against the Führer, and so did Martineau. Perhaps he'd even told the girl.

Hofer took a deep breath. "No, we can't take a chance on their getting away."

"Herr Major?" Adler turned inquiringly.

"Send an order to the pilot of that night fighter to shoot on sight. They musn't reach England."

"As you say, Herr Major." Adler picked up the microphone.

Necker put a hand on Hofer's shoulder. "You look terrible. Let's go down to the mess and get you a brandy. Adler will call us when things start to warm up."

Hofer managed a weak smile. "The best offer I've had tonight." And they went out together.

Dougal Munro was at his Baker Street desk working late when Carter came in with the signal and passed it across. The brigadier read it quickly and smiled. "Good God, this is extraordinary, even for Harry."

"I know, sir. I've alerted Fighter Command about receiving them. Where do you want them to put down? I suppose Cornwall would be closest."

"No, let's bring them all the way in. They can land where they started, Jack. Hornley Field. Let Fighter Command know. I want them down in one piece."

"And General Eisenhower, sir?"

"Well leave him until Kelso's actually on the ground." Munro stood up and reached for his jacket. "And we'll have the car round, Jack. We can get there in just over an hour. With any luck, we'll be able to greet them."

In the mail plane the atmosphere was positively euphoric as Martineau left Heini Baum in the cockpit to keep an eye on Sorsa and joined the others.

"Everything okay?" Kelso asked.

"Couldn't be better. I've made contact with our people in England. They're going to provide an escort to take us in, courtesy of the RAF." He turned and smiled at Sarah, taking her hand. She'd never seen him so excited. Suddenly he looked ten years younger. "You all right?" he asked her.

"Fine, Harry. Just fine."

"Dinner at the Ritz tomorrow night," he said.

"By candlelight?"

"Even if I have to take my own." He turned to Braun, the observer. "You said something about coffee, didn't you?"

Braun started to get up and the plane bucked wildly as a great roaring filled the night, then dropped like a stone. Braun lost his balance and Kelso rolled on the floor with a cry of pain.

"Harry!" Sarah screamed. "What is it?"

The plane regained some sort of stability and Martineau peered out one of the side windows. A hundred yards away on the port side flying parallel with them he saw a Junkers 88S, one of those deadly black twin-engined planes that had caused such catastrophic losses to RAF Bomber Command in the night skies of Europe.

"We've got trouble," he said. "Luftwaffe night fighter." He turned and wrenched open the cabin door and leaned into the cockpit.

Sorsa glanced over his shoulder, face grim and pale in the cockpit lights. "We've had it. He's come to take us back."

"Has he said so?"

"No. No radio contact at all."

"Why not? It doesn't make sense."

The JU88S suddenly climbed steeply and disappeared, and it was Heini who gave the only possible answer to the question. "Every kind of sense if they don't want us back, my friend."

Martineau saw it all then. Something had gone wrong and it had to involve Hofer, and if that were so, the last thing he'd want was to have them back in Gestapo hands to bring down Erwin Rommel.

"What do I do?" Sorsa demanded. "That thing can blow us out of the skies. I know. I've been flying one for two years now."

At that moment, the roaring filled the night again, and the mail plane shuddered as cannon shell slammed into the fuselage. One came up through the floor of the cockpit, narrowly missing Sorsa, splinters shattering the windscreen. He pushed the column forward, going down in a steep dive into the cloud layer below, and the Junkers 88S roared overhead, passing like a dark shadow.

Martineau fell to one knee, but got the door open and scrambled out. Several gaping holes had been punched into the fuselage of the plane and two windows were shattered. Kelso was on the floor, hanging onto a seat and Sarah was crouched over Braun, who lay on his back, his uniform soaked with blood, eyes rolling. He jerked convulsively and lay still.

Sarah looked up, her face surprisingly calm. "He's dead. Harry."

There was nothing to say, couldn't be, and Martineau turned back to the cockpit, hanging on as the mail plane continued its steep dive down through the clouds. They rocked again in the turbulence as the Junkers 88S passed over them.

"Bastard!" Sorsa said, in a rage now. "I'll show you."

Baum, crouched on the floor, looked up at Harry with a ghastly smile. "He's a Finn, remember? They don't really like us Germans very much."

The mail plane burst out of the clouds at three thousand feet and kept on going down.

"What are you doing?" Martineau cried.

"Can't play hide and seek with him in that cloud. He'd get us for sure. Just one trick up my sleeve. He's very fast and I'm very slow and that makes it difficult for him." Sorsa glanced over his shoulder again and smiled savagely. "Let's see if he's any good."

He kept on going down, was at seven or eight hundred feet when the Junkers 88S came in again on their tail, far too fast, banking to port to avoid a collision.

Sorsa took the mail plane down to five hundred and leveled off. "Right, you swine, let's have you," he said, hands steady as a rock.

In that moment Martineau saw genius at work, understood all those medals the Finn wore, the Knight's Cross, and a strange feeling of calm enveloped him. It was all so unreal, the lights from the instrument panel, the wind roaring in through the shattered windscreen.

And when it happened, it was over in seconds. The Junkers 88S swooped in on their tail again, and Sorsa hauled back the column and started to climb. The pilot of the Junkers 88S banked steeply to avoid what seemed like an inevitable collision, but at that height and speed had nowhere else to go but straight down into the waves below.

Sorsa's face was calm again. "You lost, my friend," he said softly and eased back the column. "All right, let's get back upstairs."

Martineau pushed back the door and glanced out. The inside of the plane was a shambles, wind blowing in through innumerable holes, Braun's blood-soaked body on the floor, Sarah crouched beside Kelso.

"You two all right?" he called.

"Fine. Don't worry about us. Is it over?" Sarah asked.

"You could say that."

He turned back to the cockpit as Sorsa leveled out at six thousand feet. "So, the old girl's leaking like a sieve, but everything appears to be functioning," the Finn said.

"Let's try the radio." Martineau squeezed into the copilot's seat. He twisted the dial experimentally but everything seemed to be in working order. "I'll let them know what's happened," he said and started to transmit on the SOE emergency frequency.

Heini Baum tried to light a cigarette but his hands shook so much he had to give up. "My God!" he moaned. "What a last act."

Sorsa said cheerfully, "Tell me, is the food good in British prisoner-of-war camps?"

Martineau smiled. "Oh, I think you'll find we make very special arrangements for you, my friend." And then, he made contact with SOE Headquarters.

At the control room at Jersey, Adler stood by the radio, an expression of disbelief on his face. He removed the earphones and turned slowly.

"What is it, for God's sake?" Necker demanded.

"That was Cherbourg Control. They've lost the JU88S."

"What do you mean, lost it?"

"They had the pilot on radio. He'd attacked several times. They suddenly lost contact and he disappeared from the radar screen. They think he's gone into the drink."

"I might have known," Hofer said softly. "A great pilot, Sorsa. An exceptional man. I should know. I chose him myself. And the mail plane?"

"Still on radar, moving up-Channel toward the English coast. No way on earth of stopping her."

There was silence. A flurry of rain drifted against the window. Necker said, "What happens now?"

"I'll leave in the Storch at dawn," Hofer told him. "The pilot of the mail plane can fly me. It's essential I get to Field Marshal Rommel as soon as possible."

"And what then?" Necker asked. "What happens when Berlin hears about this?"

"God knows, my friend." Hofer smiled wearily. "A bleak prospect—for all of us."

About fifteen minutes after Sorsa had changed course for the second time, Martineau received a response to his message.

"Come in, Martineau,"

"Martineau here," he answered.

"Your destination Hornley Field. Fly at five thousand feet and await further instructions. Escorts will assist. Should be with you in minutes."

Martineau turned to Sorsa who had his headphones on. "Did you get that?"

The Finn shook his head. "I don't understand English."

Martineau translated, then crouched down beside Baum. "So far, so good."

Baum sat up and pointed. "Look out there."

Martineau turned and saw, in the moonlight, a Spitfire take station to port. As he turned to check the starboard side, another appeared. He reached for the copilot's headphones.

A crisp voice said, "Martineau, do you read me?"

"Martineau here."

"You are now twenty miles east of the Isle of Wight. We're going to turn inland and descend to three thousand. I'll lead and my friend will bring up the rear. Well shepherd you right in."

"Our pleasure." He translated quickly for Sorsa and sat back.

"Everything okay?" Baum asked.

"Fine. They're leading us in. Another fifteen minutes or so, that's all."

Baum was excited. This time when he took a cigarette from his case his hand was steady. "I really feel as if I'm breaking out of something."

"I know," Martineau said.

"Do you really? I wonder. I was at Stalingrad, did I tell you that? The greatest disaster in the history of the German Army. Three hundred thousand down the drain. The day before the airstrip closed I was wounded in the foot. I flew out in a good old JU52, just like this. Ninety-one thousand taken prisoner, twenty-four generals. Why them and not me?"

"I spent years trying to find answers to questions like that," Martineau told him.

"And did you?"

"Not really. In the end, I decided there weren't any answers. Also no sense and precious little reason."

He pulled down the earphones as the voice came over the air again, giving him new instructions and a fresh course. He passed them on to Sorsa. They descended steadily. A few minutes later, the voice sounded again. "Hornley Field, right in front. In you go."

The runway lights were plain to see, and this time Sorsa didn't need any translation. He reduced power and dropped his flaps to float in for a perfect landing. The escorting Spitfires peeled away to port and starboard and climbed into the night.

The Junkers started to slow, and Sorsa turned and taxied toward the control tower. He rolled to a halt, switched off the engines. Baum got up and laughed excitedly. "We made it!"

Sarah was smiling. She reached for Martineau's hand and held on tight and Kelso, on the floor, was laughing out loud. The feeling of release was fantastic. Baum got the door open and he and Martineau peered outside.

A voice called over a bullhorn, "Stay where you are."

A line of airmen in RAF blue, each carrying a rifle, moved toward them. There were other people in the shadows behind them, but Martineau couldn't make out who.

Baum jumped down onto the runway. The voice called again, "Stay where you are!"

Baum knotted the white scarf around his throat and grinned up at Harry, saluting him, touching the field marshal's baton to the rim of his cap. "Will you join me, Standartenführer?" And then he turned and strode toward the line of men, the baton raised in his right hand. "Put the rifles away, you idiots," he called in English. "All friends here."

There was a single shot. He spun around, took a couple of steps back toward the Junkers, then sank on his knees and rolled over.

Harry ran forward, waving his arms. "No more, you fools!" he shouted. "It's me, Martineau."

He was aware of the advancing line slowing and Squadron Leader Barnes was there, telling them to stay back. Martineau dropped to his knees. Baum reached up with his left hand and grabbed him by the front of the uniform.

"You were right, Harry," he said hoarsely. "No sense, no reason to anything."

"Quiet, Heini. Don't talk. We'll get a doctor."

Sarah was crouched beside him and Baum's grip lightened. "Last act, Harry. Say kaddish for me. Promise."

"I promise," Martineau said.

Baum choked, there was blood on his mouth. His body seemed to shake and then the hand lost its grip on Martineau's tunic and he lay still. Martineau got up slowly and saw Dougal Munro and Jack Carter standing in front of the line of RAF men beside Barnes.

"An accident, Harry," Munro said. "One of the lads panicked."

"An accident?" Martineau said. "Is that what you call it? Sometimes I really wonder who the enemy is. If you're still interested, by the way, you'll find your American colonel in the plane."

He went past them and through the line of airmen, walking aimlessly toward the old aero club buildings. Strange, but he had that pain in the chest again, and it hadn't bothered him once in Jersey. He sat down on the steps of the old clubhouse and lit a cigarette, suddenly cold. After a while, he became aware of Sarah sitting a few feet away.

"What did he mean, say kaddish for him?"

"It's a sort of mourning prayer. A Jewish thing. Usually relatives take care of it, but he didn't have any. All gone to the bloody ovens." He took the half-smoked cigarette from his mouth and passed it to her. "Anyway, now you know. Now your education's complete. No honor, no glory, only Heini Baum out there, lying on his back."

He got to his feet and she stood up also. Someone had brought a stretcher and they were carrying Baum away, and Kelso was crossing the runway on his crutches, Munro and Carter on either side of him.

"Did I remember to tell you how well you did?" he asked.

"No."

"You were good. So good that Dougal will probably try to use you again. Don't let him. Go back to that hospital of yours."

"I don't think one should ever go back to anything." They started to walk toward the waiting cars. "And you?" she asked. "What's going to happen to you?"

"I haven't the slightest idea."

She took his arm and held on tight and as the runway lights were switched off, they moved on through the darkness together.

JERSEY 1985

17

IT WAS VERY QUIET there in the library, Sarah Drayton standing at the window peering out. "Dark soon. Sometimes I wonder whether the rain will ever stop. A bad winter this year." The door opened and the manservant, Vito, came in with a tray which he placed on a low table by the fire. "Coffee, Contessa."

"Thank you, Vito, I'll see to it."

He went out and she sat down and reached for the coffeepot. "And afterward?" I asked her.

"You mean what happened to everybody? Well, Konrad Hofer flew out in the Storch the following morning, got to Rommel and filled him in on what had happened."

"And how did Rommel cover himself?"

"Very much as Harry had suggested. He flew to Rastenburg."

"The Wolf's Lair?"

"That's right. He saw Hitler personally. Told him Intelligence sources had warned him of the possibility of plots against his life, which was why he'd used Berger to impersonate him. He stayed pretty much with the facts. If he'd gone to Jersey himself, Harry would have assassinated him. Berger was dismissed as a rat who'd deserted the sinking ship."

"I'm sure he didn't put it to the Führer in quite those terms," I said.

"Probably not. There was an official investigation. I read the Gestapo file on the case a few months after the war ended. They didn't come up with anything very much. They knew nothing about Hugh Kelso, remember, and what made the story so believable from Rommel's point of view was Harry himself."

"I don't understand," I said.

"Remember that Harry had gone to some pains to tell Hofer who he was, and that meant something concrete to the Gestapo. They had him on file, had been after him for a long time. Remember, they only just failed to get their hands on him after that business at Lyons when he shot Kaufmann."

"So Rommel was believed?"

"Oh, I don't think Himmler was too happy, but the Führer seemed satisfied enough. They drew a veil over the whole thing. Hardly wanted it on the front page of national newspapers at that stage in the war. The same thing applied with our people, but for different reasons."

"No publicity?"

"That's right."

"In the circumstances," I said, "the accidental shot that killed Heini Baum was really rather convenient. He could have been a problem."

"Too convenient," Sarah said flatly. "As Harry once said to me, Dougal Munro hated loose ends. Not that it gave anyone any problems. With D Day coming, Eisenhower was only too delighted to have got Kelso back in one piece, and our own Intelligence people didn't want to make things difficult for Rommel and the other generals who were plotting against Hitler."

"And they almost succeeded," I said.

"Yes, the bomb plot in July, later that year. Hitler was injured but survived."

"And the conspirators?"

"Count von Stauffenberg and many others were executed, some of them in the most horrible of circumstances."

"And Rommel?"

"Three days before the attempt on Hitler's life, Rommel's car was machine-gunned by low-flying Allied planes. He was terribly wounded. Although he was involved with the plot it kept him out of things in any practical sense."

"But they caught up with him?"

"In time. Someone broke under Gestapo torture and implicated him. However, Hitler didn't want the scandal of having Germany's greatest war hero in the dock. He was given the chance of taking his own life on the promise that his family wouldn't be molested."

I nodded. "And what happened to Hofer?"

"He was killed in heavy fighting near Caen not long after D Day."

"And Hugh Kelso?"

"He wasn't supposed to return to active duty. That leg never fully recovered, but they needed his engineering expertise for the Rhine crossings in March forty-five. He was killed in an explosion while supervising work on the damaged bridge at Remagen. A booby trap."

I got up and walked to the window and stared out at the rain, thinking about it all. "Amazing," I said. "And the most extraordinary thing is that it never came out, the whole story."

"There was a special reason for that," she said. "The Jersey connection. This island was liberated on the ninth of May, nineteen forty-five. The fortieth anniversary in a couple of months' time. It's always been an important occasion here, Liberation Day."

"I can imagine."

"But after the war, it was a difficult time. Accusations and counter-accusations about those who were supposed to have consorted with the enemy. The Gestapo had actually hunted down some of the people who had sent them anonymous letters denouncing friends and neighbors. Those names were on file. Anyway, there was a government committee appointed to investigate."

"And what did it find?"

"I don't know. It was put on hold with a special one-hundred-year security classification. You can't read that report until the year twenty forty-five."

I went back and sat down again. "What happened to Helen de Ville, Gallagher and Guido?"

"Nothing. They didn't come under any kind of suspicion. Guido was taken prisoner at the end of the war, but Dougal Munro secured his release almost at once. Helen's husband, Ralph, returned in bad shape. He'd been wounded in the desert campaign. He never really recovered and died three years after the war."

"Did she and Gallagher marry?"

"No. It sounds silly, but I think they'd known each other too long. She died of lung cancer ten years ago. He followed her within a matter of months. He was eighty-three and still one hell of a man. I was with him at the end."

"I was wondering," I said, "About de Ville Place and Septembertide. Would it be possible to take a look?"

"I'm not sure," she said. "Jersey has changed considerably since those war years. We're now one of the most important banking centers in the world. There's a great deal of money here and a considerable number of millionaires. One of them owns de Ville Place now, perhaps I could arrange something. I'm not certain."

I'd been putting off the most important question, she knew that, of course. Would be expecting it. "And you and Martineau? What happened there?"

"I was awarded the MBE, Military Division, the reason for the award unspecified, naturally. For some reason the Free French tossed in the Croix de Guerre."

"And the Americans? Didn't they come up with anything?"

"Good God, no!" She laughed. "From their point of view the whole episode had been far too uncomfortable. They preferred to forget it as quickly as possible. Dougal Munro gave me a job on the inside at Baker Street. I couldn't have said no even if I'd wanted to. He'd made me a serving officer in the WAAF, remember."

"And Martineau?"

"His health deteriorated. That chest wound from the Lyons affair was always trouble, but he worked on the inside at Baker Street also. There was a lot on after D Day. We lived together. We had a flat within walking distance of the office at Jacobs Well Mansions."

"Were you happy?"

"Oh, yes." She nodded. "The best few months of my life. I knew it couldn't last, mind you. He needed more, you see."

"Action?"

"That's right. He needed it in the way some people need a drink, and in the end, it did for him. In January nineteen forty-five, certain German generals made contact with British Intelligence with a view to bringing the war to a speedier end. Dougal Munro concocted a scheme in which an Arado operated by the Enemy Aircraft Flight was flown to Germany by a volunteer pilot with Harry as passenger. As you know, the aircraft had German markings and they both wore Luftwaffe uniforms."

"And they never got there?"

"Oh, but they did. Landed on the other side of the Rhine where he met the people concerned and flew back."

"And disappeared?"

"There was a directive to Fighter Command to expect them. Apparently the message hadn't been forwarded to the pilots of one particular squadron. A blunder on the part of some clerk or other."

"Dear God," I said. "How trivial the reasons for disaster can sometimes be."

"Exactly." She nodded. "Records showed that an Arado was attacked by a Spitfire near Margate. Visibility was very bad that day, and the pilot lost contact with it in low clouds. It was assumed to have gone down in the sea. Now we know better."

There was silence. She picked a couple of logs from the basket and put them on the fire. "And you?" I said. "How did you manage?"

"Well enough. I got a government grant to go to medical school. They were reasonably generous to ex-service personnel after the war. Once I was qualified I went to the old Cromwell for a year as a house physician. It seemed fitting somehow. For me, that's where it had all started."

"And you never married." It was a statement, not a question and her answer surprised me, although I should have known, by then, if I'd had my wits about me.

"Good heavens, whatever gave you that idea? Guido visited London regularly. One thing he'd omitted to tell me was just how wealthy the Orsini family was. Each year I was at medical school he asked me to marry him. I always said no."

"And he'd still come back and try again?"

"In between his other marriages. Three in all. I gave in at last on the strict understanding that I would still work as a doctor. The family estate was outside Florence. I was partner in a country practice there for years."

"So you really are a Contessa?"

"I'm afraid so. Contessa Sarah Orsini. Guido died in a car crash three years ago. Can you imagine a man who still raced Ferraris at sixty-four years of age?"

"From what you've told me of him, I'd say it fits."

"This house was my parents'. I'd always hung onto it so I decided to come back. As a doctor on an island like this it's easier to use my maiden name. The locals would find the other rather intimidating."

"And you and Guido? Were you happy?"

"Why do you ask?"

"The fact that you came back here, I suppose, after so many years."

"But this island is a strange place. It has that kind of effect. It pulls people back, sometimes after many years. I wasn't trying to find something I'd lost if that's what you mean. At least I don't think so." She shook her head. "I loved Guido dearly. I gave him a daughter and then a son, the present count, who rings me twice a week from Italy, begging me to return to Florence to live with him again."

"I see."

She stood up. "Guido understood what he called the ghost in my machine. The fact of Harry that would not go away. Aunt Helen told me there was a difference between being in love and loving someone."

"She also told you that Martineau wasn't for you."

"She was right enough there. Whatever had gone wrong in Harry's psyche was more than I could cure." She opened the desk drawer again, took out a yellowing piece of paper and unfolded it. "This is the poem he threw away that first day at the cottage at Lulworth. The one I recovered."

"May I see it?"

She passed it across and I read it quickly. *The station is ominous at midnight. Hope is a dead letter. Time to change trains for something better. No local train now, long since departed. No way of getting back to where you started.*

I felt inexpressibly saddened as I handed it back to her. "He called it a rotten poem," she said. "But it says it all. *No way of getting back to where you started.* Maybe he was right after all. Perhaps he should have died at seventeen in that trench in Flanders."

There didn't seem a great deal to say to that. I said, "I've taken enough of your time. I think I'd better be getting back to my hotel."

"You're staying at L'Horizon?"

"That's right."

"They do you very well there," she said. "I'll run you down."

"There's no need for that," I protested. "It isn't far."

"That's all right. I want to take some flowers down to the grave anyway."

It was raining heavily, darkness moving in from the horizon across the bay as we drove down the hill and parked outside the entrance to St. Brelade's Church. Sarah Drayton got out and put up her umbrella and I handed the flowers to her.

"I want to show you something," she said. "Over here." She led the way to the older section of the cemetery and finally stopped before a moss-covered granite headstone. "What do you think of that?"

It read: *Here lie the mortal remains of Captain Henry Martineau, late of the 5th Bengal Infantry, died July 7, 1859.*

"I only discovered it last year quite by chance. When I did, I got one of those ancestor-tracing agencies to check up for me. Captain Martineau retired here from the army in India. Apparently he died at the age of forty from the effects of some old wound or other. His wife and children moved to Lancashire and then emigrated to America."

"How extraordinary."

"When we visited this place he told me he had this strange feeling of being at home."

As we walked back through the headstones I said, "What happened to all those Germans who were buried here?"

"They were all moved after the war," she said. "Back to Germany, as far as I know."

We reached the spot where he had been laid to rest earlier that afternoon. We stood there together, looking down at that fresh mound of earth. She laid the flowers on it and straightened and what she said then astonished me.

"Damn you, Harry Martineau," she said softly. "You did for yourself, but you did for me as well."

There was no answer to that, could never be, and suddenly, I felt like an intruder. I turned and walked away and left her there in the rain in that ancient churchyard, alone with the past.

A BIOGRAPHY OF JACK HIGGINS

Jack Higgins is the pseudonym of Harry Patterson (b. 1929), the *New York Times* bestselling author of more than seventy thrillers, including *The Eagle Has Landed* and *The Wolf at the Door*. His books have sold more than 250 million copies worldwide.

Born in Newcastle upon Tyne, England, Patterson grew up in Belfast, Northern Ireland. As a child, Patterson was a voracious reader and later credited his passion for reading with fueling his creative drive to be an author. His upbringing in Belfast also exposed him to the political and religious violence that characterized the city at the time. At seven years old, Patterson was caught in gunfire while riding a tram, and later was in a Belfast movie theater when it was bombed. Though he escaped from both attacks unharmed, the turmoil in Northern Ireland would later become a significant influence in his books, many of which prominently feature the Irish Republican Army. After attending grammar school and college in Leeds, England, Patterson joined the British Army and served two years in the Household Cavalry, from 1947 to 1949, stationed along the East German border. He was considered an expert sharpshooter.

Following his military service, Patterson earned a degree in sociology from the London School of Economics, which led to teaching jobs at two English colleges. In 1959, while teaching at James Graham College, Patterson began writing novels, including some under the alias James Graham. As his popularity grew, Patterson left teaching to write full time. With the 1975 publication of the international blockbuster *The Eagle Has Landed*, which was later made into a movie of the same name starring Michael Caine, Patterson became a regular fixture on bestseller lists. His books draw heavily from history and include prominent figures—such as John Dillinger—and often center around significant events from such conflicts as World War II, the Korean War, and the Cuban Missile Crisis.

Patterson lives in Jersey, in the Channel Islands.

Patterson as an infant with his mother, grandmother, and great grandmother. He moved to Northern Ireland with his family as a child, staying there until he was twelve years old.

Patterson with his parents. He left school at age fifteen, finding his place instead in the British military.

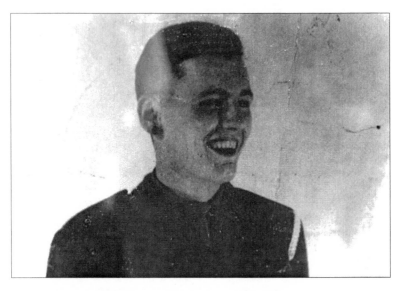

A candid photo of Patterson during his military years. While enlisted in the army, he was known for his higher-than-average military IQ. Many of Patterson's books would later incorporate elements of the military experience.

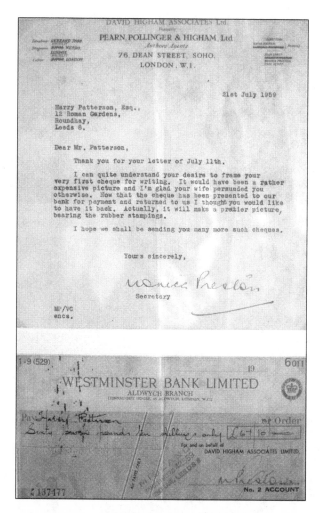

Patterson's first payment as an author, a check for £67. Though he wanted to frame the check rather than cash it, he was persuaded otherwise by his wife. The bank returned the check after payment, writing that, "It will make a prettier picture, bearing the rubber stampings."

Patterson in La Capannina, his favorite restaurant in Jersey, where he often went to write. His passion for writing started at a young age, and he spent much time in libraries as a child.

Patterson visiting a rehearsal for *Walking Wounded*, a play he wrote that was performed by local actors in Jersey.

Patterson with his children.

Patterson in a graveyard in Jersey. Patterson has often looked to graveyards for inspiration and ideas for his books.

All rights reserved under International and Pan-American Copyright Conventions. By payment of the required fees, you have been granted the non-exclusive, non-transferable right to access and read the text of this book. No part of this text may be reproduced, transmitted, downloaded, decompiled, reverse engineered, or stored in or introduced into any information storage and retrieval system, in any form or by any means, whether electronic or mechanical, now known or hereinafter invented, without the express written permission of the publisher.

This is a work of fiction. Names, characters, places, and incidents either are the product of the author's imagination or are used fictitiously. Any resemblance to actual persons, living or dead, businesses, companies, events, or locales is entirely coincidental.

copyright © 1986 by Jack Higgins

cover design by Elizabeth Connor

ISBN: 978-1-4532-9412-3

This edition published in 2012 by Open Road Integrated Media
180 Varick Street
New York, NY 10014
www.openroadmedia.com

EBOOKS BY JACK HIGGINS

FROM OPEN ROAD MEDIA

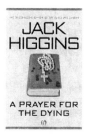

A PRAYER FOR
THE DYING

BLOODY
PASSAGE

CRY OF THE
HUNTER

DILLINGER

THE EAGLE
HAS LANDED

EXOCET

NIGHT OF
THE FOX

A SEASON
IN HELL

THE
VALHALLA
EXCHANGE

Available wherever ebooks are sold

OPEN ROAD

INTEGRATED MEDIA

OPEN ROAD
INTEGRATED MEDIA

Open Road Integrated Media is a digital publisher and multimedia content company. Open Road creates connections between authors and their audiences by marketing its ebooks through a new proprietary online platform, which uses premium video content and social media.

Videos, Archival Documents, and New Releases

Sign up for the Open Road Media newsletter and get news delivered straight to your inbox.

Sign up now at
www.openroadmedia.com/newsletters

FIND OUT MORE AT
WWW.OPENROADMEDIA.COM

FOLLOW US:
@openroadmedia and
Facebook.com/OpenRoadMedia